# The Trouble I've Seen

# The Trouble I've Seen

MARTHA GELLHORN

With an introduction by Caroline Moorehead

ELAND
London

First published by Putnam, London in April 1936
First published by Eland Publishing Limited in 2012

Eland Publishing Limited
61 Exmouth Market, London EC1R 4QL

ISBN 978 1 906011 62 8

A catalogue record for this book is available from the British Library

Cover Photograph: *Destitute pea pickers in California: Mother of seven
children, aged thirty-two. Nipoma, California, March 1936* by Dorothea
Lange (1895–1965)

Text set by Nick Randall
Printed in Navarra, Spain by GraphyCems

# Contents

To My Father

*'Nobody knows de trouble I've seen.*
*Nobody knows but Jesus ...'*

Negro Spiritual

# Introduction

IN WHAT BECAME known as Black Tuesday, October 29 1929, the US stock market crashed. All across the country – and soon across much of the world – personal income, tax revenues, profits, prices and trade all dropped, and went on dropping. By the summer of 1933, 17 million Americans were out of work. Steel plants and coal mines were at a virtual standstill. Thirty-eight states had closed their banks, and over a quarter of a million families had been evicted from their homes. In the mining communities of West Virginia, Illinois, Kentucky and Pennsylvania, children spent their days picking through rubbish dumps and fighting over scraps of food. Skin diseases, tuberculosis and syphilis were spreading and both the Ku Klux Klan and the Communist-leaning labour organisers were finding willing recruits among people reduced by extreme poverty to apathy and a profound sense of hopelessness.

To make it infinitely worse, the Great Plains of the Midwest had been hit by a severe drought. Oklahoma, Texas, New Mexico, Colorado and Kansas has become a 'dust bowl', across which rolled waves of sand and earth, filling people's ears and noses and suffocating animals. The countryside was a desolate barren stretch of dead trees and drifting brushwood. As people ceased to be able to afford their mortgages or rent, so they lost their homes. Camps were spreading around the outskirts of cities, along the dry riverbeds and railway sidings, built out of cardboard and sacks and corrugated iron, widely known as Hoovervilles, after President Herbert Hoover. There were also 'Hoover blankets', made out of newspapers, and 'Hoover leathers', cardboard soles for shoes.

While those on the right maintained that the 'losers' and 'chisellers' were experiencing the natural consequences of their own moral collapse, and developing an unhealthy expectation of handouts, those on the left argued that the Depression was caused by the excessive, concentrated power of the elites, looking out for their own interests. Meanwhile the rising number of the unemployed was overwhelming the traditional instruments of welfare, and local organisations, once able to cope with periodic economic downturns, watched helplessly as families were thrown out of their homes, fathers lost their jobs and children went hungry.

* * *

In 1932, when the economy had reached its lowest point, Hoover lost the presidential elections to Franklin Roosevelt, who came to power determined to halt all further slide into poverty. He set up, as rapidly as possible, the administration of relief on a scale never before attempted. Under a first New Deal, a Civil Works Programme was established under powers granted to him by the National Recovery Act, intended to stimulate demand and provide work and relief through increased public spending. Within four months, four million people were back in work. A Public Works Administration followed, employing people to build bridges, parks and schools. A second New Deal added social security, a national relief agency and strong stimulus to the growth of labour unions. During one of his early fireside chats, Roosevelt told Americans that the only thing they had to fear was 'fear itself – nameless, unreasoning, unjustified terror which paralyses needed efforts to convert retreat into advance'. His campaign song was 'Happy Days are Here Again'.

To put his plans for relief and the recovery of the economy into action, Roosevelt appointed a brains trust of practical and imaginative New Dealers. One of these was a crumpled, argumentative man called Harold Hopkins, whose eyes bulged and who chain-smoked and drank too much coffee. In New York, Hopkins had helped create one of the first public employment programmes in the country, before drafting a charter for the American Association of Social Workers. Roosevelt summoned Hopkins to Washington and asked him to administer a vast programme of public relief, under the name of the Federal Emergency Relief Administration. FERA was given $500 million to help states meet their relief needs, for every dollar of which three dollars of public money from other sources would be spent. A further $250 million was held as a discretionary fund for Hopkins to allocate to states where needs were too great and funds too depleted.

As an administrator, Hopkins was creative, sympathetic and driven. He was fortunate that when he arrived in Washington, there was no bureaucracy and no model for him to inherit. He could pick and choose the people he wanted and he could also experiment far more quickly and radically than other New Dealers. Until that moment, relief had been the responsibility of states. Hopkins was entering uncharted waters.

His was also one of the toughest assignments of the New Deal. He had to understand, and respond to, not only what was happening across the US, but provide data to the President and Congress, and be aware of what other New Dealers were doing. To assist him, he was given a division of Research, Statistics and Finance. Soon he was complaining that he was drowning in facts, yet knew very little about the human tragedy of unemployment, what it was actually costing in terms of broken families, alcoholism, disease and hunger. He wanted something more, something intangible and descriptive, something that would tell him what it felt like for a man to lose his job, his savings and his house and to watch his family sink into misery. Only then, he said, would he really be able to take the pulse of the country and devise a sound relief programme for the 'third of the nation' that was 'ill-nourished, ill-clad, ill-housed'.

And so, in the summer of 1933, a remarkable venture was born.

Hopkins began by hiring as chief investigator into the ills of the Depression a tough-minded, overweight, erratic 41-year-old reporter called Lorena Hickok. The daughter of a travelling butter-maker, who had beaten her as a child, Hickok left home at 14 to work as a hired girl until rescued by a cousin who helped her through school. Joining the Minneapolis Tribune as a cub reporter, she became one of the first women to be employed by the Associated Press. Hickok, who had been responsible for introducing Eleanor Roosevelt to the American public, and had since become very close to the First Lady, had bright blue eyes and wore raincoats and hats with wide brims and vivid red lipstick. She played poker and drank Bourbon with the boys. 'Don't ever forget', Hopkins told her, as he sent her out to observe and report on the effects of the Depression on the American people and the success of his relief programmes, 'that but for the grace of God, you, I, any of our friends might be in their shoes.'

In August 1933, Hickok set out from Washington in a car she called Bluette. She had been given $5 a day for her expenses, and $0.5 per mile for Bluette. 'Since we have not discussed as yet the form my reports to you are to take,' she wrote to Hopkins, 'I'm going to give you the first one in the form of a letter, telling you where I have been and what I've seen this week.' It became the model for her subsequent 120 reports.

Over the next 18 months, Hickok visited every state in the US except for the North West. It was not unusual for her to travel 2000 miles in a week, writing up her reports, which ran to several thousand words, at night on her typewriter in her motel room. Her style was breezy, evocative and free of cant; she quoted at length conversations with workers, families, reporters, employers, industrialists and union leaders. 'Cheer up. I'll be brief,' she wrote from South Dakota on November 7 1933. 'It's been a long day and I'm tired.' Normally she posted her reports, but when she encountered an emergency – as in the Midwest, where she found that drought, dust and grasshoppers had wiped out the crops – she telegraphed them.

What Hickok had to say was grim. From Puerto Rico, on March 20 1934, came a description that would be repeated, in one form or another, from states all across America.

> No one could give you an adequate description of those slums. You'd have to see them, that's all. Photographs won't do it, either. They don't give you the odors. Imagine a swamp, with stagnant, scum-covered, muddy water everywhere, in open ditches, pools, backed up around and under the houses. Flies swarming everywhere. Mosquitoes. Rats. Miserable, scrawny, sick cats and dogs and goats, crawling about. Pack into this area, over those pools and ditches as many shacks as you can, so close together that there is barely room to pass between them. Ramshackle, makeshift affairs, made of bits of board and rusty tin, picked up here and there. Into each room put a family, ranging from three or four persons to eighteen or twenty. Put in some malaria and hookworm, and in about every other house someone with tuberculosis, coughing and spitting around, probably occupying the family's only bed. And remember, not a latrine in the place. No room for them. No place to dispose of garbage, either. Everything dumped right out into the mud and stagnant water. And pour down into that mess good, hot sun – that may be good for rickets, but certainly [it] doesn't help your stomach any as you plod through the mud followed by swarms of flies and animals and half-naked, sick, perspiring humans. All this may give you just an idea of what those slums are like.

In many of the places where Hickok stopped to talk to employers, and to those who had managed to escape the worst effects of the Depression, she noted appalling racism. A Baptist pastor told her that he 'understood Negroes and loved them – as one loves horses and dogs'. 'Negroes', she was told, were 'going to get it in the neck', because as jobs vanished, 'the tendency is to throw out Negroes and hire whites, and this was only right since they are uniformly lazy and shiftless'. Hickok was not free of extreme racist language herself, at least in the early days of her travels. The 'Latins and Indians' she wrote to Hopkins, were easy-going, pleasure-loving 'simple fellows with simple needs, to be obtained with the least effort'. In Jessup, Georgia, she told him, half the population was black: 'Even their lips are black, and the whites of their eyes ... They're almost as inarticulate as animals. They ARE animals. Many of them look and talk like creatures barely removed from the Ape.' As the weeks passed, and she travelled further, she modified her tone.

Life alone on the road, constantly moving, began to take its toll. In the desert between Lordsburg, New Mexico and Tucson, she turned Bluette over and injured her neck. A doctor forced her to spend a day in bed. When it all got too gruelling she cheered herself up with food and drink, which only exacerbated her underlying diabetes. In New Orleans one evening she wrote to Eleanor Roosevelt, with whom she was in touch almost daily, to tell her that she had just put away two gin fizzes, shrimp, fish, a potato soufflé and crepes suzette, along with a 'pint of sauterne'.

At the end of 1934, exhausted and low in spirits, Hickok delivered a report summary. Its conclusion was bald. Having analysed the possibilities for the various industries, the numbers of employees, and the projected figures for further layoffs, she concluded: 'Relief on a nation-wide scale will be indispensable during the coming fiscal year.' 'And so they go on,' she wrote, describing the families she had seen, 'the gaunt, ragged legion of the individually damned. Bewildered, apathetic, many of them terrifyingly patient.' With this, Hickok returned to Washington, where she became the Executive Secretary of the Women's Division of the Democratic National Committee and spent much of her time with Eleanor Roosevelt in the White House.

Hickok had provided a highly informative picture of Depression America, but Hopkins wanted more: he needed other voices, more far-flung journeys, more up-to-date reports on the workings of his relief programmes and on the effectiveness of the women he had appointed as administrators – something of a novelty at a time when there was still considerable prejudice against women holding senior jobs. He was also very conscious of the stigma that went with accepting charity, not least because throughout the country there were people protesting against the indignity of public handouts. Was it better to boost work programmes? Should assistance take the form of cash or food parcels? And, hovering over everything was the alarming question of the extent to which communist agitators might be fomenting trouble.

Hickok's excellent reports had convinced Hopkins that the best way to find out what was really going on was to send out investigators. And so he recruited a team of 16 writers, journalists, economists and novelists, all people accustomed to listening to what people said, marshalling facts quickly, and writing it all down simply and clearly. His investigators would report to him alone and have no powers of implementation. Hickok had had all America as her beat. The 16 new recruits were assigned either a number of neighbouring states or a major city and its immediate surroundings. Their instructions were to go wherever unemployment and poverty were most acute; to talk to as many people as possible; to write down everything they saw and heard and to send it to him. Their pay was $35 a week. Those who had cars took them. The others cadged lifts from local FERA social workers or caught buses, trains and trolleys. Sometimes they went on foot. What they sent in, week after week, in carefully typed, minutely detailed reports running to many thousands of words, was a haunting picture of despair. Some, like Hickok, wrote breezily; others were analytical; others again passionate. Between them, they provide one of the most evocative – and least known – portraits of America during the Great Depression.

For some of the young investigators, their first encounter with destitution proved almost overwhelming. Edward J Webster, assigned the zinc, lead, oil, lumber and cotton communities of Missouri, Oklahoma, Texas and Arkansas, reported ever growing need: 'as unemployment continues, people become increasingly unemployable, few savings and resources run out, and people continue to move from the countryside to the towns'. The elderly and the disabled, he wrote, who had formerly been cared for by private welfare agencies or by their relatives, 'have been dumped into the lap of the Federal government' along with 'vast numbers of the socially inadequate, dwellers in shacks, shanties and vermin infested unsanitary urban hovels, who have never known anything but poverty'.

Webster remarked repeatedly on the spreading sense of dependency on relief, bringing in its wake more complaints, more mental suffering and, particularly in the 'higher socio-economic groups increasing groping, bewilderment and discouragement ... They consider themselves disgraced'. Everything must be done, he wrote, to avoid this 'wreckage of personality' and the destruction of 'those incentives without which no man or woman can carry on'. Webster had come away from the shanty towns of west Dallas, he said, 'with refreshing memories of the beggar cities of the Far East, and the somewhat embarrassing realisation that those Oriental human dumps were very, very good'.

Lincoln Concord, a well-known writer of sea fiction and, at 51, one of the oldest of the investigators, was sent to Michigan where he reported that Detroit was not so much 'disturbed as prostrated'. The banking crisis of 1932 had broken in Detroit – 'the spearhead of the Depression' – and there were 34 banks and leading citizens under indictment as a result of the crash. The feeling that these were being made scapegoats was 'hanging like a pall over the community'.

From Pennsylvania, Henry Francis wrote to Hopkins that he had been so sickened by the spectacle of the mining towns that he had fled, 'sick at heart'. The soft coal industry had been one of the first to crash; the local mines had closed, partly or totally; outside the crumbling shacks were garbage-strewn slags, closed company stores and filthy ragged children, all of them without shoes and 'losing their grip on themselves'. Some of the families who had lost their homes were now living in caves. 'Conditions on the patch are bad,' he wrote.

> Some slate roofs leak; porches are dangerously shaky, lack guard rails etc. One woman fell off a porch a month or so ago and broke her neck. The Brownsville undertaker buried her 'on credit'. I saw her son. The porch still lacked a guard rail to prevent one stepping backward to a 12 foot drop.
>
> 'Why don't you get a board and nail it up?' I asked the lad, after talking with him awhile.
>
> 'I'd be a coward to do that now,' he said. 'I didn't do it when my mother was alive, did I? Why should I do it now?'
>
> The boy was 18 or 19 years old. I understood his point of view when I learned that there was a suit against the company for damages.
>
> I saw woeful conditions in this place. Thirteen people sleeping in three rooms amid filth. Three adults in one bed is common. Bedding is terrible. Binion, who accompanied me, said, 'People might clean up a little better but they've lost heart.' Shoes, underwear, sweaters and bedding are urgently needed.

From Clarksburg, Francis sent a number of stories of particular families.

Benjamin Burdick is a former miner. He lives in Stonewall Park. Pays $13.50 for his house. Is on work relief five days a month. Had a splendid garden and has a cellar full of preserves. Commodities help out. Daughter, 19, formerly worked with Pittsburgh Plate Glass Co., but was let out four months ago. She walks six miles to the plant and return to look for work. She is going again on Wednesday and, as the Relief visitor has interceded for her, hopes for a chance to earn $12 a week again ... The daughter is ready to crack under the strain. She's intelligent, good-looking. But there's fire in her eyes.

Charles West, formerly a miner and more lately a janitor, received underwear from the relief organisation and, upon our visit, begged that it be changed for shoes for his wife. 'I can get along without underwear,' he said. 'Give the missus some shoes instead.' Mrs West shrank back in embarrassment, flushed and stammered refusal. Both are real people. Own their home. Owe two years' back taxes. Mrs West's father, an invalid, lives with them. He's eighty; they're over fifty ... The home is spotless. Clothes needed badly.

\* \* \*

The youngest of Hopkins's team of investigators was Martha Gellhorn, recently arrived back in the States from three years in Europe, and still re-covering from the end of a long love affair with the French writer, Bertrand de Jouvenel. She was 25, and the many jobs she had held since leaving Bryn Mawr had included writing articles for a number of American papers. She had been introduced to Hopkins by Eleanor Roosevelt, with whom her mother had been at university. Hopkins decided to send Gellhorn to the textile areas of the Carolinas and to New England.

Before leaving Washington, she was given vouchers for trains and five dollars a day for food, hotels and local travel. Being broke, she had no money with which to buy clothes suitable for tramping around derelict towns. So she set off with what she had brought back with her from Europe, Parisian couturier dresses once worn by models, and a brown crocheted hat with a bright plume of pheasant feathers; she wore plenty of mascara, eye shadow and lipstick.

Gellhorn, however, had a knack for total absorption in work and was soon engrossed in interviewing families. The style of her reports, typed up at night in her hotel room, was very simple, with a careful selection of scenes and quotes, set down without hyperbole. What made it so powerful was her tone, the barely concealed fury at the injustice of man and fate towards the weak, the poor, the dispossessed. In her Schiaparelli suit, with its high Chinese collar fastened by a large brown leather clip, and elegant Parisian shoes, she trudged around the slums and tumbledown shacks, recording in her notebook levels of relief, amount of unemployment, condition of houses. Above all, what fascinated and touched her were the stories of individual men and women laid low by malnutrition, illness and despair. None of the reports that reached Hopkins from his investigators during the autumn of 1934 carried more indignation and pity, though she remained acutely aware that all she was doing was sending Hopkins 'a bird's eye view – a bird flying hard and fast'.

From Massachusetts, she wrote:

> I have been doing more visiting here; about five families a day. And I find them all in the same shape – fear, fear driving them into a state of semi-collapse; cracking nerves; and an overpowering terror of the future … I haven't been in one home that hasn't offered me the spectacle of a human being driven beyond his or her powers of endurance and sanity. They can't live on the work relief wage; they can't live on the Public Welfare grocery orders.

They can't pay rent and are evicted. They are shunted from place to place, and are watching their children grow thinner and thinner; fearing the cold for children who have neither coats nor shoes; wondering about coal.

And they don't understand why or how this happened ... The majority of the people are workers, who were competent to do their jobs ... Then a mill closes or curtails; a shoe factory closes down or moves to another area. And there they are; for no reason they can understand; forced to be beggars asking for charity; subject to questions from strangers, and to all the miseries and indignities attached to destitution. Their pride is dying but not without due agony ... There are no protest groups, there is only decay. Each family in its own miserable home going to pieces. But I wonder if some day, crazed and despairing, they won't revolt ... It seems incredible to think that they will go on living like this, patiently waiting for nothing ...

Grim is a gentle word; it's heartbreaking and terrifying ...

All the investigators, travelling through the mining and textile towns or across the parched farming areas, remarked again and again on the sickly and malnourished children and the infectious diseases spreading through the population. They listened to doctors talk about rickets, chronic tooth decay, hookworm, anaemia and pellagra (the skin disease caused by vitamin deficiency), tuberculosis, and syphilis, now found in children as well as adults. It was Gellhorn who voiced their fears at greatest length; like Hickok, she sometimes allowed her sense of urgency and anger to overwhelm her natural sympathy, talking vehemently about the need for birth control and sterilisation for 'half-wits', 'imbeciles' and the 'feeble-minded'.

What has been constantly before me is the health problem. To write about it is difficult only in that one doesn't know where to

start ... Dietary diseases abound ... pellagra is increasing; and I
have seen it ranging from scaly elbows in children to insanity in
grown men. Here is what doctors say: 'It's no use telling mothers
what to feed their children: they haven't the food to give.' Conditions are really horrible here; it seems as if the people were
degenerating before your eyes; the children are worse mentally
and physically than their parents.

What horrified Gellhorn was the attitude of doctors when it came to
treating syphilis. 'Cases: a woman brought in a four months old baby; both
of them looked deathly ill and the child was paralysed. The mother thought
it was infantile; they were both plus four Wasserman. But the treatment
costs 25 cents a shot; and in that area the clinic is not allowed to accept
relief orders for treatment; they were not being treated.'

Saw a family of four; everyone had syphilis. The boy was moronic
and the girl also had t.b. ...

And they don't know what to eat or how to cook it; they don't
know that their bodies can be maintained in health by protective
measures; they don't know that one needn't have ten children
when one can't feed one; they don't know that syphilis is destroy-
ing and contagious ...

It was not the children alone who preoccupied the investigators so much.
It was also the young, and especially the young men, who seemed, as
Gellhorn put it, 'apathetic and despairing, feeling there is nothing to
look forward to, sinking into indifference'. Martha Bruère, who had
recently co-edited a collection of women's fiction with Mary Ritter
Beard, drove through Buffalo, Rochester, Syracuse, Schenectady and
Jamestown, places once prosperous with industries that ranged from
locomotives to concrete sewer pipes, from spectacles to silk ribbons,
and noted that almost none of the young men she spoke to had ever

had any work. Furthermore, as single men they had very little hope of being selected for a work relief project, since married men with families were taken on first. 'According to temperament and surroundings,' she wrote, 'they are becoming careless, listless, inert or unruly, violent and destructive.' What haunted Bruère was this spectacle of a lost generation, for whom economic recovery would simply come too late. Talking of the young, Gellhorn wrote: 'They don't believe in man or God, let alone private industry; the only thing that keeps them from suicide is this amazing loss of vitality; they exist.'

One of the clearest answers given by the investigators regarded Hopkins's basic question about the value of work programmes. Everywhere they travelled, whoever they talked to, employers as much as workers, the replies were always the same: jobs were what was needed, with decent wages; relief, in the form of groceries, vouchers or cash, was not just humiliating but often inappropriate. Thomas Steep, writing from Chicago, reported that the Italian, Jewish and black families he had spoken to had all told him that when it came to home relief, cash was better than kind, since the grocery parcels invariably contained items that one or other of the recipients could not eat.

A successful journalist and Pulitzer Prize travelling scholar with a passion for aeronautical engineering, Wayne Parrish, was sent by Hopkins to New York State and New Jersey, where he remarked on the universal longing for work, without which, he was told, there was nothing but 'futility'. Listening to applicants for relief in the FERA office in Brooklyn, he heard people blaming Hoover, or the new machines, or the drought, or bad luck – but all spoke of needing relief simply to tide them over until they could find a job again.

There was 'a young couple', wrote Parrish, 'married six months. He lost his job in a poultry concern two months ago. Furniture company threatens to take furniture, lights turned off, and things look black to them just as they are starting out in married life ... A boy who had worked in a match factory is applying for self and mother. Business bad and his two sisters and husbands also on relief. A single woman over fifty who used to work in a hospital is down to last cent and is obviously ashamed to have to apply ...' The story he heard, everywhere, was the same: when might work come?

Like Hickok, the investigators belonged to – or had become part of – middle class America, and like her they were not free of prejudice. Not one of them failed at some point to remark on the 'unworthy', the 'chisellers', the 'derelict', those who were basically 'unemployable' and for whom no amount of work projects could help. Gellhorn raged against lack of birth control, families of 14 or more where mothers and daughters were pregnant at the same time and in which children were growing up 'in terrible surroundings: dirt, disease, over-crowding, undernourishment'. 'You have to fight superstition, stupidity and lack of hygiene ... the present generation of unemployed will be useless human material in no time ... they are ignorant and often below-par intelligence ... why they aren't all dead of typhoid I don't know (it would probably be a blessing if they were) ...'

For Bruère, as for Gellhorn, it was the white-collar workers, the 'lost sheep' for whom the lack of work was a 'tragedy'. As one of the investigators wrote, 'the higher the grade, the worse the fall'. 'Almost all the work projects are Pick-and-Shovel,' Gellhorn noted. 'They do not fit into them ... Because they are a little most sensitive and keyed a little higher, they seem to break under the effects of Home Relief quicker than labourers.'

In Syracuse, Bruère went out on visits with the case workers. One American family, she reported, 'lived up a steep narrow freshly painted stairway. The clean fat wife was cooking something on a gas stove which was their only means of heating the place. Her husband – tall, lean and with a bad cough – had been a truck driver for a factory. He sat stolidly with his hands on his knees, nothing to do, nowhere to go. He had kept up his driver's licence in the hope of getting that sort of work again. He hadn't got it and had been given three days a week making concrete posts for the edges of roads. They lived on what he was paid, but he did want a warm shirt or coat or something that he could wear at his work'. Still, Bruère conceded, any job was better than nothing, for it would be 'proof that, when better times came, they were still in the game'. What was essential, she added, and the others repeated, was to avoid 'breeding a class of paupers' and to plan for the long term. 'A carefully formulated, liberal, socially progressive relief policy', suggested Webster, would find ready support. He had detected, he said, among employers the beginnings of a 'hospitality of mind'.

* * *

Sending his reporters into the field, Hopkins had also hoped for a clearer picture of how far what Bruère called the 'Flaming Reds' were gaining converts among the unemployed. Each, conscientiously, reported on the activities of the various protest groups and union organisers, but only very rarely did they find strong communist leadership. In the midwestern in-dustrial towns of Cleveland, Cincinnati and Indianapolis, David Maynard, one of the two economists in the team, and who had worked for the League of Nations, studied the meetings of the Unemployed Council, one of the more radical pressure groups. 'Intelligent leadership in these groups is rare,' he wrote. 'Most are chronic trouble-makers, known for years; others are borderline mental cases.' In Syracuse, Bruère observed in passing that 'although the surface is calm the situation is very ticklish and ... there is a large proportion of people in a dangerous mood'. In New York, Wayne Parrish, describing the increased rebelliousness of the unemployed young men, warned, 'You can't expect them to be content indefinitely.' In New Orleans, Webster reported that those on relief were not so much militant as 'stunned, confused, complacent'.

All the investigators, sooner or later, found themselves talking to 'hard-nosed', 'canny', 'tight-fisted' employers, who complained bitterly that the Roosevelt administration was 'making America a paradise for professional bums and chronic loafers'. Some of their harshest words were reserved for these uncaring, unyielding men. From Beaver County, in Pennsylvania, came a report that the Koppel Steel Car Company was withholding 50 percent of the very reduced pay packets of the few men still at work for back rent; and that from the remainder they deducted money for water and insurance. On the last day before Christmas 1932 some of the workers were given between 5 and 15 cents for a two week period.

What must have pleased and reassured Hopkins, however, as the reports reached his desk through the autumn and winter of 1934, was the praise for the way his administrators were handling the relief programmes. The women, in particular, were signalled as being both humane and efficient. Julian Claff, reporting from the paint, copper and steel town of Wilmington, though making fun of their starry-eyed 'belief in Santa Claus' and grumbling about their insane optimism and the the way that they were 'so sincere, so absurdly social minded', concluded: 'The patience and consideration displayed is worthy of the strongest commendation ... This relief show beats anything I ever dreamed of for efficiency ...'

Elsewhere, Wayne Parrish noted that in Brooklyn, the 'tactful handling' of clients was taking the steam out of the previously vociferous and quarrelsome Unemployed Councils. Gellhorn, reaching Boston from North Carolina in mid November, told Hopkins: 'Gaston County is my idea of a place to go to acquire melancholia. The only ray of hope is the grand work which our own office is doing: it's a kind of desperate job like getting the wounded off the battlefield.' Then she added: 'With all this, the employed and unemployed go on hoping ... they are grand people ... They are sound and good humoured; kind and loyal. I don't believe they are lazy; I believe they are mostly ill and ignorant ... The President stands between them and despair, and all the violence which desperation can produce ...' But, she went on, 'there is hope, confidence; something intangible and real ... "the President is not going to forget us."' Her wistful conclusion must have afforded Hopkins some comfort.

What Hopkins made of the many thousands of words that reached him, week after week, is not known, but their conclusion – that the best way back to dignity was through employment – helped him frame his campaign for work projects, old-age pensions and child benefits, and focus on longer term measures to introduce the benefits of modern technology to farmers and to put in place safeguards against anything of the kind ever happening to the country again. The New Deal was not without its darker sides, its brushes with social engineering, and several of the investigators were later criticised for concentrating too much on birth control, syphilis and feeble-mindedness, and too little on racial minorities. Taken together, however, these reports present a remarkable and unforgettable portrait of a country in the grip of economic mayhem, still living in an earlier, simpler age, one which would soon vanish before the march of industrial and technological advance. They were filed away in the archives of the Roosevelt administration and have scarcely been consulted since. The investigators, having completed their assignments, returned to their ordinary lives. Lincoln Colcord and Martha Bruère both went on to write books, but only Martha Gellhorn achieved real fame as a writer. Her reports, and those of Lorena Hickok, are journalism at its best.

By 1937, the measures put in place by the two New Deals were paying off. At the peak, in January 1935, more than 20 million people – 16 percent of the population – had been helped, and FERA was sometimes referred to as the 'heart and soul of the New Deal'. Unemployment had fallen by two thirds, and all the main economic indicators had regained the levels of the late 1920s. Though there was a further downturn that year, the worst of the Depression was over. In Washington, there was a new political alignment, with the Democrats the majority party; their ideas were liberal, and they included big-city machinery and newly empowered labour unions. A Social Security Act had been passed and programmes brought in to help tenant farmers and migrant workers. Women were at last recognised as in need of jobs and relief in their own right. The administration, intent on fending off the Red Menace at home, observed Europe's political upheavals and Japan's seizure of Manchuria and felt increasingly isolationist. Within two years, the House Committee on Un-American Activities would be seeing a communist in every trade unionist.

As for Martha Gellhorn, angry and despondent about the misery and poverty she had witnessed, she got herself fired for inciting a group of men on work relief, who were being exploited by a crooked contractor, to rise up and break the windows of the FERA office in protest. Described as a 'dangerous communist', she was summoned back to Washington.

In the mill towns of North Carolina, Gellhorn had found not just a subject for a book, but her writing voice. For the next 60 years, in slums, in refugee camps, on war fronts, in fiction and non-fiction, she would use this voice again and again, clear, sure, without exaggeration or bathos, her anger restrained and cool. Invited to stay for a while in the White House by Mrs Roosevelt, she started work on four novellas, drawn from the characters she had met and the scenes she had observed, full of the poignant details and heartbreaking stories that had no place in official reports.

The result, *The Trouble I've Seen*, is one of her finest books. Hailed as the literary discovery of the year, reviewed with respect and admiration in virtually every city of the US, Gellhorn appeared on the cover of the *Saturday Review of Literature* and was mentioned by Eleanor Roosevelt in three separate My Day columns. Writing in the *Herald Tribune*, Lewis Gannett noted that the book 'lives and dances in the memory'.

# Mrs Maddison

## I. Mrs maddison makes both ends meet

Mrs MADDISON STOOD before the mirror and tried tipping her hat first over the right eye and then over the left. The mirror was cracked and Mrs Maddison's reflected face looked a bit mixed up. But the hat was clear. It was of white straw, the pot shape that is cheapest and commonest; it had cost thirty cents and Mrs Maddison herself trimmed it, with a noisily pink starchy gardenia, in the centre front, like a miner's lamp. This flower was only pinned on (safety-pin inside, rubbing a little against Mrs Maddison's forehead) and therefore nodded as she walked, bowed before she did, and occasionally blew from side to side, petulantly. It was her best hat. With it she wore a dress of dark blue voile, with white squares printed on it, and a piece of tough machine lace making the collar. She also had white wash gloves, only one of which she wore because the other had been darned beyond endurance. Everything was very clean, very stiff; her shoes had been whitened and she had borrowed paint from one of the fishermen to rim the soles and worn heels. She got her hat on finally, deciding that straight across her forehead it looked most dignified. Peering and rising on one foot, she put her rouge on somehow; two carnation-red circles over the soft wrinkly skin. She almost never made this effort; she almost never looked so trim and certain, so easy with herself and the world; a woman who had clothes and a place to put them on nicely. She was going uptown to beg.

'One thing,' Mrs Maddison said to the hat, 'I'm certainly not gonna give anyone the satisfaction of thinking I need things. I'll get what's my right but I'll not have anyone thinking I'm charity.'

There was, in Mrs Maddison's mind, a certain doubt as to her right; for that reason she put on her best and only clothes, to reassure herself. There was also some snobbery in her dressing. She didn't want the relief people to put her in the same class with the negroes, who unconcernedly paraded their want.

She closed the front door but did not lock it, having lost the key some time ago and being, anyhow, vague about such matters, with reason.

The path went dustily beside the river, bordered on one side by tin cans, underbrush, moored house-boats, wrecks and the wide, flat, brown sweep of the Mississippi. On the land side, beneath the bluff, sat the shacks of her friends and neighbours. Next door there was Mrs MacIvor and her two boys, further down lived Lena who was a negro, but nobody cared. Then there was the Wilsons' tent: the Wilsons were not on Relief, Mr Wilson being an artist. He went about the countryside ornamenting beds, and in every negro shack, in every tenant farmer's slat house, one could see his art, gilt and black scrolls changing a worn four-poster into something half sinful, half circus. Old Maybelle lived in a box made of outworn pieces of corrugated tin roofing; these were temporary quarters. Her houseboat had sunk, and she was still repairing damages prior to moving back into her real home. Maybelle was a great friend of Mrs Maddison; some quality, casual, bright and illegal about them both, held them together.

The path wound up the hillside to town, straight from the ferry landing. Beyond the landing her own children lived and a few fishermen and some people one whispered about; they claimed they were Spanish.

Mrs Maddison waved to everyone she saw. No one asked her where she was going; her clothes announced her intentions.

Maybelle was sitting on the river-bank looking at her houseboat with love and anxiety.

'Flora,' she said as Mrs Maddison passed, 'would Alec help me with the roofing? I'll have the money next week. Tar paper. But it's my weight; I'm afraid to get up on the roof, it's kinda frail, you know.'

Mrs Maddison looked at Maybelle, smiling. Maybelle was her own age, sixty-ish, and a great woman with strength in her arms. She had a weatherbeaten man's face, rough and browned, and wore her hair twisted tight on her head. She would have shaved it, but that would mean answering questions, and Maybelle disliked questions. She had given up feeling or acting like a woman long ago; but her prestige for having once been a river captain's mistress followed her still in her old age. She was not fat, but there was a lot of her, muscle and bone; and everything about her houseboat was frail. Mrs Maddison promised to speak to Alec, her son.

The path up the hill was steep. The spring sun, already swollen and hot and ready for summer, beat down on it. Mrs Maddison stopped every once in a while with her hand over her heart, taking her breath in gulps. When her heart was quiet she wiped her forehead with the unworn glove. She did this quickly, not wanting to be seen. She knew she ought to have a handkerchief – it isn't my fault, she said to herself, crossly; I know how a lady ought to act, but what can I do?

She could see the crowds around the Relief office when she was still several blocks away. She hurried a little from excitement. There was always the chance that some commodities had come in from the north; perhaps some canned beef, or canned milk; perhaps even butter. Or clothes, maybe … she was almost running now, taking small quick steps over the cobbles, but careful, despite her haste, not to get any horse dung on her newly whitened shoes. Clothes: she had in a requisition for a baby dress for her granddaughter. The last ones she'd seen had been sweet; with pale blue French knots on them and little puckered sleeves. Now did they mean the sleeves to be like that, she thought, or was it just those fool women in the sewing-room not knowing what's the difference between sewing and shovelling coal ... it didn't matter. Those dresses had all been given away before she got in her application slip. She had to be content with three didies the last time. And did she have to lie. She enjoyed herself briefly thinking about that: about the fine scene she'd had with Mrs Cahill, her home visitor. Sticking up for her rights, that's what she'd done. Couldn't she tell a lie if she wanted to? Some country when a woman couldn't lie, doing no harm to anyone. She said to Mrs Cahill: Now you look here, Miss Lucy, I don't need any clothes for myself, I'm getting on fine, but I gotta right to clothes same's everybody else. So I'll just take clothes for my grandchild instead. Mrs Cahill said: Nonsense, you need everything yourself, you haven't a decent pair of shoes and when I put in a requisition it's going to be for you. You let that girl Tennessee scrounge around for her own child. I'll take no bossing from you, Miss Lucy, you're too young to have any sense. Mrs Maddison said, and who'd know better than me what I need? You just get me things for Tiny, like I said. Mrs Cahill objected that it was against the rules. Rules, Mrs Maddison sniffed, rules – well I never. Mrs Cahill gave up: the office was small; they had a certain leeway in allotting federal commodities and in making decisions. And she knew Mrs Maddison. A woman who wouldn't be ordered about and who only obeyed when necessary, and then you could feel her chuckling. Lord God, Mrs Maddison thought, I hope those niggers and those begging white folks don't get everything before I can push my way in.

The Relief office was an unused warehouse: it loitered over a city block, the panes out of the windows, pink paint peeling from the walls, great barn-like doors opening into damp shadows. Little grilles had been knocked into the walls and at these, separately, whites and negroes received their pay cheques, for work done on the roads or in the sewing-room. The negroes leaned against the walls, smoking pipes or stubs of cigarettes, dressed in neat white clothes, shapeless, chatty, able apparently to lean against something in the sun and laugh and talk in half sentences for hours, or days if necessary. The white people were crisper in their demands and never had to wait quite as long. If there were any seats or benches empty, inside the warehouse, they marched in and sat down. They wore their faces according to their needs for the day or their characters. There were quiet women, marked with weariness and resignation: there were angry ones, sitting stiffly as if they didn't want anyone to think they even approved the chairs in this thieving place: there were plaintive and garrulous and shy men: and Mrs Maddison, elegant with her rose, shoved into the midst of all this and settled herself on a bench, something like a bird perching and something like a ship dropping anchor.

'Howdy, Miz Crowder,' she said, bowing to the woman next her. 'What've they got today?'

'Some lady's nightgowns,' Mrs Crowder said. 'But I'm here to talk about my rent. I don't want no nightgown; they can keep their old clothes; they feel like burlap those things do. But my landlord sez they don't pay him and he wantsa put us out. And Harry, like a pretzel with rheumatism and these spring nights.'

Mrs Crowder sighed and Mrs Maddison nodded at her with bright sympathy. She turned to see who else was here, and what they were getting if they were lucky or talked loud enough.

There was that Wilkins man who ought to be shut up in jail for the way he treated Miz Wilkins. The woman was too patient; didn't step up and speak for herself. One child after another, and each year that woman looked more like something blowing down the street; an old bit of newspaper that'd been rained on. She frowned at Mr Wilkins, who didn't notice.

She saw a small girl, a share cropper's child, whom she knew by sight. Mamie was sitting beside her mother, her hands folded in patience on her lap. Every once in a while she blew off flies that circled too close about her head. Mrs Maddison did not approve of this. No place to bring children. Children shouldn't know about begging and waiting around: they should be brought up as if all this weren't going on. Or as nearly as possible. The child would get a sad old look long before she should. She'd hear things children needn't know for a while. There was Ruth Hodges crying over there in the corner: well, she had a right to cry if she couldn't help herself, but it was a bad thing to cry in front of other people, and hard times were something you managed by yourself: better to be angry about it if anything. The child worried her. She found herself getting slowly fretful, wanting to rise and sail out of this place, waving her pride around her head like a flag. She hated it. The days she came up to work she didn't mind: then she just sewed in the gloomy cavern of the warehouse and gossiped and argued when she was told to hurry and argued about not getting enough hours work. How'm I ever gonna give that Tiny orange juice, she thought, on $7.80 a month. None of their old business what she did with her money. Shouldn't spend it on Tiny, they kept saying. Lot they knew. If she didn't, who would be getting Tiny what she needed, the little smiling white radish... Why couldn't people give Bill work then, and, if they couldn't, why fuss with her about her money. Little's I've got, she thought, and it's not as if I had everything I needed for myself: I gotta right to choose if I want things or Tiny gets orange juice. Her mind turned these thoughts over, knowing each one of them, there was nothing new to think about. It was just that each week, each day, it began all over. God in heaven, she said to herself, what a stingy world it is.

'Miss Lucy,' she called. Mrs Cahill smiled to her, said, just a minute Mrs Maddison, and hurried back behind the beaver board partitions into an inner office, airless and lighted all day by bulbs on cords, where the social workers wrote reports and hung their hats. I'm kinda sorry for that girl, Mrs Maddison thought. She's getting a lot more money than I'll ever get outa this place, but she didn't used to have to run around all over this State in a Ford like a mule.

When she was little, Mrs Maddison thought … long ago Lucy Harmsworth wore a blue hair-ribbon and played on the lawn in front of a white house with high slim pillars … Mrs Maddison's son Alec was a child, too, and Mr Maddison, who had died and been missed and then forgotten, had work as timekeeper at the box factory, was it that or had they been farming? Anyhow, they had a house, and the two older boys were alive and looked as if they'd live forever, with faces like balloons and shouting their lungs out, and falling into everything and eating all day long … Timmy, the first one, had been her favourite. She'd forgotten now really what her husband looked like, since he'd been dead twelve years. But she'd never forget what Timmy was like, dying in the charity hospital of typhoid. And Rupert close after him. We all had it better once, Mrs Maddison decided. We were real folks once; we had places to live, and we had families, and we knew what we'd be doing the next year and the next one. Now, now … A familiar feeling of uncertainty overcame Mrs Maddison; a fear that everything would blow away even as she waited; things would change once again, there wouldn't even be this piddling work for her, this measly living. She jumped to her feet and walked to the back office and went in without knocking.

'I gotta talk to you right away, Miss Lucy,' she said, her voice sharp with the sudden terror she had felt.

'Yes, Mrs Maddison.'

'I gotta have more hours work. Nobody can live on that $7.80 a month I'm getting and I'm not complaining about the pay, mind you, though I must say fifteen cents 'n hour looks like nigger wages to me, and it's not much for niggers the way pork 'n' meal's going up, but, anyhow, I gotta be working more.'

'I'll see what I can do.'

Mrs Cahill was thirty; she wore a cheap and ugly gingham dress. Her hair came out in neglected strands from the bun on her neck, and wearily she shoved the loose ends into place.

Mrs Maddison was sorry for her again, and angry at herself: I didn't come here to be crying over Lucy Harmsworth, she thought; there's Tiny to be worrying about.

'No, you gotta say something sure. Now.'

'I can't, Mrs Maddison. You know I haven't got the money. It comes from the State headquarters, and first it comes from Washington. They give us what they can every month and we divide it up. If there's more money you'll get more work. I can't ...' Mrs Cahill said, thinking to herself, that proud old woman worrying her heart out about Tiny, who probably oughtn't to live, anyhow, or just won't ...

'I gotta know,' Mrs Maddison said, but her voice was dimming, and she felt tired and wanted to be sitting on her front porch watching the river but not thinking.

'Well.'

They waited in silence and a few flies buzzed crazily against the lamp bulbs, and outside the office they could hear the close droning voices of people telling their troubles, asking for help.

'Perhaps I could get you something from the Commodities,' Mrs Cahill said.

'I'm not asking you for favours, Lucy Harmsworth, I'm asking you for work. Like a self-respecting woman's gotta right to.'

'I know,' Mrs Cahill said. 'I don't mean to be giving favours. If there's anything there you've got a right to it.'

She led Mrs Maddison through a back hall to a small dark room with a counter across half of it. A young man with a pencil behind his ear, trying to look cheerfully like a grocer's clerk, presided.

'Johnny,' Mrs Cahill said, 'have you got anything?'

He rumpled some papers. And turned and looked at the shelves.

'The nightgowns are all gone. There's no clothes now, and most of the other visitors got their clients down for the food already. There's just a little canned salmon,' he said. 'About two cans left. We never got much. Would you want that?'

Mrs Cahill looked at Mrs Maddison and Mrs Maddison looked through the wall, obstinate and silent. She was thinking: if I get it we'll have something nice tonight for supper. I could ask over Tennessee and that no-count husband of hers and have a big plate of it with something on it; maybe I could earn a dime or something for some tomatoes … Her face remained stony, asking for nothing.

'Yes,' Mrs Cahill said, and signed a slip and handed the two cans to Mrs Maddison.

Mrs Maddison held them in her arms, uncomfortably, with no expression on her face. She stood looking at Mrs Cahill and said nothing. 'I know,' Mrs Cahill said, 'I know you haven't got anything against me. Go on home and get Tennessee over to supper.'

Mrs Maddison smiled at her then and went out, but tactfully, by the back door, so as not to make anybody else feel badly, and also because she knew that if Ruth Hodges was still there crying she'd have to give her one of the cans and then Tennessee wouldn't be coming tonight … A party, Mrs Maddison thought, gay at once, a party: and I'll act like I just bought the salmon with my own money, just went uptown to a store and bought it, and nobody has to give me anything.

\* \* \*

Mrs Maddison asked one of the MacIvor boys to tell Tennessee that supper would be waiting for her and Bill, about six o'clock. She sent the message like that, a casual word, not letting them know ahead what a fine supper it would be. Maybelle loaned her a can of tomatoes, knowing she'd get them back, or a can of something else, when Mrs Maddison's Relief check came on Tuesday. The MacIvors and the Wilsons and Lena instantly heard that Mrs Maddison had extra food and was going to give her daughter Tennessee and Bill a surprise party. Mrs Maddison thought regretfully of her son Alec and Sabine, his wife: she wanted them too. But she'd have to postpone that until the next successful visit uptown; or, anyhow, until next week. She was nearly out of everything: salt, sugar, flour, coffee, and the tall can of milk was suspiciously light in her hands.

She put her hat carefully on a shelf and set about making her house ready for the evening. There was very little to do. She tended it always with passionate care: she had lived in it a year now, which was a long time for anyone to have the same house. When she came to it, sent by Mrs Cahill because the rent was practically non-existent, she had wept bitterly but alone, walking up and down the river-bank, holding her hands over her mouth to keep it secret. It had been a negro cabin: three rotting rooms, the floor splintered and in places gone. Paper, plastered over the walls against the rain, hung in greying streamers, with spiders and less possible bugs crawling and crackling in the loose pieces. There was no furniture beyond a rusting stove, whose chimney gaped where the rust had eaten away a ragged hole. There were no window panes, and water lay in pools wherever it could collect, souvenirs of the last rain and a hint of what to expect from the roof. When she went up the front steps she clung to the shaking handrail, frightened of going through the steps, and breaking her ankles. After she had walked along the river for an hour, wasting her anguish over this place where she would have to live, she came back and sat down on the edge of the porch. Growing on the river-bank in front of her was a thin exhausted weeping willow, and a little to the left, amazingly, a magnolia tree. It didn't look as if it would ever have the strength to bloom again, but the leaves were glossy if scant, and stood blackly against the afternoon sky. Beside her house a wire fence shut in the water works: the drone of the dynamo was friendly and soothing, like bees, like an old woman humming endlessly to herself. She sat there quietly for hours and then decided that since she was here she would make this house fit for a person to live in. She had at that time an old trunk corded up, holding what clothes she owned, a few plates and pots and pictures of her children as babies, very starched and solemn.

From Mrs Cahill and Mrs Cahill's friends she got old magazines; and she tore out the advertisements and pasted them all over the ripped and filthy newspaper of the walls. She did this with an eye to colour, not caring much what the advertisement was about, just so it looked bright and fresh. There was, above her bed, an intimate advertisement about articles of personal hygiene for women, and she hesitated a long time about a Listerine advertisement but finally didn't use it, though the paper was nice and shiny, because the woman's face looked so anxious. Campbell's soup was vaunted on her walls, chic red-coated people smoked cigarettes, a handsome man in a polo coat drove a Packard, a lovely mask-like face, swathed like a nun, proved how clever Helena Rubinstein was with skin … It had taken her several weeks, and finally she'd gone to the public library and been eager about wanting old magazines to read. 'I wouldn't tell them I used them on my walls,' she said to Maybelle. 'They'd think I was poor and begging for something. But just wanting to read; well, that's something even rich folks do.'

Alec, who earned his living, or tried to, salvaging iron, got her a less used piece of stove pipe and cleaned up the stove. The Relief gave her a bed, and what with judicious scavenging, barter, economies and ingenuity, she'd fitted up her house. The Wilsons had been very helpful. Mrs Maddison sewed for Mrs Wilson and in return Mr Wilson ornamented her furniture. His favourite style was black and gold, but as that was fairly expensive paint he used up all his odds and ends of colour. Mrs Maddison's house had a wild brightness; two curtains on the same window being different material, each unstable chair boasting several shades of paint; but all she cared about was that it should look gay and be clean. For a year she had collected oddments, patched, painted, hammered, and now her house, she felt, was a place any woman might be proud to live in. There was the kitchen-dining-room-living-room, and two bedrooms. Some day, Mrs Maddison used to tell herself, when times are better, I'll fix up one of those bedrooms for a parlour. She knew this would never happen. Parlour furniture meant plush, and a big sideboard of some heavy varnished wood. But just saying it to herself made her happy, made her feel like a woman of property, and opened up alluring vistas of the future, when she'd be entertaining her friends in a fine room, with a big oil lamp covered by a shade, lighting them all up, and showing off the food on the sideboard …

She cared for the magnolia tree and built a support for the weeping willow, which was about to bend over into the river, the bank having been drained away and silted back, with countless floods and countless dry summers. She thought of these two trees as 'my garden'. Finally the dynamo next door became hers also, a friend, and got a name.

She called it Jennie. Some nights it sang loudly, with sudden moaning jerks: 'Jennie's got rheumatism,' she'd tell herself and fall asleep thinking what a fine house she had, and such an unusual location: with the garden and the river view, bottles floating beside grapefruit rinds, and the ferry tooting its way across to Louisiana, and the fishermen's boats put-putting up the river, and the houseboats, like dingy garages, square, stuck in the mud, helplessly tied to the shore.

'Flora.'

'Hi there, Maybelle, come right on in.'

'I brought you something. Lena made it for me. But I can't use it yet. I wouldn't have no place to put it in that box of mine. When I get the houseboat fixed, o' course – but I thought you could put it on the table tonight seeing's you got a real supper.'

Maybelle came cautiously up the steps; she was haunted by the idea that things would break under her. She handed Mrs Maddison her loan-gift. It was a new tin can, cut half-way down into fine strips. These strips had been bent outwards and twisted to resemble flower stems and on the top of each stem sat gayly a little paper crêpe flower.

'Oh,' Mrs Maddison said, and held it wonderingly in her hand. 'Oh, Maybelle, if that ain't the purtiest …'

Maybelle smiled at her. 'The house looks grand,' she said. 'But you wait till you see my houseboat. Oh, man, is that old tub gonna be a floating palace.'

They grinned at each other. 'What'ja gonna wear,' Maybelle asked.

'Why, my blue dress, of course. What did you think I'd wear; my black satin trimmed with ermine?'

Maybelle clanked her massively on the back, laughing. 'No, ma'am,' she said, 'I thought you was gonna wear a black lace nightie like that girl in your stocking ad. Well, I gotta go home. I'm making me a rag rug for the kitchen. It's a helluva job; but nothing's too good for me. We'll have a house-warming, Flora, just us two old girls, you wait. I betcha I know where I'll get some stuff. It'll be one party, all right.'

'I wisht I could ask you tonight, Maybelle.'

'Don't you think about it. You feed up that Tennessee of yours; she's looking peaked.'

'And well she might, with Bill drunk all the time and acting like a crazy Eyetalian or something, shouting at her and Tiny and I don't know what besides.'

'Well,' Maybelle said, 'you can't blame him too much, Flora, he used to be a good kid. He just don't know what to do, sitting around all day.'

'There's plenty others has to do the same,' Mrs Maddison said and her voice was cold, 'or he could help Alec with the iron.'

'Sure. There's a lotta money in that. What's Alec making now, 'bout thirty cents a day, ain't he? All he needs is a helper so's he can split.'

'All right, Maybelle.'

'Sure. You gotta think about them things. It's tough on the kids, Flora; they ain't had the fun we did.'

'I know. But I get so mad sometimes thinking about Tennessee and Tiny, and you can't only think about what Bill used to be. She ain't living with the boy she married two years ago, she's living with this here Bill, getting drunk all the time and … oh, I dunno, I'm not gonna think about it. We'll have a real good supper and I just won't think about it.'

'That's right. Well, so long, Flora. Come by for me in the mornin' and we'll go up to the sewing-room together. Have a good time.'

She creaked carefully down the stairs and Mrs Maddison could hear the great amiable voice booming to Lena on her front porch and passing the time of day with Mrs Wilson.

I'm not gonna get mad at Bill, Mrs Maddison thought: I know he's a good boy and I'm not gonna think about the rest. He just can't help himself, I guess. I won't think about it. It's none of my business. She walked lightly about her house, preparing dinner, setting the table, trying various places to put the lovely flower centre-piece Maybelle had brought. At six, everything was ready and swiftly she inspected and admired her home a last time and then went to sit in a rocker on the porch, cooling off from the stove heat and the excitement. This way, too, she could see them coming. She rocked quietly, bowed to Mrs MacIvor on the next porch, and thought to herself about Tennessee, who was her baby. That girl, she said to herself, is just too pretty for her own good. If she hadn't been such a beauty to look at she wouldn't of got grabbed off so young and she'd not be married at all yet. Nineteen now, with that child and Bill … Well, I was married when I was eighteen, Mrs Maddison thought, and it worked fine: but those were different times; that was when a man could work if only he wanted to and didn't have the rheumatism or his heart going feeble on him … It was all different, she thought; people weren't so careless of each other then: there were lots of people like Maybelle, liking to see their neighbours happy.

Well, she thought calmly, I'm getting old. It's only old women thinks such fine thoughts about the past.

She watched them coming up the path beside the river, with the dust shining around them, and the wind clicking in the sparse, dry trees. All her joy in the fine food waiting, and in the house she had garnished for their evening, faded and left her cold with wretchedness. Bill was drunk. She could see that. His head, young and nice but for the pallor and the fretful uncertain look about his mouth, lolled on his neck. He stumbled, with Tennessee holding and guiding him. Tennessee was talking to him as one would to a frightened horse or a feverish child: Mrs Maddison could hear little bits of it, in the quietness. 'No, Billy, of course she don't think you're a bum – there's no jobs, honey; we all know that – now, Billy, pick your feet up a bit, you'll be falling – no, I know you're not drunk, it's only the path's bum and you can't see in this light – hold on to me, darling ...'

Mrs Maddison took in her breath. She knew what the supper would be like: the lavish supper of salmon with tomatoes thick over it, potatoes steaming from the stove, and sweetened coffee and bread-pudding. Tennessee and she would sit in silence, choking down their food, not looking up from their plates, trying not to see what Bill was spilling on the oil cloth, on his clothes, how his hands wavered with the fork. They'd be nervous and tight, waiting for the evening quickly to finish. And from time to time, thickly, Bill would break out into argument, angry against her, and suddenly cruel with Tennessee. How can he be like that, Mrs Maddison thought: there are others with the courage to stay sober: and a young wife, she thought, watching Tennessee, half pulling Bill towards the house, a lovely young wife ...

'Howdy, ma,' Tennessee called; she couldn't wave, she was using her hands.

'Howdy, Tennessee. Howdy, Bill,' Mrs Maddison said, her voice gay. 'Hurry on up, everything's ready.'

She left the porch; she didn't want Tennessee to feel her watching that unsteady ascent, Bill with his hands on the handrail and his feet slipping. She moved about the room, lighting up the oil lamps on the kitchen table and in the bedroom. For a moment she stood and looked at her table, and Maybelle's flowers, and thought: I wish that man was dead. He's only bringing unhappiness to folks who got enough without that.

Tennessee came in first: 'Bill's not feeling good,' she said anxiously.

'Who said I wasn't feeling good?' Bill said. 'S'lie. M'feeling fine. M'feeling swell. Hi, there, Maw, how's the old girl?'

'I'm fine, Bill. Wanna give me your cap?' She took it from him and laid it on the bed. Tennessee wore no hat or coat; she stood watching Bill, leaning against the door. Her mother looked at her and thought: For nineteen that girl looks too tired, she's getting bad lines in her forehead.

Bill noticed Tennessee suddenly. 'Fine looking girl I got fer a wife, ain't she? Fine shape that girl's got.'

Mrs Maddison turned her back on him. Tennessee moved out of the light and Bill sat down heavily at the table. Mrs Maddison dished out the food. 'Miss Lucy had them cans of salmon extra,' she said.

'That's nice,' Tennessee murmured.

Bill ate in silence for a while. Suddenly he banged his glass against the table. 'Charity food, that's what I'm eating. Just old canned stuff they give to paupers and niggers. Can't git our own stuff; has to be give to us. I don't take any of that Relief; by God, I'd ruther starve.'

'It's a shame you don't take it,' Mrs Maddison said. So I'm a pauper or a nigger, she thought, her eyes smarting. 'It's about time you did, Bill Saunders. You been married to that girl two years and it wasn't only the first six months you was really keeping her like a man should. You been hanging around without jobs for a long time, long's some folks can remember. It's a fine thing to be proud but not when your own wife and baby gets skinny in the face with your old pride.'

Mrs Maddison's breath came like a clock ticking, fast and staccato, her hands were fluttering in her lap. I said it now, she thought: well, it's about time, too. Somebody's gotta. He just can't see there's anybody alive at all but him. And that girl and Tiny ...

Bill's face was getting dark with blood. 'You nagging old busybody,' he said. 'You nosey old woman, meddling in other folk's business. I'll do with my wife like I want to. Just because you're a beggar's no reason for the whole fambly to go around holding out their hats and whining for a little something to eat. I kin work and I'm not taking any of their old charity and if you don't like it.' His fist lay on the table, like carved wood. 'And, anyhow, I don't like coming here, and I don't like my wife coming here. Just to listen to you crabbing at me. So I guess we'll go. Come on, Tennessee.'

Mrs Maddison didn't move and she said nothing. She made no gesture towards Tennessee and she kept her eyes fixed on the salt cellar, waiting. Whining for a little something to eat, she thought, and felt very tired. That's what had happened to her party.

'No,' Tennessee said. 'I'm not coming, Bill. You can't talk that way to my mother, and you're drunk. How do you s'pose Tiny'd be alive now if it wasn't for ma getting her orange juice and things with her own Relief money? I don't like people who act like you. I'm not coming, Bill.'

Bill stared at her stupidly, his head a little on one side and back, as if she had slapped him. Suddenly he swung to his feet, cursing: 'Whose wife are you, anyhow?' He reached out his arm for her and she hit it away. He grabbed her by the shoulder cruelly and she twisted out of his reach: he thrust against the table to get her and she ran into the next room, and her eyes were black with fear. He didn't see where he was going and he kept talking, not words but just sounds of fury: and his hands were out before him like claws. Mrs Maddison sat in her chair unable to move; even her voice had gone. Her mind kept saying, scream out, get the MacIvors and Lena and Maybelle and everybody, help, help, but she sat staring into the next room, frozen silent. She heard Tennessee's voice lift: 'I'll throw the lamp at you, Bill. I'll throw the lamp sure's I'm standing here.' Everyone's breath sounded clearly in the house. Mrs Maddison waited. Bill came back out of the room, tearing at his cap.

'It's your doing,' he shouted at Mrs Maddison. 'It's all your doing. If you wasn't a withered ugly old woman I'd take and wring your neck.' He got down the steps somehow; they could hear him stumbling and cursing back towards the ferry landing.

Tennessee came into the room; her eyes were still wide and black but she moved listlessly. She sat down at the table and Mrs Maddison said in a tiny voice: 'Have some bread-pudding, honey.' They picked up their spoons and held them and neither touched the food.

Then Tennessee began to cry. 'What's wrong with that boy?' she said. 'He used to be a good man and I love him, I love him. What'm I gonna do?' she said and wept, staring straight in front of her.

'If he gets a job he'll be all right,' Mrs Maddison said.

'He won't get a job; there aren't no jobs anywhere. It's Mr Murdoch gets him drinks up there at the saloon; he oughtn't to do that, just 'cause he's 'n old souse hisself. Why don't he leave my Bill alone.'

'I know, lovey, I know.' Mrs Maddison pulled her chair alongside Tennessee's and stroked her hair. 'Don't fret, lamb; don't you fret. You just sleep here tonight and he'll be sobered up tomorrow.'

'I can't do that. How 'bout Tiny?'

'Didn't you leave Tiny at Alec's?'

'Yes.'

'She'll be all right there. You get some rest here, honey. It'll be all right tomorrow.'

'No, it won't,' Tennessee said, 'and you know it. And not day after tomorrow neither, or next week, or anything. Not till he gets him some work like he ought to have and takes care of us.'

'What'll you do, then?'

'I dunno. Oh, ma, what can I do?'

'Guess you'll have to leave him, Tennessee, till he gets work, anyhow. Just gotta, I guess; Miss Lucy'll take care of you and Tiny; and you kin live here.'

Tennessee said nothing: but she had stopped crying.

'You don't like him, do you, ma?'

'Not when he treats you the way he does and goes and gets drunk and lets you starve on account he's too proud.'

'You don't like him anyhow.'

'Oh, Tennessee … Remember when you got married …'

'You don't. You never did. You're lying now.'

Mrs Maddison moved a little away from her, and her hands clasped tight together. There had been hate in Tennessee's voice: my own daughter, she thought, my own daughter.

'I'm gonna leave him cause there's nothing else I can do. But I'm not coming here to live knowing you hate him. I won't do that and listen to you talking against him.'

'Tennessee, I only want you to be happy honey, I only want you to get what you gotta eat, you and Tiny …'

She was talking to an empty room: swiftly, without a word or a gesture, Tennessee had gone, and Mrs Maddison could hear her running down the path as if she hated the house she had been in, and the woman she'd left.

I fixed her up a veil outa muslin for her wedding and those pretty flowers I got at the dime store on her hair, Mrs Maddison said to herself: what shall I do with all the food that's left, nothing hardly eaten, and she looked around at the gay talkative walls, but it seemed bare and forlorn to her, and she wished it were tomorrow already, or next week, and then it might be better, or she'd have forgotten how it was, talking to her daughter's footsteps running away from her.

Maybelle sat on the ground before her box-house and smoked. It looked like a rolled leaf, the cigarette, and as it smelled pretty bad nobody had ever wanted to try one. She used to say mysteriously that she'd found the formula for making them sealed in a bottle floating on the river, and she didn't doubt but that the old Indian chiefs smoked cigarettes like hers. She enjoyed making up important stories, and then waiting very earnestly to see who'd believe them.

Mrs Maddison sat down on a keg beside her.

'I heard Bill going home last night,' Maybelle said presently. 'And Tennessee after him.'

Mrs Maddison watched a grapefruit rind fighting in the current, being whirled round, filling, sinking.

'It's bad times, Flora.' Maybelle's great hand lay on Mrs Maddison's knee. 'It's not the kids, nor it's not you. It's just the times.'

Mrs Maddison stared across the river to Louisiana, remembering how, three years ago, she'd picked pecans over there, till her back felt like something made of rusty iron. And gone to sleep in a tent with the mosquitoes droning closer and closer, and the damp air from the marshlands settling foggily in her throat. Tennessee was working in the dime store in the afternoons and going to school; Mrs Maddison could send her a little money each week, staying there in Louisiana, for the movies and marcelles: so she wouldn't feel she was different from the girls who had homes and didn't think about money all the time. I didn't do enough, she thought; somewhere I should have been better for her.

'Don't think about it, Flora,' Maybelle said. 'It don't do no good. And they'll forget, and you, too. No sense gitting moody.'

Maybelle rose and shook the dirt from her. She went behind her hut and emerged with a discoloured wheelbarrow, which had a drunken lurch when it moved, its wheels being dissimilar. On this sat a Singer sewing machine of vast dimensions and antique make.

'Well, for heaven's sake,' Mrs Maddison said, 'whatever are you gonna do with that?'

'I'm gonna trundle it up the hill to the sewing-room,' Maybelle said. 'I can't use it, anyhow, till I get the boat fixed up and I'm sick of piddling around with those flimsy things they got up there. I'm scared I'll mash the damn things every time I put my foot on the pedals. And I sez, working's fine but you gotta think of the conditions.' With this ominous remark, but evidently pleased with the effect she was making on her friend, she started the wheelbarrow limping on its way.

They arrived at the sewing-room, breathless. A crowd collected at once. Everybody wanted to know what was the matter with Maybelle, had the poor woman taken leave of her wits, and besides, pushing a thing like that, big as a horse, up the river hill, in this sun, she must be crazy, she'd have a stroke … and, anyhow, why bring your own stuff to the Government? That didn't make sense; the Government was supposed to get its own machines.

'Great God,' Maybelle said. 'Would you all keep quiet. Can't a woman do what she wants with her own stuff? I never saw sotcha commotion as if something'd happened.'

She established her machine under a light bulb. Mrs Maddison sat down beside her. Soon, above the hum of the machines and the women gossiping, Maybelle began to speak to Mrs Maddison in her booming authoritative voice.

'It's better now,' she said.

'Good.'

'This old machine I got from Captain Mike; in them days they made good solid stuff.'

'Yes.'

'I wisht that old man wasn't dead; I useta have a fine time getting drunk with him.'

Mrs Jenkins, on Mrs Maddison's left, sniffed; and young Mrs Harden, alongside Maybelle, giggled and almost stopped working, hoping she'd hear some more.

Maybelle took a deep breath, and for a minute Mrs Maddison wondered whether she was going to burst into song, a big noisy river song for men drinking.

Miss Sampson, who had charge of the sewing-room, appeared.

'Now, ladies, we've got to have all these dresses done by Friday,' she said. 'So get along, less talking, I think …'

'Well,' Maybelle said, 'we kin work better if we talk. We're likely to fall asleep if we don't. Sitting in this gloomy place doing the same old thing every time, makes you sleepy-like.'

'You ought to be glad you've got the work, Maybelle.'

'I am. Don't get yourself in a fret. I am. I'm happy like a bird. That's why I gotta talk; just bubbling up with good spirits.'

Mrs Harden tittered again and Miss Sampson left; it seemed useless to stay. The clients were dreadfully trying at times. She went into the commodities-room to check over work done: she always felt silly after she'd talked to Maybelle.

'The trouble,' Mrs Maddison said, 'is they act like they're doing you a favour, letting you work for fifteen cents an hour. Now I'm not kicking: I sez, times is bad, we gotta work for what we kin get. But work's work; it's no favour to nobody.'

'I'll have a race,' Maybelle shouted suddenly. 'I'll bet old Jemima against any of those fiddling machines you gals is working on. I'm starting on the right sleeve. I'll bet I kin get done faster than any of you.'

From all over the room the bet was taken up. 'You start us off, Flora,' Maybelle said. 'And no cheaters. Lissen, Miz Drew, you can't race, you already got one seam done. Nor you, neither, Susie Thatch. Come on, the rest of you bum seamstresses.' She bowed over her machine, like a quarterback ready to give signals, her feet poised over the great ornamental pedals.

'One, two, three: Go.'

Machines banged; women stopped working in other parts of the room and stood above the contestants, screaming over the hum of the machines. 'Damn!' Maybelle's voice shouted out. 'I broke my thread.' Furiously she fixed it; women were laughing and swearing, and those racing leaned nearer and nearer the cloth. Negroes collected outside the wide open doors and watched and laughed. Suddenly Maybelle's voice went up like a rocket. 'I'm done! I won!' All the women jammed around her to see the sleeve, to look at the wondrous and titanic Jemima which was a sturdier implement than any of the Government's contraptions.

Miss Sampson walked into this bedlam. She spread order like a nurse, driving the children away from a pillow-fight and back into bed. Everyone was quiet, a little guilty and thoroughly subdued, except Maybelle and Mrs Maddison. Mrs Maddison leaned over her machine and laughed up and down the scale, wiping her tears away. 'If you could of seen yourself, Maybelle.'

'That's enough,' Miss Sampson said. 'This isn't kindergarten.'

'But you wanted them dresses done quick,' Maybelle said, trying to look wide-eyed and abused.

Mrs Maddison went on laughing. 'It's worth losing the job,' she said, 'just to of seen you. I never saw a woman look like that. You big old mountain, shaking like a jello over that fool machine of yours ...'

Mrs Cahill watched the two of them, thinking what a pair: they'd find some way to amuse themselves if the world was blowing away. They'd probably bet on which trees would blow off first.

'Tennessee came to see me this morning.' Mrs Maddison stopped laughing at once. 'She said she was leaving Bill and she made out her application for Relief.'

Mrs Maddison nodded.

'I'm sorry about it,' Mrs Cahill said. 'But I don't think there was anything else she could do. We'll get her on Relief as fast as we can.'

'Where's she gonna live?' Mrs Maddison asked, ashamed she had to find this out from Mrs Cahill, and trying to seem casual about it, as if she didn't know because she hadn't had time to see her daughter yet.

'She's moving in with Alec and Sabine.'

'That's a small place.'

'We can get a bed for her; I think she'll be all right there. They're happy to have her.'

'Yes.' And so would she be happy to have her; and she had a bed, and a fine bright room waiting. Alec's house was falling to pieces and the damp came through the walls in wide brown patches, and Sabine was no good as a housekeeper, she was too young to care or to know how pretty a house could be. 'Yes; well, that's fine,' Mrs Maddison said, wearing her pride all around her.

Mrs Cahill paused and then said: 'Would you like to help mother this afternoon? She's starting her spring house-cleaning and she'd like somebody who wouldn't wash them into holes to clean up the curtains. She'll give you a half-dollar, I guess ... if you've got the time.'

'That'll be fine, Miss Lucy. I'll go right over from here.'

Maybelle had been listening, and when Mrs Cahill moved away she said: 'Anyhow, Flora, she's leaving Bill and that's better for her and you wanted that.'

'Yes.'

'And you kin see her just as much as you want at Alec's.'

'Yes.'

'It's better living alone when you're old, Flora. Young people's so messy, and Tiny and all.'

Mrs Maddison looked at her, saying nothing.

'All right, Flora, I know it's lonely and you want her but don't break your heart over it, she'll get over this in a week, you just wait.'

Mrs Maddison smiled and thought even a week was a long time …

With the fifty cents she bought a quart of milk and some cream of wheat and oranges, and stopped by Alec's on her way home. She called at the door but no one came and no one spoke. She left the package on the step and went home. Her arms ached from scrubbing the curtains, and she refused to think about Tennessee. She ate quickly, almost nothing, and then, in the evening cool, she sat on her front porch and rocked and brushed her hair slowly in long soothing strokes.

After a while Mrs MacIvor came out and nodded, and then presently the small gay stars appeared over Louisiana. Mrs Maddison went indoors and got her harmonica and came out on the porch and began playing the few tunes she knew, sad lazy music that had been floating over the river as long as she could remember. Mrs MacIvor moved on to Mrs Maddison's steps and Lena wandered over with Maybelle. Mrs Wilson came and was given a seat because she had rheumatism. They burned some rags against the mosquitoes and no one talked, and softly, insistently, the music curled over them in a thin streamlike smoke. The dynamo hummed in the power house, but gently, making no interruption of the quiet, and more stars came out. The weeping willow swished above the water, and the old women sat on Mrs Maddison's porch, resting after the effort of having lived another day.

## II. MRS MADDISON RETURNS TO THE LAND

In the Relief office they had read the bulletins coming from Washington via State headquarters, and they had received a good many visitors called field supervisors and field representatives. Under pressure and feeling theirs-not-to-reason-why, they had shipped unemployed families back to the land. It was a programme, which made it vast and important, possible of endless interpretation and confusion, and above all it had to be done quickly. Some of the Relief workers, who had lived long in these parts and knew conditions and what you had to have to farm, and what kind of land they were putting people on, and what the houses meant in ill-health, shook their heads grimly but in wise silence. Rural rehabilitation: in itself a magnificent idea. A chance for men to be again self-supporting; their own masters; captains of their destinies, souls, pocket-books. 'It's a fine idea,' Mrs Cahill said, 'only nobody seems to have thought much about those negro shanties we're putting our folks in.' Mrs Lewis, who worked out towards the sawmill district, said it certainly was a fine idea, but she thought there'd be some trouble about medical aid: she also shook her head. 'The malaria,' Mrs Lewis said. Miss Ogilvie, who had a sharper tongue than the others, and used to lie awake at night furtively being ashamed of herself for having such a nice bed, said: 'It sez, in the bulletins, $105.80 a year is the average cost to the govment for rural rehab. families; for everything personal. Lissen to me,' she said, with the sun shining on her eyeglasses. 'That just isn't human. And to think those northerners made all that fuss about slaves. I don't think they got their heads screwed on right up there.'

Mrs Cahill brooded over the present and future of Mrs Maddison and her children. She realised that Mrs Maddison was starving herself, doing some very fine and tricky work with her Relief money in order to coddle Tiny. She liked Mrs Maddison and thought Tennessee was stupid, sexually awake only, selfish, and that Tiny had so few chances of being a decent or healthy citizen that Mrs Maddison's sacrifice probably came under the heading of heroic if senseless gestures.

She wanted very much to get Mrs Maddison away from Tennessee's dis-affection, and she also liked Alec, and thought he could do with something to eat for a change. But rural rehabilitation … Something about the name upset Mrs Cahill, who was fairly simple and usually said what she meant. It was such a vast sound, such a stupendous and splendid idea, and when you got right down to it, it was a chance to live in an abandoned negro shanty or a badly made, too small, new house; without adequate water, heat or light, with inadequate provision for staple groceries or clothes or medical care: and work until your back broke to raise a crop for which there might or might not be buyers. Obviously it was easier to be in debt to the Government than to private landowners. The Government, being so much bigger, sometimes got a little entangled and forgot to collect on time or just lent you more money to pay back with. But the idea distressed her, still.

She talked this problem over with the local administrator and finally she approached Alec, calling on him one day when he was sitting on the river-bank fishing quite hopelessly, but fooling himself into feeling busy.

'Alec,' Mrs Cahill said, 'have you ever thought about farming?'

'No'm.'

'Would you like to go on a farm?'

Alec thought. He thought about farms as he remembered them and they seemed not unpleasant. Anyhow, a lot better than this overcrowded hut he was living in. And vaguely he had an idea that his mother had baked pies. There would, of course, be a catch in it somewhere.

'I'm not gonna take no Relief,' he said rather sulkily.

'It isn't Relief, Alec, it's a loan the Government makes you and you've got some years to pay it back. They give you a certain amount of stuff, farm animals, and tools, and feed, and fertiliser, and seed, and groceries and such; and you make a crop and you pay some money back to the Government.'

'Like on shares,' Alec said.

'Well.' Mrs Cahill was a little embarrassed. She knew that most enlightened people did not feel the share cropper system was all that might be hoped. However. 'Well. Sort of.'

'Who'll go, just me and Sabine or all of us?'

'Well, I thought if we could arrange it, you and your mother and your wife would go – the houses aren't very big and Tiny's so small, it might be better for her to stay here with Tennessee.'

'Where'll they live then? Tennessee can't live way off down here with that drunk husband of hers around.'

'No, I thought Tennessee could take Mrs Maddison's house while you're on the farm. That way it'd be all right.'

'I'll think about it.' Alec was careful not to show pleasure or surprise; he mistrusted the Government, and all employers, deeply. It always sounded better than what you got in the end. No sense acting happy; then they'd cut you down even more. But a series of new ideas started in his head: satisfactory images and plans. The first picture he evoked was one of a table groaning with food, home-made preserves and things from the garden and fried chicken from their own backyard and pitchers of milk and corn bread and good pale butter. He tightened his jeans around him and wandered back to find Sabine and tell her warily about the future.

Sabine was sick of their cabin and especially now that Tennessee and the baby were there, and it was so crowded she couldn't properly wash things out, or cook, or ever be quiet. Without saying anything to Alec or comparing notes she too had a vision of wonderful food. And maybe a good dress for coming in to town after the first crop; and some new silk stockings and even a permanent. She said casually that it looked all right to her and better ask Mrs Maddison.

Mrs Maddison's reasons were very simple: Tennessee and the baby would have a nice house if she left and then she wouldn't have to go around acting to the neighbours as if she and Tennessee saw each other and behave as daughter and mother should. When, in fact, Tennessee didn't speak and Mrs Maddison felt more and more lonely and unwanted every day. And she was getting headaches from the sewing-room; her ten cent store glasses didn't seem to be so good after all. And then again, food. And maybe a garden. She saw the house in her mind: a neat little white house with roses all over it and several large magnolia trees and things on shelves in jars, very good to eat, which she had made herself, and curtains at the windows.

The Maddisons agreed. Mrs Cahill wangled. Many papers were made out and signed. Mrs Maddison had a grand time rushing up to the Relief office, panting and flushed and clamouring for her rights and being stern and saying, I know Mr Roosevelt wouldn't mean for us not to have oil lamps.

Finally after a month of negotiations they were put into a Ford truck with whatever baggage they thought necessary or pleasant, and driven to their new start in life. They returned to the land.

\* \* \*

'Oh,' Mrs Maddison said. She stood with a rolled patchwork quilt under one arm, and in her other hand, a market basket full of oddments, notably an alarm clock, a potato masher, two bars of laundry soap and some rope for hanging up the wash.

Sabine stared too but she could find nothing to say; and behind her, alarmed but not realising the extent of the disaster, stood Alec with his mouth open.

'Gimme a hand bud,' the truck-driver said. 'I'll help you get the big pieces in but I gotta hurry along; I got some other famblies moving out today.'

Alec helped lift down the rusted stove they had brought from his shack; bed-posts; a table; a chest. He went in the house finally, with a chair resting over his head, and stopped in the middle of the floor, looking about him. He didn't know what to do. His instinct and his first desire were to cry out to this man, who was going to leave, 'Don't go, don't leave us here.' And then quickly, he thought: if only we could go back with him … They were so far away; they were so alone and so helpless. What would they do here; how could they live in this place. Suddenly he realised that farming was not a job like salvaging iron: you had to know what to do, and when. And also you had to know what to expect.

Sabine was crying softly behind him. 'They shoulda told us,' she kept saying. 'It ain't right.'

Mrs Maddison was still outside; she had not moved. She didn't notice that the handle of the market basket was eating into her hand and that her arm and shoulder were getting stiff, holding the quilt. These things took time: when you had made a picture, clear and neat in your mind, it took time to erase it. She saw plainly the house she had imagined: white, with roses growing untidily all over it. There should perhaps have been a grey cat asleep on the doorstep in the sun. The curtains would already be up … Mrs Cahill had been very uncertain about moving white families into abandoned negro shanties: these houses weren't even desirable for negroes she had felt, and that – by local tradition – was saying a good deal. It's got a tired look, Mrs Maddison thought, tired and worn-out and dirty. The kind of place you thought you'd die in, on the days when you were blue. Mrs Maddison felt that it was too late to start again; what kind of God was it, who was after her. Driving her from one filthy rattle-trap shack to another, driving and driving. She had a right to be tired; she had a right not to try any more.

'Where's Ma?' Alec said.

'Outside.'

'C'mon in, Ma,' Alec shouted, and there was irritation and despair in his voice; 'c'mon in and see the fine house your Relief got us.'

She waited a moment longer. It would take a little more courage to go inside, though she could imagine how it was. And she thought: they're young and they're not used to things. I'm the one's got to say something cheerful.

She climbed up the rickety steps. There were two front rooms, both having doors on to the porch. Behind one of them there was a lean-to addition, for a kitchen. It was the simplest form of house. She looked at both rooms and bent a little getting through the low door into the kitchen.

'Well,' she said.

They waited. Somehow they felt this was her fault. She was older. She should have known the kind of place they were coming to. They looked at her without kindness.

'Well,' Mrs Maddison said, 'I reckon Sabine and me can fix it up so's it'll be all right. It'll be all right in a coupla years.'

Alec laughed: 'We'll be dead first. We'll freeze in this place in winter. Look,' he said. Angrily he ripped more of the torn paper from the walls; light showed through gaps in the wall. 'Rain,' he said, 'we'll be washed outa bed, that's what. And how're we gonna git warm in a place like this.' Sabine, catching his anger, kicked her heel hard against the floor and the planking splintered and went through.

'Don't do that,' Mrs Maddison said. 'You don't have to show me. But we gotta live here. We don't have no other place to live. So we better get busy about it.'

'Your Relief,' Alec said in fury. 'It's your Relief's doing.'

Mrs Maddison put down her bundles on the floor. She stood up before him, a thin, old woman with her hair tightly drawn over the top of her head, sharp-faced and tired, her cheeks fallen in where teeth were missing.

'Lissen to me, Alec Maddison. Don't you talk like that to me. And don't go on saying foolishness. I'd of been dead if it warn't for that Relief. And Miss Lucy's a good woman. And Mr Roosevelt's a fine man. He's got a good kind face and he's doing what he can for us. Only it takes time. They gotta make mistakes like everybody. But don't you go blaming everything on them. And you jest get busy and set up that bed there, and put the stove where it belongs, and get the pipe fixed up on it, and Sabine, you get busy with a broom and clean out this place and don't look like somebody's stole your last penny. If we gotta live here, we gotta live here. No sense talking.'

Resentfully they obeyed her. Mrs Maddison unpacked what china and pots and pans they had; put clothes and odd bits of linen into the chest. She sang thinly as she worked. She made a lot of noise, too, trying to keep a silence from settling on the house. It's up to me she thought, they're too young yet. They get discouraged. It's up to me. Suddenly she felt a great pride that their three lives and their happiness and success depended on her: that she was the one who would keep things going, and somehow make a triumph out of this gloomy and decrepit house. It had to be done; it was another job. One more thing to get through before she died. She'd manage it too. The worst thing, Mrs Maddison decided, would be ever to admit that you didn't have any hope left at all, and that living was too much for you.

* * *

Alec was a bad farmer, and Sabine an unwilling housewife. Mrs Maddison, with love, sought to make excuses for them. It was true that they had little to work with. The mule named Thomas was old, embittered and weary. It was no joke ploughing up the field, holding the plough down with blistered hands, behind that languid and uncertain animal. Thomas had a tendency to wander off, suddenly bored by the straight line. It was also true that Alec had to haul water on a crude handmade sled, from a well about fifteen minutes walking down the road. There was no well on the place: they rationed water as if they were on a raft, with the salt ocean swelling ominously about them. And she and Sabine had to take their clothes to a pond over the hill, a greenish pond, where mosquitoes sang their welcome, to wash them. And there were no screens, and no mosquito-nets for the beds, so that sleeping was uneasy, a drugged, resentful fight against the whining pests. And the house; oh yes, Mrs Maddison told herself, it's bad. But still. She could not keep herself from singing, a thin monotonous song, as she worked. In the evenings she sat on the porch alone, beside her pot of evil-burning rags, and looked over the land. With contentment, and a kind of proud peacefulness that Alec and Sabine found maddening.

Alec was planting cotton: it was the only pay crop (if there were buyers) and the Government demanded this. The farm was twenty acres in all; and he intended to put in eight acres of cotton. By turns, and depending on his anger or where he'd been ploughing, he said: the land's clay ... it's nothing but sand, no cotton nor nothing else'll grow ... rocks, rocks, God I oughta be ploughing with dynamite ... The vegetable garden became Mrs Maddison's affair: turnips and squash, peas, beans, beets, carrots, lettuce, potatoes, corn and suddenly, from nowhere, mysteriously, she produced flower seeds: larkspur and asters and a few brown, frail-looking rose plants, carefully embedded by the porch pillars. Mrs Maddison saw everything green and rich already. Later, she thought, when we've made the crop, we'll buy chickens and a cow. The fullness of life. There might be money for paint too, and new planks to nail over the rotting floor boards, and windows later, and yards of bright print for curtains. It would be a home. She'd live long enough to make it into a home.

Sabine would get up in the morning, with a fretful look on her mouth, and say 'T'aint no use doing anything with this house.' In silence Alec hitched the plough behind Thomas and set out for the fields. Sabine and Alec worked against their disgust, wearily, and came back at nights to hate this place where they had to live. Mrs Maddison could find no words to encourage them. Now, before the garden came up, they had to live sparingly on corn bread and sorghum and turnip greens which she bought at the crossroads store five miles away: and the coffee was thin, trying to use as little of it as possible, only coloured water: and the milk was oily and yellowish from the can ... But in June the garden would be coming on, and there'd be flowers on the cotton. And all summer afterwards they could eat their own things, the fresh green things from their own land; and by September – only five months, only five months – they'd be picking cotton. And then. Maybe Miss Lucy could get them a cow before then. She dreamed as she worked.

There wasn't much to do about the house. The grey, unpainted walls, darkened in places from smoke, always seemed dirty. But, being spring, the broken windows didn't matter so much. She thought about them a good deal and finally wrote a letter, with difficulty, to Mrs Cahill, saying that there were five windows in the house and all broken: now if she could get some cheesecloth to tack over them, that would anyhow keep out the flies, and maybe when next Alec went to town he could pick up a few boards for shutters in case it rained. And so maybe it would be best if she just knocked out the windows altogether, since they were jagged-like and ugly; and could Mrs Cahill maybe get her some cheesecloth. The cheesecloth arrived, together with a box of tacks, and Mrs Maddison was as excited as if she'd suddenly been given velvet curtains to hang sumptuously over French windows ...

She dug up the garden and planted the seeds. Alec and Sabine together planted the cotton seed in the brown narrow furrows of earth in the fields. Mrs Maddison was alone in the house all day. There wasn't much cooking to do, because, finally, it always seemed to be pan bread or corn bread and sorghum and whatever else she could find or invent or afford, to eke this out. She wanted the garden to be big and the Government had been generous with seeds. She wrote a few letters, almost drawing the words as if each one were a picture, asking for magazines – she would again paper the walls gaily and cleanly. Mrs Cahill, who could not forget the old woman in that evil, decaying shack, sent her several yards of cheap print in startling colours. Mrs Maddison made curtains and bed spreads, and hung a length of it over the low door to the kitchen, which at least shut off the sight of that place, if not the smell.

It grew hot. Alec was working without a hat in the fields and he would come back at noon ominously white with the heat. Sabine made a bonnet for herself from newspapers; she worked in bent, broken, high-heeled slippers, the heels catching in the earth, suddenly jerking her ankle sideways. Before they drank the last of the water that they'd hauled in a keg, it was warmish and had a grey flat taste. Mrs Maddison tended the garden with passion and delicacy, almost luring the seeds to take root and grow. She lay awake at nights thinking of the feathery short green things that would be coming out of the earth. She particularly thought of the flowers. Alec's and Sabine's room had the walls papered now with adver-tisements: there weren't enough magazines, despite Mrs Cahill's efforts, to do both rooms. In the winter, Mrs Maddison thought, when there isn't so much work outside, Sabine and I can make rag rugs so it'll be warmer underfoot. In two years, in three years, this place would be a good place: safe and quiet, with things in jars for the winter and, every summer, plenty in the garden, and a little money coming from the cotton for extras. Safe and quiet: Tennessee and the baby could come too. They'd save money for timber and put up another room. She'd have her family around her. If only they could live it out until the first crop got sold. There were days when her head ached and the garden went black before her eyes: I'm getting old she thought. And then too she was so sick of the food they ate that it was hard to swallow; it rested uneasily on her stomach. She was thinner.

Alec and Sabine were hoeing now, cutting out the plants that grew too close together, weeding, keeping the grass off, breaking the light dry crust of earth that formed over the plants after rain. They never talked: all three of them lived in an agony of fatigue, hurrying, trying each day to keep ahead of the land which didn't want to be worked over and driven; caring for the seeds which seemed animate, each one with its own fragile and demanding life. At night after supper, Alec and Sabine went to bed. And Mrs Maddison, too weary for sleep, sat on the porch, leaning against one of the thin posts that held it up, trying to ease the aches in her body before she lay down. For a while she would sit quietly thinking of nothing; but only identifying the places in her body that meant pain: the shoulders, the centre of her back, her knees, her wrists. She waited for the aches to stop being sharp and separate, knowing that they'd merge into a general weariness that was not hard to bear. And then she could look out over the fields, and her garden beside the house. And look at the sky. Things seemed sure to her now: her life and her children's lives were no longer dependent on other people, on the strange fancies of employers, and the rules and regulations of the Government. Yes, they were in debt: but the Government was going to give them time to pay. It wasn't like being on shares or a tenant, when you never knew where you stood. As long as we grow things, Mrs Maddison thought. She liked the emptiness of the land before her. It's good land Mrs Maddison said to herself, and we're making something to last. Something for the children. There's nothing wrong with being poor Mrs Maddison decided proudly, if you've got your own place, and no one coming to holler about the rent and throw you out; and if you know there's food in your garden, and you don't need to go begging around at every store. It's the begging and not knowing where you're going to be next. 'And work,' she said suddenly aloud, 'Land's sake, no one's ever gonna call my chilrun no-count loafers.'

\* \* \*

A man came and talked with Alec about the cotton; he said he was the farm supervisor for the rural rehabilitation families around here. A woman came and talked to Mrs Maddison about groceries and what they needed in the house: she was the home visitor out this way. The callers made Alec mutely angry. He didn't want anybody butting in his business. Even if they acted nice about it. He could get along. Next time they came Mrs Maddison could just tell them to get the hell out; he'd manage his own farm. Mrs Maddison, who had an entirely personal conception of Government, was encouraged by these visits. For her, simply, it meant that Mr Roosevelt and Mrs Cahill were not forgetting her. If they couldn't come themselves they'd send their people. She was glad of this: she knew Miss Lucy wasn't forgetting her because there was the cheesecloth and the print. But those things were gifts and had nothing to do with the Government. The Government was supposed to be interested and come around every once in a while and ask how you were getting on and ask if they could help. Government was like that. She had been rather boastful with Miss Blythe, who was Mr Roosevelt's representative out that way. She'd shown off her not yet producing garden and her house, and extended her arm largely to exhibit their land, the acres which were theirs, which made them respectable, steady, rooted people with a future. Miss Blythe had been flattering about the house and said she'd try to get their grocery order raised. 'Of course,' Miss Blythe said, 'if you can manage with it being so small – well that's just that much less money to pay back later.' Mrs Maddison liked that too; she was borrowing money, she wasn't begging.

Mrs Maddison told Alec that Mr Roosevelt had some right nice people working for him out this way; but Alec was neither interested nor pleased.

Sabine and Alec were more than silent; they were sullen now. They hated everything about the farm, and they had no faith in it. Alec used to say bitterly he knew his cotton would be bad, or it'd rain too much later, or there'd be boll weevil; or no buyers. He didn't believe anything could come of this; he saw the future as a long half-starved drudgery, slaving for nothing. And the silent days and the silent nights. Sabine saw herself growing ugly, her hair straight and unkempt, her hands coarse; no clothes, no finery, no fun. No girls to gossip with and no dances or any of the things she wanted. At least, in town, they could get together with their friends and have a little drink and somebody could always play a fiddle and they could go uptown and look at the stores anyhow. But this: working yourself to death and nothing to show for it. Those hateful ugly selfish little cotton plants.

Mrs Maddison was going calling. She was in such a good humour that she had to share it. She walked over the dusty reddish roads, with her hat sitting up on top of her head, where it would shade her, but not press down and give her headache. Her gingham dress was darned till it seemed to be covered with white sores. None of this worried her; she was going graciously to pay a call on Mrs Lowry and pass the time of day, and talk brightly of the future.

Mrs Lowry was sitting on her porch fanning herself. She was about Mrs Maddison's age. Mrs Maddison said, 'Howdy, Mrs Lowry, fine weather we're having' and they sat down to talk. Mrs Lowry said it was a treat, she never saw anybody for a month of Sundays and she'd have come to see Mrs Maddison but they were that busy. 'Farming,' Mrs Lowry said; 'you just gotta keep at it every second till you die.' But she seemed proud of it on the whole. Mrs Maddison liked her. She thought it would be nice in the winter, when they had more time, and she and Mrs Lowry could swap recipes and patterns for crocheting. Later, when the vegetables had been canned and the cotton sold.

Mrs Lowry had been in her house a year. 'Lawd knows it's nothin' to look at,' she said. 'But you ought of seen it when we come. Dirty, I never seen such a place. Now we got our own vegetables put up, and suchlike; we're gettin' on all right. It's worst the first year.'

Mrs Maddison agreed.

'The bad thing is the young folks,' Mrs Lowry said. 'There's no fun for them. And they don't have no patience, poor things.'

'Later,' Mrs Maddison said to Mrs Lowry, her eyes shining with the thought of it, 'when we're all fixed up and everybody's not working so hard, we'll get together and have a barn dance. I see you gotta barn here, and we could sweep it out and fix it up pretty, and everybody bring a little something themselves, and have a real party.'

She had said this breathlessly, hurrying before the vision failed her. In her mind, the barn was filled with young men and girls, dressed as she had been dressed when she was young and went to a party. They'd be doing square dances, and the fiddlers thumping with their feet on the floor to keep time. And apple-bobbing. And blind man's buff. All the neighbours there together, being gay and serene, and every man sure of his home, sure of tomorrow, and easy with today.

Mrs Lowry understood her excitement. 'If only the young folks'll wait,' she said. 'We'll have a good time yet before we die.'

\* \* \*

Alec lay in his darkened room and Sabine talked to Mrs Maddison in savage whispers.

'We're going,' she said. 'Soon's he can move we're going. We're not gonna stay out here to get ourselves killed. Sunstroke,' she said, and her whisper was shrill. 'He'll be laying in the fields dead next. And me with the malaria. What kinda life is that? They can't make us stay. We hate this place 'n' we're going quick; 'n' we're never coming back. So.'

Mrs Maddison twisted her hands in her lap. There were roses now, climbing up the door posts, and even if the posts were unpainted and the house grey and streaked behind them, these were real roses. Next year there would be more and maybe paint, too. The garden was green and just looking at it made you feel rich and safe. She'd been serving her own vegetables now for weeks. Next year, if they had a cow, there'd be butter to put on the new tender carrots and the beets, and the fresh green peas. The cotton was coming out thinly in the fields, but it was only the beginning.

She'd gone down and picked a boll, and held the soft white fluff in her hands gently. This was money; of course there'd be a buyer and fine prices. This was more lumber for another room, and shoes, and a buggy, maybe. The worst was over. Things were growing. Larkspur and roses and squash and potatoes and cotton. This was what life meant, if life was good. She'd even gotten her room papered in advertisements now. With money, they could buy boards, make furniture, a solid roof, a whole floor, and paint to make it clean and gay. They had only now to live a little carefully and everything would come to them. They were safe now and what lay ahead was more safety and even ease. In the winter, when they couldn't work after dark and there was nothing much to do anyhow, there were the neighbours. All the things she'd planned and dreamed.

'Sabine,' she said softly, 'he'll get over it in a day or so. 'N' you'll get over the malaria. Miss Blythe said she'd send some quinine. We done the work, Sabine. You can't go now. The worst is all over.'

'We're going. And don't you try to stop us, neither. You're old and you don't expect to get any fun outa life. But we're young. And we're not gonna stay around here and kill ourselves.'

'You won't have any fun back in that old shack of yours. You won't even have stuff to eat. What kinda life is that, then? Sabine, we worked so hard,' Mrs Maddison said. There were tears in her eyes, but she was not looking at the younger woman. She was looking out the door, at the roses. For the last month it had seemed to her that not only Mr Roosevelt and Mrs Cahill were remembering her, but God also. The things she wanted: a home, and roses, and food, and quiet when the work was over, and a place to live and be. Tennessee could come in the fall; when they had a little money, too. She was an old woman and she was a lucky one: she had everything she could want.

She cried out against this dreadful and wanton thing they meant to do: leave the land when things were growing; leave the cotton unpicked and the garden going to weeds and waste. And the house they'd made into something like a home; let it rot back again into a worn-out negro shanty. But she knew they wouldn't listen to her. Miss Blythe came and argued and so did the farm foreman: he even threatened Alec, saying 'You'll never get a loan again' and 'You're a low quitter, that's what you are.' Alec was ill, and hysterically obstinate; something had happened to him. He hated the land beyond any explanation. He would rather starve than stay there; it was a slavery to him and a bleak, empty, exhausting life, with none of the things that made for pleasure. Sabine chattered with chills and burned with fever, and cursed the home visitor and the farm foreman and Mrs Maddison, and said she'd crawl to town on her hands and knees if she had to, but she wasn't going to stay out here in this hole and kill herself, and get ugly, and go crazy with the work, and no fun ever, ever, ever.

The entire neighbourhood got drawn into this, and Mrs Lowry stood on the porch with Mrs Maddison, one day at sunset, looking out over the white beginnings of the cotton, and the greenness of the garden and said: 'It's a sin and a shame, Flora. They'll be sorry, too.'

Mrs Cahill drove out in her uncertain Ford and tried to talk to Alec, who wouldn't listen. Mrs Maddison could not stay on alone; the work was too much for her. She couldn't keep the cotton cultivated and do the garden too. 'You'd be having sunstroke next,' Mrs Cahill said and smiled.

'He did have a sunstroke,' Mrs Maddison said abruptly. 'It was a real bad sunstroke and he was sick's a baby.'

'I know.' Mrs Cahill put her hand on Mrs Maddison's shoulder. The old woman would defend those no-count children if they did murder.

'Would you like to take home some roses, Miss Lucy, or some larkspur? It's all gonna be wasted now.'

She stood beside her flowers weeping quietly and helplessly. 'All wasted,' she said. 'It all come to nothing.'

'Alec deserves a beating,' Mrs Cahill said furiously. 'He's selfish, and he's being stupid, too. Sabine's a fool and you couldn't expect anything else of her. But Alec. I'd like to get some big strong man to give him the beating of his life.'

'It's only that he's not hisself. He's still weakish from that there sunstroke. But it's gonna be too late when he sees what he done. We'll of lost the place then.'

Mrs Cahill put her arm around Mrs Maddison's shoulder. 'You've done your best, darling. Nobody'll ever blame you. You made a fine place here and somebody'll be lucky to get it, and they'll know what a good worker you are. We'll see you get taken care of all right in town. I'm sorry. I'm sorrier than I can tell you.'

'We were all fixed,' Mrs Maddison said. 'We could of lived like real people again. Well,' she said, 'how's things in the sewing-room, Miss Lucy?'

Finally Mrs Cahill drove Alec and Sabine back with her. She thought it would be easier for Mrs Maddison to have them out of the way. The driver would come with the truck tomorrow or the next day and move Mrs Maddison and their possessions back into town. The land couldn't be wasted; someone would have to work it and try to profit by it and pay back the debt. Mrs Cahill drove in angry silence. Once Sabine started to talk to her and she turned and said: 'You're a no-count girl, Sabine, and you've got a no-count husband, and I don't want any truck with you. You've broken that poor old woman's heart and you deserve anything that comes to you. I'll drive you to town but I won't act friendly with you.'

Mrs Maddison had something to do. Before it grew dark, before she slept. Now that her son had really done this thing; gone away, not caring for the land or the money he owed. She got out a block of ruled paper and a stubby pencil and began: Dear Mr Roosevelt:

It was a long letter. She explained Alec's sunstroke and Sabine's malaria, and how hard it had been for over four months, working with so little and the house cheerless and such poor food. She told about everything which excused Alec in his desertion; but loyally, she said too, that the garden was fine now, and the cotton coming up. She hoped he wouldn't be too disappointed in Alec, but Alec was young, and when you were young you were foolish, and did bad things without knowing. She hoped he would excuse Alec. She was grateful for the things Mr Roosevelt had done, and she would work to pay back the money they owed but she was afraid it would take a long time. Work was so hard to get and money so scarce. She enclosed a short spray of larkspur because she wanted him to know that it was a fine place she was leaving ...

She sat alone on the front porch and watched the stars come out. It had all come to nothing. The safety and the ease that was ahead, and the good times, and having a place and being someone. Nothing. The land was fine and beautiful she thought, and she could smell the roses in the dark.

## III. MRS MADDISON AND HER CHILDREN

Alec and Sabine were going to give a party to celebrate their return to the land of the living. Tennessee had moved to their shack, as soon as she heard her mother was leaving the farm. All three of them invited their friends. It was going to be a fiddling party. Dancing was impossible in Alec's home, both because of space and because of the weakness of the flooring. But people could stamp time, and sing; and somehow, without visible explanation, there would be whisky in jugs. Both Alec and Sabine were thin and still frail from their illness, but they were in fine spirits now. At last, something that was fun. After that hated farm, those barren months which seemed years, and at the same time were almost forgotten.

Mrs Maddison returned to her own house, the day of the party: but she was not invited. It was a young people's party to begin with, and besides that, her children did not feel tenderly towards her.

Bill had disappeared, and Tennessee, knowing this had to be, still held rancour against her mother, as if in some mysterious way, Mrs Maddison was the cause of Bill's drinking. Someone had told Tennessee that Bill was looking for work in Biloxi. If only he found a job. He was her man anyhow: her mother didn't have a right to judge him.

It was dark, and guests began to straggle along the narrow path to their cabin. They could hear voices first and then people calling: the first arrivals were the fiddlers.

The men stood around outside, a little shy, stamping their feet and laughing and talking with Alec. Then they came in: a young man and two old men, one with a stubble of whitish beard on his face. They had their fiddles under their arms. Some strings were always missing. And there was no certainty about the tuning. But they made a grand gay noise. Couples began to drift in: one young woman brought her child, a baby of about nine months, and put him on the bed, under the mosquito netting with Tiny. The children slept quietly through all the noise. There weren't enough chairs to go round; some of the guests sat on the floor and others leaned against the wall, or huddled together on the second bed. Water was dipped out of a bucket. The men passed the whisky jug around and swigged it straight; there were a few cups and these were given to the women and a little water was mixed with the whisky. There were fourteen people in the cabin by the time the last guest came: and it was hot.

Outside in the darkness, mosquitoes droned over the swampy land where the river had receded; and the thick rushing sound of the Mississippi slurred over all other noises. Two oil lamps lighted the cabin: there was only one room. Tennessee stood by the water bucket, and passed the whisky jug when it was required. Her face gleamed with sweat: it was sun-browned and now had an oiled shining look. She wore her hair to her shoulders, loose and thick, held herself well, and her body was firm and inviting beneath her gingham dress. She was barefooted as was Sabine: the other women had shoes over bare feet, because they had been walking through the woods to get here. One man suddenly ripped off his sweat-soaked shirt, and sat with the lamp-light picking out little threads of sweat on his naked chest. The fiddling went on.

Someone called out the name of a song and the young fiddler said humbly that he wasn't good enough. And they all said: 'Sure y'are Jakie, go ahead Jakie. Attaboy, you kin play that fiddle.' Another man took a few straws from a broom and settled himself beside Jakie: Jakie laid the fiddle on his knees. It was a quick tune; the straws were to keep the beat, and to syncopate it: they whined against the wood of the fiddle as Jakie plucked the strings. Feet thumped faster and faster. When it was over everybody had another swig from the jug and told Jakie how good he was. The music was making them dizzy, the music and the heat and the whisky. Now all the tunes were fast, fast and yet whining, the strange melancholy music of the river. They had a hypnotic quality, the insistence on one phrase, monotonous swift music. The women swayed a little as they tapped their heels against the floor. Tennessee lifted her arm slowly to push back her hair and the young fiddler watched her with covetous eyes. Everyone was getting drunk. A man sitting beside his wife on the bed, leaned across and kissed her at the opening of her dress, and they all noticed this almost as if it were a signal given.

The children slept without moving. The fiddlers were getting a little tired, so they played slower music and everyone sang the verses; the long saga-like songs, with the refrain always the same. Tennessee began to think about the young fiddler; he had black hair curling close to his head and a fine strong neck. She moved across the room to him, as if she were walking in her sleep. The young fiddler felt her coming: he stayed bowed over his fiddle, slowly plucking at the strings, as if he were calling to her that way. She sat down on the floor beside him and watched him. The jug went the rounds again.

Someone named another song; and the old fiddler took out a dirty red handkerchief and ran it all over his face and head, and asked for some whisky before he began.

Tennessee, softly, as if he and she were alone in the room, her eyes a little glazed from drink, moved alongside the young fiddler and leaned her back against his leg. He pressed his leg against her: he felt as if his whole side was suddenly against coals, burning, but not hurting. The fast music started again. Alec held Sabine on his lap, holding her back against him, a little stretched out, so that the cloth of her dress was tight over her stomach and legs. The men who had come without women were beginning to look enviously around them. The young fiddler dropped out, leaving the two others to carry the tune. He reached for the jug and took a long unhesitating drink. He wiped his face with his hand and shook the sweat from his eyes. Then slowly, he looked down at Tennessee. He leaned over her suddenly, putting his hands around her, on her breasts, and kissed her where her throat joined her shoulder. Tennessee didn't move: her body felt limp and easy. The young fiddler stayed so a moment, bent over her.

A voice from the door, a thick furious voice, said: 'Git your hands off my wife.'

The music stopped.

The young fiddler straightened up and Tennessee fell backwards from him, supporting herself on her elbow. Bill stood in the door. Bill was drunk obviously. His eyes couldn't seem to look straight at anything, but he had seen enough. His face was red and ugly; and he stood there in the door as if uncertain where to begin, as if he couldn't decide where to start his vengeance.

'You dirty whore,' he said to Tennessee; but nobody minded talk. 'I'm taking you home with me. I'm gonna give you such a beating you'll learn to go around whoring. I'm gonna beat your skin off of you. You seem to of forgot,' Bill said very carefully, 'I'm the one's your husband.' There was a silence. 'Any guy that thinks different can say so,' Bill said staring at the young fiddler.

Bill started across the floor towards Tennessee and no one stopped him; it was true, she was his wife, he had a right. He stood above Tennessee who watched him with black fascinated eyes, and suddenly he brought his fist smashing down on her bare shoulder, at the place where the young fiddler had kissed her.

'Alec,' Tennessee screamed, 'he'll kill me, he'll kill me.'

No one moved: they seemed all helpless with drink, confused, and unable to manage or direct their bodies.

Bill pulled her up from the floor by the arm, roughly, and started back towards the door. 'Alec, Alec, you won't let him, you won't let him, he'll kill me.' With the back of his hand, Bill struck her across the mouth to silence her. But Alec had finally understood. He shouted at Bill: 'Leave my sister here. Here's her home. Git on out; nobody told you to come here.'

Bill turned; it was the young fiddler he wanted to kill, but no one was going to tell him what he could or couldn't do with his wife.

He told Alec what he thought of him in short ugly words. Alec was drunk too, and anyhow no man could talk like that to him, and no man could beat up his sister, right in front of him too. He crossed the room to Bill and got him by the neck of his shirt and pulled him away from the door and from Tennessee. Quietly, people began to drift out of the cabin, into the darkness, with no words. This was a family fight. The old fiddler found his violin case under the bed and picked it up and got out; the young woman lifted her baby from the bed and holding the child as if he were a flour sack, dropped from the cabin to the ground, by the back door, and started home. No use getting mixed up in trouble. Someone took the young fiddler's arm and led him away; he was pretty far gone anyhow. He'd gotten mixed up about the fight; the only thing he could remember clearly was Tennessee's breasts.

Tennessee kneeled on the floor and watched; the men did not fight cleanly or well, they fought with their nails, kicked, butted with their heads, and cursed rhythmically, but not wasting much breath on it. Blood ran from Alec's mouth and Bill's shirt hung from him in shreds. They knocked over a lamp and Sabine screamed and hurled the water bucket on it; the men fought through broken glass, crunching it back and forth across the floor. Suddenly Bill reached for the whisky jug, grabbed it by the handle and swung it over his head. Tennessee rose like wind and pushed him from behind, at his knees so that his balance was lost and Alec flung himself against Bill with all his weight and Bill crashed backwards and sideways, dropping the jug, and fell with his head against the stove. He didn't move and nobody noticed him. Sabine went to Alec and tried to wipe off the blood and get him to lie down on the bed; and Tennessee, picking her way carefully over the broken glass went to the bed where Tiny slept and crept in beside her. She wanted to close her eyes and sleep. There was nothing more to worry about now; for the time being she was safe.

Alec looked at Bill, though the room was dim with only one light burning, and said: 'He'll come around in the mornin'.' He threw a few cupfuls of water down on Bill's head, without bending, or looking closely and went to bed with Sabine. The house was quiet in a few moments: they had all drunk a lot that night.

In the morning they found that Bill was dead.

* * *

Everyone knew of it before Mrs Maddison. It was decided that Maybelle should break the news to her. Maybelle didn't like the job and put it off until afternoon. By that time, many things had happened. Tennessee had called on Mrs Cahill for help: she had sent a telegram to Bill's parents in Jackson and gotten an answer. She was to take the body there for burial: and she was to take Tiny with her and stay. In a crazy despair – because, if he beat her or not, he was still her man, and now he was dead – she turned against Alec, screamed at him, accused him of murdering her husband, said she never wanted to see any of them again, she hated them, she hoped the law would get them. It was her Bill; he was the one she loved; and now they'd gone and killed him. Mrs Cahill's face twisted with disgust: she thought it would be a fine thing for everyone if Tennessee did leave for good. She thought of Mrs Maddison and arranged for the Relief truck to take Tennessee and Tiny and the coffin (covered with tarpaulin so as not to scare the negroes en route) to Jackson. The less accusing Tennessee did, the better. Alec was quiet, helpless and stunned. The worst was that he couldn't be sure he remembered things clearly. But he did know that he hadn't killed anybody. Not really killed. Killing was when you went at a man with your hands or a knife or a gun and tried to finish him. He'd been fighting. He knew that. The sheriff came and took him to jail and locked him up. 'For safe keeping,' he said soothingly to Sabine who was almost as crazy as Tennessee.

By afternoon, things were quiet again on the river-front. Alec's shack was empty because Sabine had moved to her family's house which was uptown behind the box factory. Tennessee and Tiny had gone. And Alec was sitting in jail, looking at his hands, saying to himself, 'I never killed him. I couldn't of.'

Maybelle explained it all to Mrs Maddison. She started in a rush and finished lamely, with pauses between her words. It was hard to say that Tennessee had turned against her brother, and gone away without saying goodbye to her mother. And that Alec was already in jail.

'He didn't kill him Flora,' Maybelle said. 'Nobody thinks that, not even Sheriff. It was fighting; that's different. He fell and hit his head. That don't count the same. Even lawyers say that. It'll be all right Flora.'

Mrs Maddison said nothing. She should at least cry, Maybelle thought, or get up or something. This silence frightened Maybelle. Her friend looked old; she looked like a thin, old woman who is too tired to think or feel.

'They got Alec in jail?' Mrs Maddison said finally.

'Yes, honey. But sheriff knows it ain't like murder.'

'I gotta get a lawyer to talk for him,' Mrs Maddison said.

With what money, Maybelle thought, how's she gonna get money for lawyers and such. That costs; poor people don't have lawyers.

'Sure,' she said, without conviction.

Mrs Maddison sighed. 'Well,' she said, 'what's gotta be has gotta be.'

Maybelle wanted to cry. This was worse than she had imagined. This terrible weariness. She put her hand gently on Mrs Maddison's knee. 'If I kin do anything, Flora,' she said.

Mrs Maddison shook her head. Then she made a great effort and re-membered Maybelle, and patted her hand, and smiled at her.

'The willow's grown since I was on the farm,' she said. 'I'm surprised it's so green. I kinda thought it would git all burned up, what with the heat. It's sure pretty. I'm lucky I got such a nice place to live in.'

Maybelle rose to go then.

'You're a fine woman, Flora,' she said.

Mrs Maddison smiled as if she hadn't heard: 'I'll be seeing you in the sewing-room. I'm gonna start work again tomorrow.'

Mrs Maddison dressed with care and climbed the hill in the sun. She stopped every few minutes, with her hand on her heart, breathing deeply, waiting for the heartbeats to slow. She couldn't understand yet, clearly, what had happened: and maybe I never will, she thought. I'm only a plain woman and maybe these things are too big for me to understand. Maybe I wasn't meant to. For, surely there seemed no reason why this trouble should come to her family; they were not wicked people. She thought, with sorrow, of Tennessee. The girl was too young, she hadn't learned enough yet. It's your own fault, Flora Maddison, she said, you should never of let her marry Bill and we'd all be happy today. She hurried now: poor Alec, sitting there alone. She wouldn't let herself think of Tennessee turning against him.

Alec looked at her silently: he wasn't going to ask her the question; he didn't dare. What if she said …

'No, honey,' Mrs Maddison said, 'you didn't kill him. He just killed hisself. He fell back on the stove and killed hisself. I'm gonna get a big lawyer from Jackson to talk for you. Don't you worry, honey. We'll git everything fixed up fine.' She kissed him on the cheek and sat with him quietly for a time, holding his hands in hers.

'Sabine?' he said.

'Sabine's fine,' Mrs Maddison said, though she knew nothing about her. 'She knows he killed hisself too, honey. Sabine'll be right along now to visit with you. We all love you, son.' And she thought, with pain, of Tennessee, who was too young to know what she was doing.

* * *

September was viciously hot. There was no call for it, decently the summer should be over. Heat hung over the river-front, and only the river moved, swift, thick and brown between the caked mud banks. Mrs Maddison sat on her porch until late at night, almost until dawn, waiting for a little freshness to come into the air so that she could sleep. She played her harmonica very softly, cupping it in her hand. She didn't want to disturb Mrs MacIvor, who had the toothache. If only I could sleep, Mrs Maddison thought. I'm that tired. I'm old, she decided, but she had excuse enough for weariness. She found washing to do, fifty cents for a great bundle, bending over the tub in the heat; sometimes having to go and sit on the porch, without moving, waiting for the blackness to pass from her eyes. She made some children's dresses for a lady uptown, sewing at night by the oil lamp, until she couldn't see the stitches and stopped, knowing the lady wouldn't be pleased if the work came back with great coarse stitches like basting, just because Mrs Maddison's eyes were old. She helped as an extra with the fall house-cleaning in the druggist's house and at the preacher's. People gave her work, if they could. They knew why the old woman was always on the streets, walking fast from one job to the next. Every nickel counted, every nickel was saved, there was Alec waiting …

The heat came at her like an angry hand, pushing up against her throat. It's cool in the jail, she thought; anyhow, there's that. Hurry, hurry. She had some curtains to make for Mrs Guthrie, who ran the hat shop. After the curtains were made, she could probably get some more cleaning, or washing. But how much money did she need? What if she could never get enough; lawyers cost a lot, more than doctors or anybody. Or so she'd heard. She'd never had use for one before.

Maybelle said: take the bus to Jackson and go and see him. Mrs Cahill had mentioned a Mr Everett, who was a fine lawyer and would talk well for Alec, if they could get him.

'But I'll use up my money.'

'You gotta do it, anyhow. You can't write such things to folks. Besides, lawyers, you gotta talk a long time and tell them everything.'

She thought this over for a week, and finally decided to go.

Mr Everett received her in a dim room, which seemed cool and rich to Mrs Maddison. She was badly frightened. What if she could never get enough money? She blinked her eyes, getting used to the gloom, and slowly she told him the story. She told him many things he had no use for, but he let her talk. He watched her, desperate and still too proud to beg for help, and keeping, somehow, a control and restraint on her voice.

'You can pay me later, whatever you can manage,' he said. 'It doesn't look like a difficult case.'

At best, they'd get a verdict of justifiable homicide based on self-defence, and an acquittal; at worst manslaughter, and a lenient judge – Mrs Maddison would make an admirable witness – only a light sentence; ten years, maybe, or even less.

He encouraged her: 'It really isn't a bad case at all, Mrs Maddison. I'd be very surprised if he weren't acquitted. You just go back home and don't worry. I'll do everything that's necessary; and I'll get in touch with you, whenever I have to. Tell the boy to cheer up, too. I'll drive over and see him next week. There's not a thing to worry about.'

Mrs Maddison rose uncertainly and thanked him. She wanted to tell him that she loved him; that all her life she would never forget; that she would work until she dropped to get money to pay him. But she could never thank him for this feeling of being saved, of having someone kind and helping, now, when she was almost exhausted, almost unable to endure her trouble. She could find no words.

'God bless you,' she said, and Mr Everett looked at her, touched and a little amused. She was being a good deal more grateful than he deserved, he thought, but it was nice, anyhow. It made him feel fine. He shook her hand and led her to the door.

Mrs Maddison caught the bus that left at five. It rattled off dustily, and honked and barked through the twilight. She was safe again. Once more she had managed, somehow. She looked at her hands, and knew how old she was; but she had won, anyhow. Until tomorrow or until the next trouble. Her boy would be talked for: and some day Tennessee would learn the things she should know. Indomitably, Mrs Maddison made pictures for herself again: pictures of a reunited and contented family; of plenty, of a home, a garden, things on the shelves in jars. Soothing and strengthening herself with the future, which never came, but was at least always there to dream about.

Dust hung in amber gauze shreds over the road. Trees so close together that they all seemed to grow from the same roots. Here and there stagnant water shone like oil and mosquitoes hummed in the dusk. Negroes got on and off the bus, laughing, their arms full of brown paper parcels, corn meal and flour and a can of sorghum squaring out the bundle. Everybody talked to everybody else; droning like weary flies. 'Here you are, auntie,' the driver said and handed down her parcels to a gaunt, root-gnarled negress. She stood, bent beside her parcels, in the dusty road and waved, and the bus lurched on. Towns made up of a gas station and two stores at a crossroads, and dust and wagons waiting, and negroes dressed in dusty overalls and straw hats, and white men squatting close to the pavement in the shade of the stores, smoking or chewing a long piece of grass …

I'm safe, Mrs Maddison thought, I'm safe for a little while; anyhow, till tomorrow. She leaned her head on her hand and the bus creaked and swayed over the rutted roads, and she fell asleep as it grew dark.

# *Joe and Pete*

WIND BLOWS FLAT and strong across the city and carries the rain with it. The sky is grey green: early November. Ferryville looks as if it had been made hastily by people who had their minds on something else: supply and demand, perhaps, how best to ship the stuff out ... A small radius around the city hall appears to prosper: those few squares where people eat, shop, go to the movies and otherwise spend money. Beyond the city hall stretching to the river, are rows of small houses looking alike. The workers from the factories live in them. They are silent and the rain spatters and bounces on the cracked pavements.

The larger factories lie on a narrow low strip of land beside the river. The Minton soup factory is the biggest. In common with most big factories it hesitates in appearance between a hospital and a prison. It seems to have grown by some curious elementary process of nature: like the amoeba perhaps, dividing and multiplying. Parts are old, ramshackle, clinging to the new bricks and concrete. Runways span the street, the buildings weave and sprawl, dim, unshakable. Doors, like mouseholes, unreasonably pierce the walls anywhere; and faintly, distantly, one can hear the rattle and hum of machinery, see the windows vibrating ...

Not today.

The picket lines were small, groups of men standing at all the thirty entrances, chaffing their hands, moving from foot to foot, mostly silent or saying something briefly to laugh.

'Some job,' a man said. 'Now, if only it was Florida. The next time I strike, I'm gonna do it in summer.'

'They'll be around soon with the coffee.'

'How much longer?'

'Two hours this shift.'

'One thing you gotta hand Joe, he sure has organised this thing. Jees when you think of it, thirty doors you gotta watch all the time, and men to feed and relief pickets and Christ knows how much stuff besides. And the stuff to the papers,' he said, his voice wandering with admiration.

'I wouldn't want Joe's job.'

'He sure knows how to do it.'

A negro with a red muffler tied over his cap, around his ears, came up. He had a water kettle full of coffee, a sack of clanking tin cups (everyone's tin cups), and a bag of sandwiches.

'Hi there.'

They hurried towards him, asking questions. 'How're the other guys, any trouble, anything doing, anybody go home, everything okay?'

'Sure,' the negro said smiling. 'Sure, sure. Everything's fine. You leave it to Joe. You leave it to me. I bring the coffee and Joe got the ideas. Hey, you, leave them sandwiches, one apiece like Joe said. Them sandwiches gotta feed 25 and 27 too.'

A man put one back. 'All right, Jakie.' They swatted him on the back and he walked off, lopsided, careful not to spill a drop of coffee. 'You keep it up till summer,' he said, 'and I'll bring you ice cold beer.'

'Yah!'

'Hey, Jakie, didn't you hear they were gonna have a meeting today, and we're all gonna get forty a week?'

'Listen to him,' Jakie said, laughing in his throat, 'listen to him. When we're daid man, then the Lord's gonna come up to us and say: "You boys get together and make a union and I'll give you what you ask for ef it's in reason.'"

They laughed and moved about the door, stamping their feet, asking each other occasionally what time it was.

Presently the relief crew came up; Joe was with them. They could hear his voice, quiet, very sure, telling some joke about the manager, what the foreman had said when he passed the picket at 17.

The waiting men forgot the cold for a minute, gathering around Joe. 'What's the news, Joe, anything new, everybody all right, nobody went home yet …?'

'I heard the Labor man from Washington would be here tomorrow,' Joe said. 'They'll have to talk then. It'll work out fine. They say those Department of Labor men are okay. They say they can get this stuff straight. How're you? Cold? We sure picked a fine time for our strike, didn't we? We could a had it just as well last spring.'

'Any old time,' one of them said, cheerfully, 'any old time practically since this here plant opened.'

'Well, Joe, we're betting on you,' one of the pickets said, 'you talk straight to them when they get here. You tell them how it is.'

'Yes,' Joe said. They all looked at him a moment, serenely. Their confidence, believing he alone could do what he knew none of them could do, not all of them together, frightened him. 'We gotta keep everybody's spirit up,' he said, 'that's the main thing. Do you hear anybody talking?' he asked.

'Hell no, we're behind this union.'

From nowhere, suddenly, still and swift as a bullet passing, came the word. Scabs. It was a whisper first, a rumour. They must have felt it, standing there, even before a man with red-rimmed eyes, shapeless in his coat, came up to them and hinted it; wondered what now, what shall we do Joe. They stood; Joe waiting, almost as if he expected to hear thunder, his eyes squinting, half shut, and his mouth tight.

Then it came, from the other side of the buildings, angry, deep but clear.

'Scabs! Scabs! Scabs!'

They had all started running, Joe ahead, and over his shoulder he kept saying: 'For God's sake, don't do nothing violent, it'll only hurt us, they'll only lock you up, we can't get away with it. For God's sake,' he said thinly, his breath failing, 'for God's sake, keep your shirts on.'

Around the door of 17, the men had crowded together shouting; there were only gestures now, fists black against the grey green sky, shoving, churning, cursing at a narrow line of men, walking in to the factory with their heads down, each one looking at the other's heels. A double row of police stood by, with their clubs ready, suddenly looking warier, thinner, more dangerous than they ever did on traffic duty. Behind the pickets, more police, the blue coats trim against the grey formless mass of strikers.

From every corner and at once, men came. They left the other doors hurrying to see, their faces strained and furious. Men like themselves, workers like themselves with as little as they, as much to want, coming here with police thick around them, to steal work, to break this strike. After three weeks of this cold, of waiting, of fear at night and the wives doubting, they should come to break the strike, people like themselves. There was a quality of wonder about their anger. This was something they had been prepared for, but could not believe. They could understand that the police were against them, the management, and the newspapers. But not others like themselves.

Joe was there, running between the police and his own men, taking an arm here and saying: 'For God's sake, don't, don't.' Pushing someone back, shouting: 'Don't give them a chance, this is what they want.' Pleading: 'Wait, the men from Washington will be here, we'll lose everything if ...'

A policeman pushed him, said: 'Get out of the way, youse, step back.' For one still moment, Joe's arm swung up, crisped, waited. Then he let it fall. 'No no,' he shouted. 'That's what they want. No, stop, will you,' he said to a man behind him, a man whose eyes had gone blind and bright with anger.

No one knew where it came from and it went wild. It must have been iron, a crowbar perhaps, from the clattering noise it made, breaking through a window pane and falling inside on the concrete factory floor. Then it was useless. Joe saw it; said to himself helplessly: 'They got us where they want us,' and around him he saw, felt, heard bodies thudding against each other, the sharp crack of clubs on bone, the bright swift smack of fists.

Sirens howled. Policemen were thick as dust over the street. On the kerb at the end of the block, were people, the public, half afraid, half curious, not knowing what to think, for whom to shout. Behind the crowds, the strikers' women pushed, trying to get through, crying for their men, fighting their way.

'Kill him, kill him.' Who was saying it? One of his men. 'No, for God's sake,' he said and suddenly, in gladness, with joy, he saw a policeman coming for him, the club high above his head. Joe let his fist go, hard for the blue-coated stomach, shouting not words, just sound, free and glad at last, not caring what happened now. 'Good,' he grunted, 'good,' and pushed through, striking crazily, half blows, sometimes hitting something that gave, felt soft, went down …

When they threw the first tear-gas bomb, it was all over. Blinded, dazed, bruised, they were packed in the wagons on top of each other, and the street cleared.

'I wonder if the scabs got in,' Joe asked, speaking to no one.

The silence was like sound itself, and final.

\* \* \*

Pete was having a fine time. He didn't know what it was all about but now that didn't matter. He hit out with his arms, crazily, spinning like a weather-vane, and big and useless as a scarecrow. All the time he was saying: 'You sonuvabitch, you goddam bastard, you': but it was a song, it was glad and exulting. Then, from nowhere, a policeman's club clicked on his left temple, slanting and swift: and he fell. Many people walked over him unintentionally; there was very little space and it was full of men running and shouting and trying to hit each other. Presently, tear gas smoked over the crowd between the factory walls and the houses opposite, and there was panic and people stumbling helplessly, cursing. It ended rapidly, with the noise of police wagons, bells clanging, backfiring, shrieking gears. Pete came to in jail. His experience of a strike had been exactly three weeks of peaceful picketing and then this sudden hot exulting fine business of being able to hit back or hit all around him, for a little while at least.

He was in a cell with several other men. They were packed in carelessly because, any minute now, with perhaps a few words about being Reds or perhaps not, and maybe a bit of bruising (but that also was dictated by personal taste) they would be released. His head hurt badly, both on the temple and at the back, at the base of the skull, and his eyes seemed very small and painful to him. He was half-leaning against the wall of the cell, and he sat up and felt his temple softly and passed his hands over his eyes and shook himself a little and looked around. He had never been in jail before but then he had also never been in a strike. He wasn't unhappy about it; beyond the pain in his head he remembered those few minutes when he, Pete Hines, had seemed to be a powerful man, a free and dangerous man, hitting out for himself and everybody else. It was cheap at the price.

'How ya coming, brother.'

He smiled vaguely at the man next him and said: 'Okay.' Across the cell, a man was sucking his mouth carefully, two teeth were missing in front and he kept running his tongue over the empty bloody space and his face looked surprised. Some of the men were not marked beyond scraped knuckles or tears in their clothes: four others besides Pete had bruises on their heads, bruises that were drying now, into red, dirty-looking welts, and would soon be darkly coloured, blue and purple and later yellow and greenish. They all seemed to Pete to be feeling fine about it, the way he was.

'Jees,' he said, suddenly, to no one, 'that was swell. I'd do that again. That was good all right.'

A few of the men listening, smiled back at him.

'Wonner where they got Joe,' someone said.

There was silence: saying that name made the strike again something that had a purpose, something that went from definite decisions to gestures, and was intended to have a final result.

Joe Barrow was the one who'd had the idea long ago, and talked about it at home, and then later, with other men at Dick's saloon and written away for information and advice, and finally organised the local union. He was the man who did the thinking. Pete considered him. He had nothing new in his mind, despite this surprising experience of feeling so fine and hitting out for himself. He still thought what he had the first time he listened to Joe talking to a meeting in the small hall of the Labor Temple. He thought what Joe said was true and he liked how he said it, and the way his face changed as he talked. He understood every word Joe said and, from what he could remember of listening to other people talking on platforms, people who wanted to get elected to something, he had either not clearly understood or not quite believed any other speaker before. It was enough for him that he liked the way Joe looked and that he believed what Joe was saying.

'You can put me down,' he'd said that night, leaving the hall; and he shook hands with Joe, and he had gone home feeling he was in with good guys and that things would be better now.

When the strike was called he went out with the others and reported where he was told to report, and did picket duty as instructed and helped at odd jobs – mostly errands or getting coffee and sandwiches around to the men at night on picket duty – anything they told him to do. He didn't talk much because he felt shy to ask questions, and he had no opinions about the strike, beyond believing in Joe.

A man with raw knuckles said: 'What the hell happened?'

A man whose head looked something like Pete's, and whose eyes were bloodshot, said: 'Some guy threw a brick, or a crowbar, or something.'

'Those goddam cops.'

'Yeah, but I bet they say it was Joe or one of the union.'

'We'll win anyhow.'

Pete thought about that. He knew they were striking because they had to work too fast, and one man had to do two men's jobs and didn't get paid enough for half a man. And then, too, he'd heard Joe explain this, they were striking for the right to organise and be a union. He liked the union very much. He felt safe with these men, and he'd had a fine time picketing. Kind of walking around and talking to your new friends, or listening, and he had a little money saved up, so it wasn't like some of the men that had to go on Relief. When you had to go on Relief it wasn't fine any more: you didn't feel the same.

'They got you good, didn't they boy,' a man said to Pete.

He said 'Yeah' modestly. He was feeling fairly proud of his clouted head, and he was still wobbly and dazed, but glad to have been there when the trouble started.

'I hope Joe's all right,' someone said.

'Oh, sure.'

Presently a policeman came and unlocked the cell door and let them all out. Minton's Soup Factory wasn't too popular locally: the Mintons spent their money some place else. The policeman was pretty nice about it all and the cold air of the street felt good to Pete. A man he had never seen before, who had a cut on his face, linked arms with Pete and said: 'Let's go to Dick's and get a beer.' Most of the crowd from the jail straggled off to Dick's to find out what the latest news was and what Joe was saying. Pete had a little money on him and everybody seemed to be buying everybody else beers, as if it were a holiday or late Saturday night, and soon he was pleasantly drunk and feeling light and happy.

He was crazy about the union. He hadn't known what swell guys he worked with before, or how good it was to feel surrounded by friends and safe because there were so many of you. He kept thinking, Ferryville isn't such a bad burg after all; though he'd lived there all his life, and even in the same house for the last fifteen years. But he'd never found himself thinking about it, one way or the other, before.

'They say the Labor guy from Washington's gonna be there to-morrow.'

'I bet Joe'll fix up that arbitration committee okay.'

'They say Bignose is gonna talk for Minton on that committee.'

'Didja see the *Evening Gazette* yet? It says the strikers rioted. Hell, none of us slung that brick.'

'When we win this strike, I'm gonna get my little woman a new coat to celebrate. We'll get paid like we should then, I'm telling you.'

Pete drank beer and smiled and said 'Sure' whenever he was called upon to make any answer, and felt fine about everything. They'd win the strike and then he wouldn't have to tear his arms out and break his back trying to dip twelve of those stinking 115 gallon cauldrons of soup into the machine, every hour: and Mabel would get a new coat too, or that electric washing machine she was always talking about, and he could go to union meetings at night and listen to the boys who knew how to talk. He went home unsteadily and late, singing. He thought he was having about the best time in his life.

He'd forgotten about Mabel. But she was waiting in the front room, wearing a lavender flannel wrapper and her face was hard with anger.

'So that's what your old union is for: to make you go out and fight with cops and get your dumb head cracked open and then make you go out and get drunk. It's a fine union, that is.'

He didn't want to argue with her; he was still feeling warm and pleased.

'Now Mabel,' he said dimly.

'Now Mabel, nothing. You act like we got money to burn. And how about the rent, Pete Hines, and how about the food for the time your damn old union keeps you from working and how about a lotta other things? I hate that union,' she said, 'everything was fine before that big loudmouth, Joe Barrow, begun to shoot off his face.'

'Lissen,' he said, and his voice was not nearly as conciliatory.

'I will not lissen. Who do you think I am. You go out and get yourself drunk and me sitting here, never going to the movies, or anything I wanna do, and scrimping and saving and washing my hands to the bone with the laundry and everything and all because of that union.'

'The President,' he said with dignity, 'told us we should strike.'

'Yeah. I bet.'

'He did. You couldn't know because you never read the papers or go to meetings or anything. But he sure did. He said in that NRA we could all get together and make unions, and if we couldn't get the right wages and stuff, then we could strike. The President's on our side. He knows a lotta guys like Joe.'

'Yeah. I betcha. I bet Joe goes and stays down there in the White House with him, and he sez: "Joe, what would you do if you was me?"'

'You lissen, Mabel ...'

'You lissen yourself, Pete Hines. You're a damn fool and you're drunk and you better go to bed and sleep it off. And tomorrow you can stay home and help me some instead of running around with those fool union men and you'll be a lot more help here with the furnace than all that stuff about picketing. And if you ask me, Joe's a big-mouthed liar. And if you wanna know where this is gonna end, it's gonna end with us on Relief.'

He laughed at her. After all she was only a woman and what could she know about unions and strikes, and Labor people from Washington, and committees, and the NRA and things like that. How could she be expected to know that the union was fine and there were a lot of men in it, practically everyone, and they'd get what they wanted. She was only a woman and women didn't get around much. 'Relief,' he said, laughing. 'Say, I never heard such boloney. I'll be working when I'm sixty.'

* * *

Joe went in to them quietly, the last. Before him, he herded the other two men, his members of the arbitration committee. He wore a blue shirt with a lavish wine-red tie, satin, and a small dingy diamond tie-pin. He saw the bare important-looking room and the other men around the table, thinking about something else. If we get mad, he thought, if we get up and get sore, then it won't go. He was glad there were no Italians on his side: they got excited, they spoke bad, quick English, and had a way of shaking their fists. Samuels and Harding slinked in ahead of him and found seats. Their hands looked absurd, afterthoughts tacked to their sleeves. They looked at the other men, their heads a little down, frowning. The Government man sat at the head of the table. Joe was surprised to see how young he was, just about his own age, thirty-five perhaps, not soft-looking, not seeming to be a man who had simply sat all his life waiting for the money to roll in. He looked tired too, and Joe found himself glad of this; thinking, if he's tired, he'll understand better about us, he'll know about work.

Curley, the plant manager, was there, and Daniels, floor foreman, and the owner, Mr Minton. They seemed nervous, given to sudden smiles, as if to show that they were easy with this, knew they were right, as if the workers were being foolish, unreasonable, like spoiled but dangerous children.

The Government man was named Stevens. He greeted the strikers' committee and got to work, sorting papers before him, speaking abruptly with no words he could spare.

'Yes,' Joe would say. 'Yes, that's right. Yes, you got all that straight.'

Then it was Mr Minton's turn. He said: 'Mr Curley will speak for me, I don't keep up with the details of the management.' And then he made a little speech about the factory, its ideals, what it meant to the workers. They all listened impatiently, Stevens with his hand over his eyes. Joe thought: The worst of it is, the poor old cluck probably believes all that drip he's saying.

Presently the case was outlined, stood agreed between them, the points of the dispute singled out and named.

And then it began. Joe thought, in the week that followed, that he had spent the best part of his life in this room, angry and exhausted by turns, hopeless, harried, trying to keep Samuels and Harding quiet, sane, attempting in the intervals between meetings to still their anger, their desire to blow up the plant, everything, stay out on strike until they all starved, kidnap Minton, anything, anything. Would this haggling never end?

He knew himself, early, that they had lost; they would gain nothing from this except Minton's fear, Curley's bitterness, a growing palpable desire for revenge. Within himself he wondered how he would face the men, after those cold starved weeks, after all the hope and strain, and say: 'Boys, I got you this,' holding up between thumb and forefinger a crumb.

At last, because he saw nothing else for it, knowing they had no money left to fight, there would be no coffee, no sandwiches, no groceries to take home at night, knowing the men were tired and the women frightened, he gave in. He thought: I've failed them and what else can I do? This is only the beginning, this is nothing, but how can I tell them that or give them patience or anything to go on with.

They agreed on a raise of three cents an hour; and on certain operations it was decided to add another man, to lessen the strain of the stretch-out. No one would be fired for belonging to the union, for striking: and they could hold meetings, grow, continue.

The men went back to work, not glad but relieved. Joe watched them file in, in the morning with the sky grey, high and frozen, their faces still smeared with sleep.

He thought: Back to your nine dollars, twelve dollars, your fourteen dollars and the machines driving you, living through the day to provide for yourself a little house with the basement flooded and the rain coming through broken windows, and Sunday a day to recover from it, a day to be limp and asleep.

The men greeted him as they passed. 'Hello, Joe,' they said, friendly and confident, 'you sure told it to them all right. You sure got us a raise, boy; you know how to handle this stuff all right ...'

Finally Joe went in, to the dark, smooth machines where he worked, too ashamed to stand there and take thanks for nothing.

* * *

Pete sat in his front room reading the papers. He rocked back and forth and held the paper close to his eyes, frowning. Finally he began saying the words over with his lips. He had bought all the papers and he had read everything they printed about the strike and the arbitration committee, once. But he was not sure he understood. Newspapers said things so strangely, as if they were writing about dead people or people some place else. This was, of course, his strike, and Joe's, and all the other men's, the ones in jail and the ones on the picket line. But the small black print seemed very remote, the words were cold and indifferent, and he could not be sure he had really understood.

Mabel watched him from the kitchen door. 'You might keep your shoes on in the parlour,' she said. 'You won't be having shoes soon enough, and we're not bums yet, anyhow, Pete Hines.'

He felt around under the greyish over-stuffed sofa for his shoes and put them on. 'Wouldja like me to wear my coat too, and my collar, and maybe I should even have a diamond stick-pin?'

'You can still try to look like somebody with a job,' she said bitterly and went back to the kitchen.

He sat with the paper on his lap and stared in front of him. He was looking at the Age of Innocence, framed and unbearably sweet against the mottled wallpaper, but he did not see it. He saw nothing of that room which had been brought together, object piled on object, for the last fifteen years: their married life. Their wedding picture and both their parents, the baby who had died, the calendar with an Indian girl and a vast American beauty rose on it; the table covered with a fringed cloth, and topped by a marble lamp, the straight chairs neat against the wall, the lace curtains with plush drapes over them: he knew it was all there. His front room, the place he felt prosperous and sure in. The kitchen behind it, with something Mabel called a dinette, where they ate; and the bedroom, with a kewpie-lamp on Mabel's dressing-table. He was better off than a lot of men who worked in Minton's, having all these things. All these solid and different things, proving how long and steadily he had worked, in one factory or another: and showing also that after the baby who died there had been no others. He was proud of his home: it gave him a feeling of being somebody, having a handsome place like this to come back to. He liked Mabel to get herself up, too, when they went to the movies or to a church social or a dance at Holliday Park in the summer; that showed also what a worker he was, that he could make money and provide a fine house for his wife and fine clothes. It wasn't possible that he had understood the papers. He began to read again.

'The arbitration committee, presided over by Mr Guy Stevens, special representative of the Department of Labor and formed of six members, three designated by Mr Minton of Minton's Soup Inc., and three chosen from the local Canners' Union, today reached a decision satisfactory to both parties, which terminates the Minton strike at the beginning of its fifth week. Mr Curley, plant manager at Minton's, and a member of the arbitration committee, expressed himself as perfectly satisfied. Mr Barrow, speaking for the Canners' Union, stated that he "hoped it would all work out all right according to the decisions of the committee". Certain changes in work loads will be agreed upon later. An increase in wages of three cents an hour was decided on. The Canners' Union is recognised …'

Three cents an hour, Pete said to himself. Pete fingered the paper and felt afraid. Of course, if the union was recognised, that meant Joe would go on talking with the bosses and trying to get something better.

He rocked back and forth and tried to understand all this. Of his $105 savings, only $35 was left. That money had been saved for sickness; or if there wasn't any sickness, it was supposed to add up slowly and some day buy him and Mabel a good funeral with coffins lined in quilted pink satin. He was glad to spend it all right for the strike: but what did it all mean? It didn't sound as if the strike had come to much. And still there were so many guys in it and they'd been so strong. He remembered the fine feeling of hitting out, and how important he had been for just a little while and how happy. He thought perhaps he'd better go over to Dick's and listen to what the boys were saying, because sitting here alone this way you got mixed up and didn't really understand things. It seemed suddenly lonely to him in his front room and he was uncertain of himself and the things he had so clearly believed. It would be better to go and see what the boys were doing. He felt hurried. The room was too little and too dark and he knew nothing, he understood nothing. He got his coat and hat and was putting on his collar and tie before the mirror in the front room when Mabel again came from the kitchen. She had flour on her arms and she looked hot.

'Where you going now?'

'Down to Dick's; I wanna see what the boys gotta say about this arbitration committee.'

'And get drunk, I guess; and talk all night and then what've you got?'

He said nothing, yanking at his tie, hurried and nervous, needing a crowd of men about him, all taking assurance from each other's voices.

'You lost your strike,' Mabel said slowly. 'I always knew you would. Your fine friend, Joe, lost your strike and used up most of your money and now what're you gonna do?'

He pulled on his coat and, with his hat in his hand, went swiftly to the door. He turned and saw her standing there, arms crossed, hot from the stove, but not angry, only final and warning. He slammed the door behind him, to blot her out, because he was afraid she told the truth.

\* \* \*

It seemed that the human body could no longer endure these relentless days, with the cold clawing through to the bone, the boredom, the grey same hours. December, Joe thought, is a month for dying. The union meetings went on, but differently. There was fear in them somewhere, as the men came to the bleak little hall above the tyre shop. And they talked too loud, raising their voices against an unnamed threat.

One day Mr Curley called Joe; he went to the plant manager's office with his overalls on, his arms stained by grease.

Curley's smile was in his eyes, and beneath his skin; he was too wary to let it come out, spread, glow; and his voice was hearty like red apples, jovial and deep.

'I'm damn sorry, Joe, but we got to lay you off for a while; just nothing doing in your shop, slack season you know. We'll let you know when things pick up. We have to reduce the entire staff, about a third, I guess. Tough times ... the depression ... sorry ...'

Joe took a pack of cigarettes from his pocket and lit one and flicked the match up towards the ceiling. It made a brittle noise, dropping on the floor. He stared at Curley and breathed the smoke out in long twin streamers.

'I certainly hope Mr Minton'll manage to make both ends meet,' he said, and smiled and went from the room.

* * *

Pete lay in bed acting as if he were asleep. He waited while Mabel paused, not sure whether she ought to wake him – mainly from spite – or whether he would be less trouble in bed, out of the way. She got up and he heard her in the kitchen, making a lot of noise with the coffee-pot and the frying-pan. He screwed his eyes shut and lay rigid. He knew that today, sometime, he would have to go to Minton's and see Bignose Curley and get his job back. He didn't want to. His legs writhed under the sheets. He was nervous and dimly resentful. It seemed to him it was like having to apologise and make up, without really doing that, but at least implying it. He felt licked and embarrassed. He felt as if he had been caught at something. Suddenly, he had the dreadful idea that Bignose might laugh at him and the union and say: 'Well, you guys sure thought you knew a lot ...' By now he was sweating with humiliation. He'd postponed going back for a week: there were men you didn't mind seeing when you felt you had the worst of it, but not Bignose.

All right, he said to himself, get up, you cluck, and go and see Bignose. What the hell's the matter with you; scared you'll get your tail spanked or something?

Mabel gave him breakfast dourly.

Now he found that it was harder and harder to face this interview. He walked out of his way, towards the centre of Ferryville, past the shops. He had on his work clothes. He was walking with his head down and his shoulders hunched, not conscious of where he was, but stalling for time. He turned and saw himself reflected in a shop window and stopped dead and looked at himself. He went closer to the window. He hadn't thought about how he looked for years, not since he used to go for the girls. He saw a tall man, not old or young, thin and loosely and carelessly hinged together, who held himself stooped, with one shoulder higher than the other. He couldn't make anything of his face: it seemed to him like everybody else's face, like all the faces on the street. But what worried him now was the way this man, himself, walked. 'My God,' he said, softly and aloud, 'I'm walking like I was unemployed.'

He turned and went very quickly towards Minton's, his chest out and breathing like a locomotive, with effort.

It was eleven-thirty and the factory shrieked outside the wood partition. He could hear steam escaping, the rolling thunder of the belts, the heavy metal clanking of the iron containers dragged over cement floors. He waited on a bench for a chance to see Mr Curley. He twisted his cap and scraped the floor with his toe and felt himself to be damp and hot all over.

A stenographer opened the glass door and said: 'Come on in.'

Curley was busy with some papers and didn't look up. Pete stood there. He felt, suddenly, as if his arms were unnaturally long, like an ape's, hanging way down to the floor and loose. He couldn't make himself stand up straight, grin, and look the way he wanted Curley to think of him.

Curley looked up, very vague.

'Hullo, Mr Curley.'

There was a silence. 'I'm Pete Hines. I'm a soup dipper in number three.'

'Oh, yes.'

'Well. I just come to report back for work, to tell you like, you know, to get on the payroll again. Now the strike's over and everything.'

Curley wanted badly to say what he thought of strikers; disloyalty, Russian ideas, and the whole dirty pack of them. But he couldn't. On account of those Government snoops sticking their noses into business and making a mess of everything. Fool kids or college professors or something, they were always sending around from Washington. On the taxpayers' money too.

'I'm sorry, Hines, but we won't be able to take you back right now.'

Pete looked at him, stupidly.

'What,' he said, this was as bad as the newspapers and the arbitration committee and everything else. Nobody said anything simply, or anything you expected.

'Naturally, we had to get in other help during the strike to keep some of the plant open and, of course, those people get preference now and, of course, right after the strike, a lot of people came straight back and some new ones too, and we had to hire quickly to try to make up for all the lost time. I'll take your name, of course, and let you know as soon as anything comes up.'

'Oh. Sure.'

'Just leave your name with Miss Jones when you go out. It's probably only a temporary lay-off,' Mr Curley said and began to turn over the papers on his desk again.

Pete got out of the room, mumbled his name and address to Miss Jones, and somehow found himself again on the street, walking with a more pronounced stoop than before. But I'm outa work, he kept saying to himself, stupidly. I'm outa work. And it isn't the good season, either. I'm never outa work. I been working since I'm twelve. I don't see how it can be like that. I'm a good soup dipper; they never complained of my work. And I been there six years. Besides, the President said we should make unions, and if the bosses didn't act like they should, we could strike, and then the Labor men would come from Washington, and then we'd go back to our jobs and they'd fix everything up in Washington. By God, he thought suddenly, Curley can't fire me. The President won't have it. It's against the law.

\* \* \*

They sat in Joe's office, which was a corner partitioned off from the main room of the union headquarters. A chipped soup plate was full of cigarette butts and chewed cigar ends. It wasn't very warm but the air was old and heavy. There were three folding chairs and a kitchen chair behind the desk, at which Joe sat. Joe passed his hand over his eyes, his face, trying to wipe off the weariness.

'I can't explain it to you, Pete,' he said. 'We'll get this stuff before the Labor Department whenever we can. I'll write the people in Washington. We got to keep the union going. That's all. It takes time. Everything's slow,' he said and hated the sound of his voice: flat and stale like the air he was breathing, toneless with discouragement.

They sat in silence. Everything's too slow, Joe thought. Sometimes, it seems like there must be millions of people not doing anything but waiting; all of them waiting for something to happen, or somebody to say something. And nothing does happen. Things just go on.

'It's cold too,' Pete said into the silence. 'People gotta have coal.'

'I know.'

'What'll they all do; all the guys got fired?'

'Relief.'

Pete shook his head mulishly. 'Not me. I'm as good as I was when I was twenty. I'm only thirty-nine now; men that ain't sick can get work.'

'There must be about twelve million guys in this country then, sick as hell.' He grinned at Pete. 'Lissen boy, go on out and try. You might be lucky.'

'What're you gonna do?'

'I got some life-insurance I can cash in. That'll keep me a coupla months. And I'm gonna hold the union together.'

Pete stood up. 'I'm gonna go out and get me a job.'

'Good luck.'

'Same to you.'

Joe opened the window and stood by it, looking over Ferryville. The city lay shapeless and murky before him, sloping to the river. It was late afternoon. He thought about the places people lived, and his own home: that would have to go now. He'd send his mother to his brother in Boston who still had work. And give up the flat and move into a furnished room. And save and do without and, somehow, manage for a while. All the men like Pete – whose names you couldn't remember because they looked alike – who didn't understand anything and were helpless, he was bound to them. He'd started the union, and he was responsible. It was going to be hard. Not the business of living in a dump and all that, but just having to sit here and wait for them to come in and ask questions he couldn't answer. He'd have to act cheerful, no matter how he felt. It wouldn't do them much good to know that they were licked now, and perhaps for a long time.

There are more of us, he thought. But we're like a long freight train without a locomotive. If he'd been to school more … if all the others like Pete knew what was happening around them, and knew how to get together and obey and give orders, for a while. If they could even see what was happening. We get lied to, he thought, we're the easiest people there are to fool. He thought of how he and Samuels and Harding, at the arbitration committee meetings, had been impressed by the way Mr Minton and Curley and Daniels looked: their clothes. The way Minton especially, sat and talked, as if he were used to having people listen to him and do what he said. The Government man was the same: education did that, and clothes, and having enough money, so cops could never tell you to get a move on … Suddenly, he felt infinitely alone, and without a world, knowing that he was not really one with Pete and the others, separated from them by the few things he knew and the many more things he wanted. And as for the other world: he thought grimly, and not quite with laughter, of the kind of tie he wore and the kind of tie Mr Stevens wore; and the way his voice sounded, and his accent, and the way his hands looked, and how he walked … I got to keep them going somehow. We've got to be building something up all the time and learning stuff, and how to fight back, and we've got to learn all the tricks they know. It's slow, he said to himself, and again he stumbled over the word. But what about me, he thought, what about my life. From somewhere in his mind, came a phrase: all men have inalienable rights to life, liberty and the pursuit of happiness. He leaned his forehead against the cold window pane and tried, hopelessly, to laugh.

* * *

The trouble with Joe, Pete thought, is, he's discouraged. Then, too, Joe was in a tough spot: everybody'd be coming to him saying, 'What'll I do.' That was dumb: the thing to do was go out and get another job. No use crying over spilt milk. Any guy with a good work record and muscles and some sense could get a job: maybe have to look around a little. But that was nothing.

By now, Pete was enjoying himself. Life was simple again. He didn't have a job and he was going to get one. That was easy. Not like all the things he'd been trying to understand: the union and NRA and things. All he had to do was go around and tell his name, and what he could do, and then go back to Mabel and say 'Well, kid, I'm working for …' Pause. For whom. He began to make lists, in his mind, frowning. It had been so long since he'd thought about all this, six years. He felt that probably, even when he was working for somebody else, he'd start out in the morning, dopey-like, and begin walking towards Minton's. Well. There was the Orpheus Victrola Company, the Susie Sweet Biscuit Company, the Florida Cigar factory, the Bridle Leather Works, the Parisian Shoe Company (he dismissed that; shoes had always seemed to him especially skilled work somehow, so he wouldn't even bother). And the Beverley Underwear Mills. That was about all in the way of factories. There was the Lampson Trucking firm though, and probably a lot of other jobs like that, driving a truck or hauling stuff or something. But he was a factory worker, always had been. Better stick to the factories. He went to the nearest: the Susie Sweet Biscuit Company.

There wasn't anybody in the office. He waited a while and then wandered off to look for someone. He found a clerk and said he'd come about a job. The clerk laughed at him. 'Lissen, brother, we wouldn't know how to act around here if anybody got hired. All we do here is make "necessary re-trenchments". You better go somewhere else.' Pete thought the clerk was being smart, but it didn't matter. There were a lot of other places.

He walked across town towards the Orpheus Victrola plant. It was cold and he hurried. Probably going to rain. No sense getting there soaked and looking like a bum. He was a little breathless when he arrived. At a desk, behind a counter in an empty room, sat a man with a green eye shade. Pete leaned on the counter and said: 'Hello.' The man nodded. 'Anything doing,' Pete said. The man looked up at him. 'Nope. You can leave your name there on a piece of paper, if you want. I'll let you know.' There was neither sincerity nor warmth in the man's voice, and Pete thought it would be a waste of paper.

He pulled his coat collar up, when he got on the street. These refusals had happened so fast that he didn't have time to think about them, or be in any way distressed. He said to himself, guess people don't buy so many victrolas, now it's the depression, and set off again, zig-zagging across the town.

It was dark now, and he thought he'd go to the Parisian Shoe Company, anyhow, because it was nearest. It'd be too late to do anything more today. It was raining too.

He went into the office without knocking; it was a small room, lighted by one electric bulb hanging on a cord. Rain smeared against the windows. There was a woman in there, talking to a man, or pleading with him. Pete only saw her back: a broad, middle-aged woman, hatless, the dark hair knotted loose at the nape of her neck. She was leaning over a table behind which the man sat, holding herself up with one hand and beating on the table with the other, as if not knowing what she did. She was crying and her voice came out in the choked, unclear way of someone who has been crying and talking for a long time. The man looked nervous and unhappy.

'I'm sorry, Maria,' he was saying. 'You know I'd take you on if I could. But we're not taking anybody. Later, for the Easter trade, maybe. I swear I'll get you back the first chance I get.'

'It's too late,' the woman said, 'I can't wait for Easter. I gotta have money now. It's Raphael, he's sick. The little one. I gotta have milk and oranges and the medicines the doctor says. He's so skinny,' she said, her voice suddenly rising, and the free hand fluttering against the table. 'You gotta give me work. He's sicker today than he was yesterday. Please, Mr Atkins, I always worked good here, I never done nothing wrong, I always worked steady. I'm fast too. You gotta …'

The man spread his hands in a gesture of helplessness; his face was lined and distressed. The woman was not talking, now, only making stifled sounds, with a handkerchief against her mouth.

It might be Mabel, only she's got brown hair, Pete thought, shocked and silent. So this was what it was coming to, women were crying to get work, women were crying like they might at home, but for only their husbands to see, in front of strangers … And they couldn't get work anyhow. He turned, fumbling for the door-knob. He ran most of the way home, running and walking, with the rain falling now in long thin curtains over the empty streets. It might of been Mabel, he thought.

He got up early and he didn't wait for breakfast. He was at the Florida Cigar Company before it opened. He watched the workers straggling in, sombre in the cold smoky morning light. He thought they were lucky, just to be working.

The day's crop of applicants had collected before the employment office door. Pete held himself a little apart; he wanted it clear that he was used to working, and not at all used to hanging around factory doors. He filed in, in turn. But he didn't have a chance to say anything. A bored and sleepy voice told him: 'Nothing doing today, come back in about two weeks or leave your name and address.' A voice reciting doom and failure, as if it were announcing a weather report: but nothing nearly as important as a baseball score. None of the men who had come in the morning cold waited about the doors. Were they going some place else, Pete wondered. How long did a man keep it up. When did he just decide to stay in bed because what was the use anyhow …

That day, fearfully, he canvassed every factory in town. Between stops, he went into stores and asked if they needed any help – a grocery store, a café, and finally a garage. His feet ached, and he was beginning to worry about his shoes. How would he get them fixed, once they were worn-out. He was hungry until about two o'clock, and then just weak, with a headache pulling and buzzing behind his eyes.

Presently, he noticed that he wasn't even walking any more. He was shuffling his feet over the pavement, sagging and exhausted. Nothing was clear to him now: he couldn't understand why he should be doing this, how it had all happened. Towards the end of the day, he went into offices mutely, and looked at some man behind a desk or table and that man, in equal silence, shook his head. They didn't even bother with words. There was nothing to say.

At dusk, he went past the Lampson Trucking Company and noticing the lighted office, entered. He said to a man he could hardly see, being dazed now with weariness and despair, 'Need a driver?'

The man looked at him and said carelessly, 'You're too old.' He stood swaying on his feet, but the man had nothing more to say.

Very quietly, Pete left the office. He didn't know in what direction he was going, and he couldn't even feel his body. Old, he kept saying to himself, too old. But yesterday or years ago, he had walked firmly around the city, conscious of his muscles and all the good years ahead for a man who knew how to work. Old. Old. He must get home now, quickly. He must get inside among his own things, where he would be safe.

It was later than supper time, and Mabel opened the door, ready with anger. 'Late again,' she said. 'Your union, your fine union. It makes you lose your job, and you're never home like a decent man, and the supper spoiled, and you don't care what happens to me. You don't care about anything except your old union.'

He stood blinking in the light. They won't give me work, he thought. They say I'm too old. Suddenly he was terrified and lonely, and he wanted her to put her arms around him, the way she had when they were young, and kiss him and tell him he'd find a good job tomorrow or the next day. Tell him something. And hold him against her, and make him feel that it wasn't true about his being old, and no one needing him for work. He stretched out his arms, awkwardly. And Mabel, thinking he was perhaps drunk again and crazy – everything was wrong since the union – imagined he was going to strike her. She put her hand out to hold him off and shouted at him: 'Don't you touch me, Pete Hines, I'll call the cops. Don't you touch me, you bum, I won't take that from you …'

\* \* \*

Pretty soon, Joe thought, this place will stop being a worker's union, and turn into a club room for the unemployed. Practically no one, who was still working at Minton's, came to the union office. Even men who had daughters or wives, employed in the factory, stayed clear of the union, fearing to endanger other jobs besides their own. Afraid, Joe said to himself, everybody's afraid. Afraid and waiting. He felt no anger for this: and made no effort to force employed union members to meetings. I haven't got the right, he thought. There's rent and food and the children: you can't ask men to be brave every day in the week.

And besides, he added, I couldn't do it if I tried. They don't think enough of me any more. They're beginning to blame me, somehow. Perhaps that was to be expected: but still. Some days, when he sat alone in the office and only a few men came in, and then usually to talk to him as if everything were his personal fault, he had a hard time with his temper. Being what the newspapers called a union leader, Joe decided, was not a bunch of roses.

He heard the outer office door opening and some men coming in; they were stamping snow from their feet, the grey, slimy wet snow of a city. One of them called: 'You in there, Joe?'

'Yup. Come on in.'

There were three of them, and they took the folding chairs and tilted them against the wall for comfort, and asked for cigarettes.

'You got it soft here,' one man said.

'How d'you figure that?'

'You kin stay indoors all day.'

'Yeah, and not have to go around to the agencies and have the guys laugh in your face.'

'And you're not on Relief, neither.'

'And you ain't got a wife hollering at you, or kids you gotta feed when you can't even feed yourself decent.'

'Say,' Joe said. 'Cut it out. Any of you guys can have my job any time you want it. Right now. Just step up and take it.'

'What's a matter with it. Looks good to me.'

'Yeah? I guess you think I'm getting a big salary from the union, too.'

'Aw Joe, nobody said nothing about you making any money out of it.'

'Well, lay off of me. I'm not on Relief yet, but I will be, soon's my life-insurance money runs out. And I couldn't get a job around this town, not if they hired everybody in the place, starting tomorrow. And I'm so goddam sick of this room and sitting around here writing letters to Washington, I could puke. I said I'd do this job and I will. But I'm not gonna take any of that you-got-it-soft stuff.'

They're beginning to hate me, Joe thought with wonder. Not long ago, they thought I was the finest man in town and they all said: How's-the-boy-Joe and you-sure-know-how-to-manage-this-stuff. They'll probably accuse me of using the union funds for myself, next. And he thought: there's nobody to talk to. There isn't anybody who'd know what I was talking about if I said that I'm going crazy here. That I know nothing I do is any good, and I have to do it anyhow, so we won't look as licked as we are; and so things will go on. He lit another cigarette, he was smoking several packs a day, and he had to make an effort now, holding the match, to keep his hand from shaking. Funny, Joe thought, I guess a man can live with just about nothing, but he's got to have friends.

Some more men came in, they brought chairs from the outer room and one of them sat on the corner of the desk. The conversation became general.

'Didj'a know the bakeries dump the loaves of bread with torn wrappers out on the city dump-heap? A guy told me that, downtown yesterday. I went out there this morning, and I got two loaves, and kinda washed them off …' 'The Relief moved us, on account we can't pay our rent where we are. Jees, you oughta see them houses they put you in. The bedbugs crawl around on the ceiling and fall on the floor and make a little click. My wife has to put pans of water under the bed posts, and she's gonna have a baby in two months …'

'Didj'a hear about Sam Garvin's daughter. She got so sick sitting home and couldn't have any clothes or anything, so she went out on North Main Street on Saturday night and she got a coupla guys. And somebody told Sam, and he beat the hell out of her …' 'They're cutting wages over at the Parisian Shoe. They got a system about piece work, now, so they can gyp you outa lot of money; but you gotta sign the payroll like you got code wages …'

A man came in; he pushed the door so that it slammed back against the wall, and he came straight over to Joe. 'I gotta have a dollar, Joe. My kid's got a abscessed tooth and she's screaming off her head, it hurts so bad. And they don't have that Relief Dentist Clinic till Friday, and anyhow there ain't no time to sit around there and argue, and wait for a doctor's order or any of that. She's gotta get it pulled quick. She pukes up all her food and she can't sleep, and it's awful. The dentist won't do nothing till I pay him. Joe, lissen …'

'I'm sorry as hell, Bert. I haven't got it.'

There was a silence. The man who had come in stared around the room at the other people there, but not seeing them. He didn't know what to do, now. He turned slowly to leave, saying nothing. He would have to go home and watch his child. The other men looked at Joe, with disgust. He didn't have the money: he was living on $3.50 a week for himself, two meals a day, and spending $6 a week of his own money on the union, the rent and heat and light for the office, stamps … It wouldn't last long anyhow. The union came first.

'Say, Bert,' a man said slowly, and he was looking at Joe as he talked. 'We can help you I guess. This whole gang'll go over there to Relief now, and just push in together and make them give you that dentist order. There's ten of us. You won't be coming, will you, Joe?'

'I'll go alone with Bert and talk to them,' Joe said. 'I think I can get that order.'

'Maybe it'll be better if we all go with Bert: things don't always come out like you think, Joe. Maybe we'll be better at it than you will. I guess Bert'll be better off with us.'

Joe half rose and sat down again in his chair.

He lit another cigarette and said: 'Suit yourselves. I gotta lot of work to do here, anyhow.'

Without goodbyes, they filed out of the room. One of the men had his hand on Bert's arm. Bert himself seemed surprised by all this, not knowing exactly what had happened, or why, suddenly, the attitude of the men had grown cold and menacing. But what mattered was a medical order for his child. He let himself be led away.

Joe put his head down on his arms: his shoulders were flattened against the desk, and light coming from the window behind him picked out the frayed and shiny back of his suit. He thought: what is it makes men really love you for a while, and then turn away, with their faces closed and hating. Why am I doing this. Why not go away. I'm only a little man anyhow, why not give up this idea and go off somewhere and start over and take what comes my way and not think about it. What is it in me that keeps me here. And how about myself. I've got a right to something for myself, too, something like being happy.

A woman's voice said: 'Excuse me.'

He looked up, flushing with embarrassment. 'I was feeling sick,' he said uncertainly.

'Sure.'

'What can I do for you?'

'Nothing much. I'm a member of this union. I just was going by, and I came in to get warm. It's cold out.'

That's something we're good for here, anyhow, he thought.

'Where I live, they ran out of coal lately. It's a helluva life,' she said brightly.

She pulled a chair close to the radiator and sat hunched up against it. Any minute, Joe thought, she'll take off her shoes and stockings and hang them up to dry. She doesn't know I'm here. She looked a little blue around the mouth; her hands were clumsy with cold. She was not especially young, and not very fresh. Small and dark; with an imitation fur coat, that had never been rich or handsome and now showed the marks of time. Her make-up was on badly, and her face was curiously pallid with cold, around and behind the crooked geranium-red cheeks. He thought she was probably running out of everything, even rouge. Funny, how much sadder and poorer women could look. She took off a brilliant blue beret and began to smooth out and almost caress a long straight quill that stuck from it. The snow had dampened and softened the quill and it looked bad. Her face was wrinkled with concern, her mouth pursed up to make a little sound of dismay or despair, which didn't come out. She must be about thirty, he thought, or thirty-two, and every year had done something to her.

'You been in factory work long,' he asked.

'Nope, I was a stenographer till three years ago. But I couldn't get any more work in that, so I been peeling potatoes for a couple of years.' She smiled at him. 'Wonderful experience for a girl,' she said.

'They fired you at Minton's?'

'No, laid-off.'

'Because of the union?'

'Oh, no. They're just cutting down: one girl should do the work of two now – you know how it is. I don't think Curley ever got the idea I was a big Labor agitator. Just laying people off, you know. Happens all over the country.'

'What're you doing now?'

She looked at him with a bland stare. His questions were beginning to annoy her. After all, she had once paid her union dues, in fact three times, and she'd only come in to get warm.

'What's it to you?'

'I'm sorry,' he said. His voice was reassuring; he hadn't meant to snoop, he was only interested or concerned for her. That was his job anyhow, he was supposed to keep up on union members ...

'Well, I'm on Relief. I live like Riley,' she said. 'I get two dollars a week to live on and the Relief pays my landlady $1.75 for my room. I have just the swellest little life.'

He was beginning to like her. Thinking it over, he liked the arrogance of that stiff, upstanding feather in her hat. And she didn't seem to expect anything of him. She hadn't come to tell her troubles, or blame him for them.

'It's getting late,' he said. 'Do you want to go out and get something to eat?'

'Gee.'

'What?'

'Us girls don't usually get offered a dinner first.'

He was angry now. He hadn't planned anything about her; the offer of food had been his tribute to her hat and her spirit. Because he liked her. All right, if she wanted to act that way.

'What do the boys usually give you, sister?'

'Girls like me get a beer, if we're lucky,' she said. 'But then, that's nourishing, too.'

\* \* \*

Pete pushed the door open and both of the women stared at him. Mabel had not expected him to come home so soon. Usually, he was out all day, looking for work. She had an idea, now, that he didn't often go to a factory or a store and apply for a job. She imagined that he was more likely just walking about the city, in that new way he had, dragging his feet. Every once in a while he would stand and stare at a shop window or read the signs in front of an employment agency. She had seen him once, when he didn't know she was there watching. Perhaps he even stopped people on the street and said: 'Could I clean your front steps? Could I wash your car …?' She didn't want to think of that. And when he came home, nights, there was no use asking him what luck he'd had. The way he held himself told enough, and the empty unfixed look in his eyes.

When she had used up the last coffee, when the lard pail was empty and there were no more potatoes or flour in the house, she had gone alone to Relief headquarters in the City Hall and made an application, marked urgent. Now the lady had come to visit, the social worker. Some part of Mabel had stopped thinking or feeling, and she was only glad that Miss Merton was being so polite about it. She had already accepted the idea that Miss Merton should be here, asking what questions the Relief thought necessary. And she was answering them, in a flat, unmoved voice. It would be all right. They'd get Relief. And Pete wouldn't be home until after Miss Merton had gone.

She looked at him feeling frightened; she couldn't remember when she had done anything important without asking him about it first. And she knew he did not want Relief: he had said he was able to work and no one was going to make charity out of him. Miss Merton inspected him uncertainly. He hadn't shaved for some days, his shoes were muddy and wet and he looked at once exhausted and desperate: as if anything would send him off into a raving anger against what he had become.

'This is Miss Merton, Pete.'

'Pleased ta meetcha.' He didn't gather who she was, or why she was there. He was tired. He wanted to lie down, rest, close his eyes, perhaps sleep a while and not think about anything.

He went past them into the bedroom and shut the door. Mabel sighed. 'We'll just talk low so's he can't hear,' she explained. 'He takes all this awful hard.'

'Yes, I know. It is hard. Now would you mind telling me, Mrs Hines, have you any life insurance, you or your husband?'

'No.'

'Have you any relatives who could help you now?'

'No.'

'Would you mind giving me a list of your nearest living relatives and their addresses?'

Mabel pulled from her memory some ignored cousins and an aunt. People died or moved away. One was very alone. She felt tired, too. She knew this only had to happen once and she hoped that it would be quickly over.

'May I look?' Miss Merton said, jotting things down in a little black notebook. She went towards the kitchen. Had to make a more or less complete inventory of what these people owned: to see if any of it could be sold, if there were any resources they hadn't yet used up. Mabel misunderstood. She made a despairing gesture and she did it quietly. She opened the bread box and the ice box and the kitchen closet. 'Nothing in them,' she said.

'Oh, yes. Yes, of course. By the way, here's your Relief order for the week, Mrs Hines. For food. You can take it to your regular grocer, he'll accept it as if it were money.' This was always the most nervous part: Miss Merton looked at Mabel anxiously through her glasses. Sometimes the clients got very upset about these orders. They were dreadfully small.

But Mabel didn't look at the amount; she held the slip of paper in her hand and said: 'Do I take that to Mr Burg? This piece of paper?'

'Yes.'

'But then, he'll know I'm on Relief.'

'Well.'

'But I been buying there for over ten years regular. He knows me. He knows Pete, too; and the way we always lived and everything. I don't see how I can ...' Her voice trailed off into miserable silence. She saw herself sneaking into Mr Burg's store and waiting until everyone else had been served; she, who was an old and favoured customer. Mr Burg always came out cheerfully wiping his hands on his apron and said: 'Well, Mrs Hines, and what will it be today? Fine weather we're having.' He always waited on her himself. She wasn't like some that went to the store in any old clothes. She always wore a hat and fixed up before she went, as a decent woman should. A woman who was buying properly for her husband; and had a nice house and a bright clean kitchen to cook in. For years she'd been doing this. Always. And now. She looked at the grocery order and saw that it was for $3 and raised her eyes to Miss Merton, blankly.

'For a week,' she said, 'three dollars?'

'Yes, I'm afraid so,' Miss Merton said quickly. 'That's the budget for families of two, now. Of course, your coal and rent and medicine and all that is extra. It's only for food.'

Mabel folded the green slip. There wasn't anything more to say. There was nothing even to think or understand or be sure of.

'What is the rent here?' Miss Merton asked.

'Twenty.'

'Oh, dear.'

'Why?'

'Well, I'm afraid that's more than Relief allows for rents. I'm afraid you'll have to find a cheaper place; unless your landlord would accept our usual rates or just give you credit until Mr Hines gets a job.'

'We'll have to move?'

'Well, I don't know. We'll have to work out something. That's more rent than we allow, you see.'

'But we can't,' Mabel said, and now she had forgotten Pete and her voice rose. 'We can't. It's our home. We been here since we're married. It's our place, it belongs to us. What would we do if we had to go somewheres else? Give it up,' she said, the tears sticky on her face. 'Give it up.'

'Who says we're gonna give it up?' Pete stood in the doorway of the bedroom in stocking feet, looking strangely thin and pale. 'What's that about our house?' he said.

'We were just discussing the rent,' Miss Merton said, and Mabel wiped at the tears with the back of her hand.

'Why?'

'Well, I'm from the Relief, you see.'

'Get out,' Pete said. It was just a statement.

Miss Merton looked perplexed and a little hurt.

'Get out,' Pete said. 'This is my house. I don't want nothing from the Relief.'

Miss Merton walked towards the front door. Mabel went with her. 'He'll get over it,' Mabel whispered. 'He'll hafta. I don't see what else. I'll come and see you at City Hall. But you better go.'

'Yes. Well, goodnight, Mrs Hines.'

'Did you get her here?' Pete said.

'What else could I do? There's nothing to eat in this house, Pete Hines, and no more coal. We can't starve, can we? We can't lock up the house and die, can we?'

'Maybe not and maybe so,' Pete said darkly, 'but I won't have strangers coming in my house poking around. I can work,' Pete said. And then, suddenly, he shouted it, waving his arms crazily over his head. 'I can work! I can work!'

Mabel sat down in a rocker. She was too tired now to argue this thing. What did it matter, anyhow? There were only a certain number of reasons for living, and when you didn't have them any more. 'What's the differ-ence?' she said slowly, and Pete stared at her, frightened by the dead quiet of her voice. 'We haven't got the baby, so it don't matter. We don't have to do all this. We don't have to.'

'What're you talking about, Mabel?' he was whispering to her, but he didn't know it.

'What've we got, anyhow, now? We'll be old, soon.'

'But I been working all my life,' Pete protested. 'It oughtn't to be like this. I can still work. For a long time, yet. I don't see,' he said.

'We had some good times, anyhow, Pete.'

'It's not all over, yet, Mabel.' But he was begging her to comfort and reassure him, to promise him a future he couldn't see.

'We had fun that year we went to the beach for a week.'

'Mabel, it isn't over. Don't act like that. Oh, Mabel, Mabel.'

Suddenly he was down on his knees by her chair, with his head on her lap, crying awkwardly and trying to stop himself. He wept in terror and she stroked his hair, saying to him dimly: 'There, there, Petie, it'll be all right.' He had his arms around her, and her hands were gentle. They stayed there as it grew dark, not talking, because neither of them could think of a comforting lie for the other to believe.

\* \* \*

They had found out a lot about each other over a thirty-five cent plate dinner. And finally, when the waitresses grew restive and lights began to go off in the back of the restaurant, they left. It was cold, with the wind blowing sharp and foolishly from different directions. Every once in a while, as if by mistake, a gust of rain would curl over the streets. They walked for a while. Then Joe said: 'I've got a room; it's pretty bad but it's warm. If you want to come.'

Now she was taking off her hat and then placing her hands on the radiator and blotting herself against it, and saying: 'This is Roxy's compared to my place.'

He looked with distaste around the room; the patched, not too clean linoleum on the floor, yellowing lace curtains, and the bedstead, chipped. He had a liking for clean things, at least, and some place to put the books he'd gotten together during the last years.

'Where I lived before,' he said, and stopped. No. Tonight, just tonight, now, he was going to forget. He was going to live tonight as if he wouldn't have to wake up and go back to that lonely and hostile office; as if he didn't hate this room; as if life were good. He was going to think of himself, tonight, and what he wanted: something like happiness.

'Are you warmer?'

'Yes.'

'You're a good kid, Anna.'

She looked at him, smiling. It was as if she said, you don't fool me, but I'll play any game you say. If we're going to tell lies tonight, okay by me. And she thought to herself, there's nothing to lose and probably there's nothing to gain. But that doesn't say we can't try to have a good time …

'Do you like me?' Joe said.

'Sure.'

'Enough?'

'I couldn't tell you yet.' She was smiling again.

Joe didn't realise that he was standing in front of her, grinding his teeth the way he did when he was thinking, and frowning. I've got to put it up to her some way so she can get out of it if she doesn't want to. She's probably had guys getting tough on her: I don't want her that way. If it's going to be any good …

'Listen,' he said. 'I don't want to do anything you don't want to. It's up to you, see? I don't want you to think I expect anything. I mean, I'm not that cheap a guy.'

'I know you're not.' She stretched out her hand towards him. 'You're a dope for being straight. You'll never get thanked for it. Not even from your union buddies.'

'I don't want to talk about that. Not now, anyhow.'

'Sure. Like I don't want to think about Relief. Or what the hell I'm gonna eat tomorrow. I know. To night's out.'

Joe waited.

'Come here,' she said.

He took her in his arms and had the surprised feeling that his arms were empty. He kissed her on the mouth harder than he meant to, but she didn't draw back.

'Put out the light,' she said.

He went to the switch by the door and came back towards her in the darkness. But she wasn't there. She was sitting on the bed and dimly he saw her bending over as if she were taking off her shoes. She said nothing. He waited. He could hear himself breathing. But insistently, and he could not escape it, he thought, she had me turn out the light so's I wouldn't see her underclothes, so I wouldn't see how poor and old they are. She's thinking about that, too. He pulled his mind away from this. He got his clothes off quickly, throwing them on a chair, and found her again in bed.

For one moment, with his blood beating behind his eyes, he felt lifted and reckless. Whatever reasons had moved him to bring her here were forgotten: her poverty and his, and the senseless waiting of their lives. He held her body with his hands, and drew her towards him. And then, suddenly, he realised without wanting to that the bones of her naked body were an outrage. This was a half-starved woman, no matter how crisply and mockingly she might talk of her life. Hungry, he thought: great God, the girl is probably always a little hungry. He was not reckless and excited any more. He was back in something he knew, something that pursued him. People not having enough. He caught his breath and it was almost a sob. I can't think about it, he told himself, not now, not now. Let's have this at least. Let's get drunk on this and forget for a while; for the night, anyhow.

She had felt or guessed what he was thinking: it was for this she had wanted the lights out, and the protection of darkness. I'm getting old, she thought, and God, I must be ugly. In despair she reached for him, and in despair he took her, brutally, trying to crush from both their minds the knowledge that this was no glad and easy and fortunate coupling. This was just two people in the dark.

They lay beside each other quietly; he had his arm under her head.

'Thank you, Anna.'

'You don't have to.'

'You're a swell kid. I mean it. I'll remember.'

'It's no use, is it?'

'No,' he said. 'No, I guess not. Not for people like us.'

After a time she moved and said: 'I got to be going. Don't get up.' In the darkness she dressed. He could hear her feeling around the floor for her shoes, and then a rustle as she pulled her dress on. He lay in bed, looking at the ceiling. She came over to the bed and stood beside it.

'I'm going now,' she said.

He took her hand and held it against his mouth.

She waited a moment, looking down at him, and then she said, shakily: 'Cheer up, dearie. All you gotta do is think how fine it's gonna be a long time after we're dead.'

The door closed softly behind her and he could not hear her on the stairs.

\* \* \*

The man who had called to him on the street was a miracle. He'd had to call twice because Pete couldn't believe it had happened. But the man actually wanted the gravel raked on his drive and the garage cleaned out. Pete had looked so stupid when told this that the man almost sent him away. It was just surprise. It was the first work Pete had been offered in four months. The man said he'd give him a dollar and Pete tried to keep from crying, or singing, or doing something he'd be ashamed of.

'We're not gonna spend it on groceries, Mabel,' Pete said. 'Can't you see it's my chance? I gotta start out in business. I gotta sell stuff. I'll make a lotta dough and pay it back to Mr Aarons. If I can get him something before the fifteenth we can stay here.'

'Business,' Mabel said. 'What kinda business?'

'I'm gonna sell shoe strings and chewing gum. I seen guys doing that. A lotta people need shoe strings and everybody chews gum. You can't lose. I can get the stuff wholesale.'

'Why don't you sell apples? Then we can use them if they don't all get sold.'

'Naw, they're not selling apples any more. That was way back. This is serious stuff. This is business.'

Mabel made him a tray from the top of a cardboard box she begged from the cleaners. She found some old ribbon and hung the tray from Pete's neck by a bit of dusty pink satin. She spread the shoe strings and gum out neatly and Pete shaved. He was terribly excited. In his mind he had it all worked out. This was the break he'd been waiting for. It had to come. Probably business was better than factory work, anyhow. He saw the rent paid, and the two of them safe again in their home. But that was only the first step. After that he saw people crowding around him, on Main Street, all buying. Then he'd enlarge his business and sell Hershey bars and maybe cigarettes. He'd be off Relief by now. God, he thought, off Relief. For a moment there was no need to go further. But then active, and hopeful, his mind plotted the now luminous future. He could probably get a store before he was through. People had to buy things; had to. He knew about that. Groceries. Or meat. Something like that. Or shoes. He saw himself working again, from morning until dark, regularly every day, and coming home to good hot dinners, and Mabel wearing fine clothes at Holliday Park in the summer. He walked towards Main Street holding his tray carefully against him, considering his shoe laces and his chewing gum with love.

Then another thing, he thought, there's not so many of them on the tray, so that looks like they've been bought and that'll encourage people.

He started on the corner but found people were too hurried here, too interested in the traffic lights and ducking under the street cars. Only the newsboys did business. He moved to the middle of the block, and stood in the sun. It was pleasant just being there. Having something to do. A working man; a business man you might really say.

A woman came by: she wore a fur coat and she was young. She hesitated. She walked a little past him and then walked quickly back and with embarrassment dropped a quarter on the tray and fled.

'Here's your gum, lady.' He held it out, running after her.

'I don't want it, thank you,' she said over her shoulder.

He came back to his place and thought this over. It wasn't right. She must have made a mistake. He wasn't begging. Anybody could see he wasn't begging: he had things to sell. He was somewhat angered, but on the other hand two bits was two bits. He put it in his pocket, first making sure that his pocket was whole.

Nothing happened. He hadn't known how hard it was to stand still in the same place. He moved back and leaned against a wall. And then decided that wasn't proper: it didn't look wide awake. Have to stand out from the wall; maybe talk to people.

'Shoelaces?' he said to a man. 'Need some chewing gum?'

The man pushed him aside, roughly. He had used a stiff arm with some energy behind it.

'Say, you,' Pete started to follow him. What the hell kind of guy did he think he was, going around shoving folks on the street. But then he thought, no. Might get in trouble with a cop. Maybe he ought just to stand and not say anything to people.

In the course of five hours he sold twenty cents worth of gum. He was desperately tired. He ached from his heels in straight shooting pains up to his neck. It's only that I haven't built up a trade, he thought, takes time to get regular customers.

He was hungry too, but he couldn't face the idea of going home to Mabel with forty-five cents, for his day's work. Somehow, he felt Mabel would be too upset about it, and they'd sit that night, as they had uncounted nights before, silently, in the front room, not doing anything, just waiting for it to get late enough to go to bed.

He had planned coming back tonight with $1.65, all sold out, and ready to buy more gum and shoelaces for tomorrow.

He was thinking about this and putting words together in his mind, for Mabel. To keep it from seeming bad to her, he'd talk about how you had to build up your regular customers and everything and explain it that way …

Suddenly, he saw a man farther down the block, standing, as he was, against the wall, and sharply profiled in front of him was a tray, like Pete's own. Goddam the bastard, Pete thought, here I been standing around all day getting this place for myself and building up my trade and now that guy comes along. There's not money in it for two, he said to himself, and he was already angrily walking up the block towards his rival. The ache in his back hurried him on, his hunger and his disappointment sharpened his anger. I'll smack him one, he decided, sneaking up on me like that and stealing my customers. Taking the bread outa my mouth. Couldn't the guy go somewheres else; he must just be mean, just be wanting to get in there and grab off the people who'd be buying from Pete otherwise.

'Hey you,' he called, but the man did not turn. That made Pete angrier. Trying to high-hat him was he, trying to act innocent-like. His fist shut, tight and hard. I'll paste him one, I don't care if the cops run me in or not, no guy's gonna get away with that. He saw his business destroyed, everything gone. He ran forward and grabbed the man by the shoulder and spun him around, his fist up, ready to smash him between the eyes, cops or no cops. And he found himself staring at a quiet, blank face, with sealed eyes, the eyelids close and shrivelled over the iris, and a small, hand-drawn sign on the man's chest said: 'I AM BLIND.'

He let go the man's shoulder and his fist fell. He stood there, trying to find some words to say to this man, to explain, but he couldn't. He, Pete Hines, was doing a blind man's job, he was stealing from the blind; he was a strong, healthy man with eyes, and the only thing he could get to do was blind man's work, and this man would be hungrier because of it. Blind man's work. What kind of world was it; what kind of country were they running anyhow. Something seemed to be screaming inside him, but there were no words, only a murderous fury and a feeling that this was the last time he was going to get caught and cheated and shamed. The last time. He was against them now, them and their world. He was against them as long as he lived, with the only thing he had – hate.

He tore the pink ribbon from his neck and dumped his shoe laces and gum on the blind man's tray. 'Here buddy. You take 'em. You sell. That's your work. I'm not blind, buddy,' he said protestingly, to convince the man, to make the man realise that it was a mistake for him to have these shoelaces and gum at all, they didn't belong to him, it wasn't his kind of work, my God, he wasn't blind.

\* \* \*

Joe had known this would happen some day. But only in his mind. His heart rebelled against the idea, against the stupidity and injustice of it, and the waste. He looked at the men standing in front of him. Probably it was only his eyes, tired from writing there in the ill-lit office. The men seemed unusually tall, all the same height even, and black and they stood tall and strong like trees. There had been no shuffling or uncertainty, they'd come in together firmly, stood grouped around him with none of the coughing nervous sounds of unsure people, waited, given him time to understand what was happening before any words were said. And then Frankie Zaleski spoke for them. They didn't want him any more; he wasn't the man they wanted to represent them and talk for them and guide them. They didn't trust him. He'd muffed the job. He wasn't really trying. He didn't have the guts. They could run the union better without him. They had their own ideas. So he better just get out.

He hadn't the strength to stand up and at least talk to them on their level and he felt himself at an unconquerable disadvantage, seated there before them. He felt weak and sick, and he kept thinking, there's only one on my side. But there were things he'd have to say. If he took it silently, it would seem that he agreed, that he admitted what they accused him of. It would seem that he was a man who had been caught mismanaging other men's affairs, and now that he was caught, he was scared, and would slink off. He would have to say something; but he couldn't speak in his own defence. That would be an apology, and there was no apology to make. He had done his best. And he was the only one who knew how little any man could do.

His voice disgusted him; it sounded quavery and thin.

'All right,' he said. 'You take it over and run it the way you want. You'll anyhow know what you're talking about, then. I been working at this steady for months, and there's no more a man could do. But if you don't see it like that.'

He felt his shoulders sagging. I've got a right to be sore, he thought, I've got a right to get up and curse them to hell. The fools. Who'd have done this work like I have, for nothing, putting his own money in it. None of them. But he wasn't angry. He was only tired.

'We elected Frankie to take on the job,' a man said.

He smiled at that. Frankie was a good guy, but he'd have a fine time trying to write a letter, or make a speech, or keep the dues straight, or argue with the bosses, or any of that stuff.

'Okay,' Joe said. 'If you come around tomorrow morning, I'll show you where all the stuff is, Frankie, and what you gotta do.'

'I guess I can figger it out all right by myself,' Frankie said.

Suddenly he was angry. That was extra, that was like kicking a man for the fun of it. That unneeded hint of suspicion and the blank crazy stupidity of it. He stood up now, leaning on his desk.

'Lissen, you poor half-witted cluck. You'll never figger it out. None of you. You haven't got enough brains all of you together. You'll sure make a fine business of this union. You'll make a joke of it; they'll sit around Washington and laugh like hell every time they get a letter. And Minton'll be so happy he'll probably buy you an office. You might as well close this place up and stop thinking about it. The union's bust. Now. And besides which, get the hell out. I pay the rent. I'll get my stuff out and you can come in tomorrow and run this union any way you want. I don't give a goddam. I'm through. You can make any kinda goddam fool of yourselves you want. But I'm not gonna sit here and lissen to a bunch a horses' behinds like you talking about stuff you don't know about. The door's right behind you. I'll take the whole bunch of you on if you don't get outa here in three seconds flat.'

They stared at him; it was a quick change.

'Say, who d'you think you're talking to?' Frankie said, and stepped out from the others.

'To you. You heard me. Get the hell outa here.'

'You can't get away with that, Joe Barrow. You been sitting here running this union cockeyed, and not getting a damn thing for us and playing in with the bosses, and a lotta things we don't think's so hot. And now you talk like you was God-a-mighty. What you need is to get your face smeared.'

'Yeah. Well try and do it.'

There was just that quiet breathless moment which heralds a fight, that single instant of uncertainty for both sides to decide and to start.

A man put his hand on Frankie's arm. 'Come on, Frankie. Leave him be. It'll only mess up the office. We'll come back tomorrow.'

The others muttered agreement. Frankie dusted his hands together as if he had already hit Joe and the fight was triumphantly finished. They left more awkwardly than they had come.

Joe sat down again, with his hands stretched out open on the desk in front of him, staring at the door. So this was how it ended. This was what you got for it. His anger, which had protected him, dropped. And he thought: what do I do next. There was nothing left, not the union, nor his friends, and the feeling of being wanted, not work. There was no place for him now. His life which had fitted in with other lives, was now something needless and limited. It was as if he didn't have a name any more. His mind babbled helplessly: what am I going to do, what am I going to do next …

Someone kicked the door open and the glass in it rattled as it hit against the wall. He jerked up straight. Frankie coming back to get his fight.

'Lissen Joe,' Pete said.

So Pete was sticking with him, Joe thought, there was Pete anyhow.

'You tell Mabel,' Pete said. 'I'm not gonna go back there. You tell her. You tell her it was blind man's work. They can't do nothing more to me. I'm gonna get out. You go and tell her. Tonight. So's she won't worry. But tell her I'm not coming back. I can't do nothing for her, and tell her goodbye. You'll do that Joe?'

'What're you talking about?'

'It's the way they're running this country,' Pete said and his voice fell. There was terror in his voice. 'They're trying to make us crazy. They're trying to make us do blind men's work. They tell you you're too old. They don't act like we was men. I'll show 'em,' Pete said, and Joe was frightened of the man's eyes, 'I'll show 'em if they can get away with that.'

'They all came in here a little while ago,' Joe said, 'and they told me to get out. They said I ran this union cockeyed, and they didn't want me around. They told me to get out.'

Pete focussed his attention on this, something else that had happened: they were against Joe too, then. 'They did that,' he said.

'Yeah.'

'The bastards,' Pete said wonderingly.

'Sure.'

'What're you gonna do.'

'Don't know.'

'You can come with me. We'll show 'em.'

'No,' Joe said, and was surprised himself that he had made this decision. That would after all be best: go away. Forget it. Stop trying to do anything.

'You'll tell Mabel?'

'If I go,' Joe said, talking for himself, 'they'll be sure to say I took some union money; and the whole union'll get a dirty name. Somebody'll make it out crooked. I still gotta stay,' Joe said to himself, and he was amazed to discover this, that there was a role left for him, something important which he had to do.

Pete was at the door. 'Goodbye, Joe. Make it all right with Mabel. Tell her it's blind man's work.'

The moon had come up: a raw wind drove streaky clouds over the sky. People were indoors now, eating. People with the rent paid, Pete thought.

He was going away from this: this place had been his home, and now it was strange to him, and full of cruelty. But he understood nothing. He was walking bent against the wind, towards the river, and his mind churned with these things he knew he would never understand. I worked all my life he kept saying: I was only in jail once. I paid my taxes. At the street corners, the wind sprang out at him. Where did guys sleep that didn't have a home? And all the other men, the ones he'd seen mornings asking for work at the factories, the people standing in front of employment agencies. What about them too? Suddenly it frightened him more than he could bear, to think of the others who must be like himself. It made it worse. There was nothing you could be sure of.

He was walking with his head down and now he was conscious of an extra darkness, shutting out the moon. He looked up and saw the great unformed mass of the Minton factory, silent and empty. There was no one on the streets. It looked as if the factory had been abandoned for a long time, in this light: as if no men ever came in the doors, lumpish with sleep in the morning, and went home in the afternoon, glad to be leaving. He stopped and stood with his head back, studying the overgrown outline of this building, like carelessly piled boxes against the sky. And then he had a thought. It grew so swiftly that it was no longer an idea but a plan, something he had been waiting for and always wanted to do. The last thing he could do.

He went back along a side street: they were repairing a tenement and he remembered a small pile of bricks lying before it.

He picked a brick, a whole one, holding it up for the moon to shine on, to make sure it was solid. He held it in his hand and amazingly it felt warm. He hurried to where he saw the factory, big and black over the surrounding houses.

'I'll show you,' Pete shouted: his voice was close to him and sharp and not very real. 'I'll show you if you can get away with it. You and all the others.'

He raised his arm to throw, and it stuck. The brick stayed in his hand, above his head. There was no one on the street, no cop's voice calling to stop him. Nothing. But he couldn't do it. This was the last thing for him, to show he was a man anyhow, and they couldn't cheat him and kick him around and make him crazy. But the factory was too big. He tightened his hold on the brick, but he couldn't throw it. He let it drop and it cracked on the pavement.

Then, close under the shadows of the factory, he ran towards the freight yards, where the trains crawled slowly all night, going someplace else.

# *Jim*

## I. JIM COMES HOME

CLIMBING UP THE dirt track to the house, he could hear them: his father and his sister, Clara.

'I'll go out with anybody I please, anywhere I please, anytime I please,' she said, her voice heavy and slow with anger. 'What do you think you are, anyhow? What gives you a right to order me around? What do you do for me? I don't care about that, but don't try to stop me doing for myself.'

His father's voice rumbled: 'I'll teach you to talk to me like that.'

'If you touch me I'll get the police.'

Jim stood at the door, watching them. His father standing above Clara with a milk-bottle in his raised hand; his mother in a corner mending, not noticing the noise or the scene, which she knew by heart, anyhow. Nothing had changed. Why should it; he had only been gone six weeks.

'Happy days,' he said cheerfully, to his father's back and his sister's suddenly turning, surprised face.

'Jim,' Clara said. 'We didn't know you'd be coming back so soon.'

'Hello, son.' Mrs Barr crossed the room and kissed him on the cheek. 'You're looking fine. Did they feed you good at the farm?'

'Yeah. It was fine. Hello, Dad.'

'Hello, Jim.'

'Well, that's lucky. You won't be getting much here. I don't understand that new Relief lady, she gives $8 a week to Mamie Hodges and her family and there's only three of them and she only gives us $6.50; it just ain't right…'

Jim patted her arm. It made it even worse to whine about it. Bad enough to have to take it, to be helpless, to be waiting in a line, interviewed, questioned, handed things with kindness. It made it even worse to whine. That way it looked as if you were accepting the gift all right, only you wanted more. He didn't accept, not in his mind. Nobody had to keep him, he was Jim Barr and young and could work and take care of his family … Mrs Barr was talking again, about her heart and how she'd have to get a medical order from the Relief to go to a doctor … 'Clara,' Jim said, despairingly, turning away.

'Oh, ma, when he just comes home,' Clara said. 'When he's just come in, can't you think of something cheerful to say?'

He put his arm around Clara and they walked into the next room. He shut the door. 'Got a new steady?' he said.

'Yeah, Joe Bartlett, the boy who works at the grocery downtown. He gets good money, too; $10 a week. But it don't do him much good; he's got his mother and sister there to take care of and he don't get help from the Relief because he's working.' She was silent a moment. 'Anyhow, I'm glad of that. Even if we can't do much, me and him, I'm glad he's working. I'm glad he's not on Relief like us and always arguing, or hanging around with the other boys by the garage or somewheres.'

'Sure.'

'God, he's a swell guy, Jim.'

'What's the old man got against him?'

'Oh, he says Joe's got a name with the women; says he got that blonde girl over by Henderson – you know, her name's Lucy something – in trouble.'

'Did he?'

'I dunno. What if he did? He's not that way with me, anyhow.'

'Well,' Jim said.

'I made a little money while you were gone, taking care of Miz Newton's baby when her maid went out. And I gotta job for the winter doing the housework at Miz Carter's, before school and after, board and room.'

'Pay?'

'Two dollars a week, that'll be enough for spending money and books and clothes. I'm fixed all right.'

'Jees,' he said.

'What's wrong?'

'Two dollars.'

'Better than nothing.'

'I know; me, I can't make two cents.'

'Oh, now, Jim.' She put her hand on his arm. 'Sure you can. What'd you make on the harvest?'

'Thirty-one plunks; I got about twenty-seven left, for school and stuff. I only got three weeks pitching oats; been walking around the rest of the time. You know – asking ...'

'It'll be fun going to school together. We can pass notes and play around.'

'You bet. I'm twenty-one. You're a girl and you're only seventeen. And we'll be in the same class. It'll be lotsa fun.'

'Jim, nobody thinks you're dumb. Everybody knows it's just 'cause of money. And you trying to work for the family. Don't let it get you down, about being older, I mean.'

'Oh, hell, no. It's fine. I should care. When I'm forty I'll graduate from college with big honours. And when I'm sixty I'll be out of medical school all ready to start life and have a swell practice. When I'm seventy I'll give you a high-class wedding with a white satin dress.'

'What's the use, Jim?'

'It's a joke.'

She looked at him. 'I almost never laugh,' she said.

\* \* \*

Clara took him to school the first day. She was already staying at the Carters' and already, even before her school work started, she had purplish circles under her eyes and she moved limply.

'It isn't hard,' she said. 'It just never stops.'

He met her at the corner, smiled, and said: 'Don't leave me alone, Ma.'

In the hall, boys and girls came up to Clara to say hello, ask each other questions about classes, teachers, teams, parties, and laugh without knowing why.

'This is my brother ...' 'Pleased ta meetcha.' One boy Jim knew – Dick Manfred's younger brother: too young to be included in their talk or plans when he went to Dick's house. Considered a pest, somebody to take care of unwillingly.

'Hello, son,' Jim said. Sam Manfred frowned: so did Clara.

'He's in your class,' Clara whispered. 'You can't treat him like a baby.'

'Oh.'

'Come and pick your desk,' Clara said.

They went to the study hall: a great square room smelling already of feet, damp sweaters, stale candy. The boys shoved, trying to sit near to or far from the present love. The girls giggled and coyly said I'm gonna sit here, and waited for a stampede and said it again louder: if nothing happened they chose their seats near someone else more favoured.

There were innumerable small worlds here: each living, centred around a mystically selected individual, glued to and following that lead. Each group pyramided up the one led by a few senior girls whose fathers had money, owned stores, cars, securities. Each world secretly or openly despised the others: each one had defined positions in its own hierarchy; special names; a language. Everyone was eager; there seemed to be a purpose in their movements, guided, perhaps, by last year and the friendships of last year or things done together in the summer. Jim stood alone in all this: where he sat made no difference. He didn't want to whisper behind his desk lid, sigh down his lady's neck, throw spit balls at his enemies. He only wanted a place to keep his books: all the desks were alike.

'I'll sit near you,' Clara said. He smiled at her: how kind she was. Anxious and careful with him: wanting him to feel he belonged here, wanting to identify him with these kids whose faces even seemed to him soft and unformed. Could two years make all this difference. It had been two years since he'd come to this study hall and put his books in a desk and even then he was older, but it didn't seem to matter. There was Dick Manfred then, also nineteen, a senior. Dick had worked in Seattle, and been in a longshoremen's strike, and jerked sodas in San Francisco, and ridden the rails, and women had taken him in, too, and fed him, and been good to him, and he and Dick could talk about what things they understood. It seemed to him he knew something none of these babies knew: he knew it was hard to get work, he knew you couldn't get it at all most of the time, and when you did it was by the day, the week, using your muscles only as if you didn't have anything but arms, as if your head was just stuck up there for looks. He knew what it was to be saying to yourself, it's going to be like this all the time: people like me finally die hanging on to a shovel. Or a pitchfork. He knew also that his only chance was this high school, and after it college, and even that wasn't sure: but without it he could see nothing. He had to have an education: something that changed him enough to fool employers, so that the men behind desks wouldn't always write down after his name: common labour. What did these kids know?

He chose a desk without thinking: on his left sat a fattish boy in a plaid lumberjack shirt, already busy aiming something at somebody's head: on

the other side was a little girl who must have been a freshman – all classes
studied together in a muted shuffling, sighing tumult – a nice, quiet, shy
little girl with long yellow braids. He smiled at her and she smiled back,
blushed and quickly put up her desk lid and rummaged around inside.

'But I'm over there,' Clara said, standing above him.

'That's all right, kid. You go on over and play with your friends. I'm fine
here: I only came to this school to study. Don't you worry about me.'

'But, Jim, you won't be happy if you don't get in with a gang.'

'Happy,' he said. 'That's a good one.'

* * *

He had been in school a month: already his imitation leather coat, bought
carefully with the harvest money, was scratched. Already he drew in
against the cold, walking fast in the mornings. And still he could bring
no order into his mind. Even sitting quietly like this in the hot stuffy hall
was hard. He had to tell himself every day: it stops at three. Three isn't
so far off. Nine to three is a short working day: better than factories or
the docks or the farm. Better than sitting home. His shoulders twitched
and he kept looking out the window: he had been painfully aware of the
fall, quickly come and now almost gone. He thought he had counted
each leaf falling from the tree outside; sometimes he thought he had
heard them. And he was old, older than any of these kids, shabby and
poor, getting thin again at home and feeling his body slump. He sat
and waited for three o'clock and then unhurried, weary, disgusted with
himself, he wandered home.

He kept saying to himself: It'll all come back. But his eyes strayed, and
his mind handled half-remembered phrases thoughtlessly, like a woman
shopping for something she doesn't want. Nothing focussed. He sat in the
study hall with a worn blue book before him: American history. There were

things here to be learned: the teacher had assigned twelve pages for the day's lesson. The civil war: where was it, anyhow; a part of the country he had never seen, some people from the east and others from the south, fighting about negroes. He didn't know much about negroes. On the whole he thought they were nice, cheerful and stupid. People paid them less and arrested them quicker. They had been freed: there was a war about it. Would there be a war, for instance, to free the unemployed, who were slaves too, in a way?

I must learn this, he thought, and imitated unconsciously the bland dead look of his classmates and moved his lips, saying again and again, Lee lost the final battle of the war at Appomattox on April 9th, 1865. He had been doing this for perhaps ten minutes: he stopped and enquired of himself what he had been saying, something about Lee, a battle ... He passed his hand over his eyes, ready for tears, or furious flight. What's the use, he said, I can't do it. I don't give a damn for that stuff. That civil war is all over, long ago. And then he thought: is knowing about Lee and his battles what gets you jobs? Because that's what I want: the hell with everything else, I want a job. A good regular job you can count on all year, that isn't going to kill you before you're forty and you can live like a decent man, not the way they do at home, not like some kind of animal that feels and talks about it ...

The bell rang. The boys and girls shoved each other getting out of the room: shoving was a special sport, preferably one shoved a girl, one's favourite girl. Jim had spoken of this once to Clara, seeing her gay and argumentative, being pushed along by a boy whose hands on her shoulders, then hips, were possessive, interested.

'Why not climb into bed,' Jim suggested to her. 'It's more fun.'

She was angry with him, saying that he had a dirty mind and they were all friends here, just kids, they didn't mean anything by it. He had said nothing but he was ashamed, thinking perhaps she was right and they were all too sappy to know what they were about. Anyhow, Clara had so little that made her eyes bright, or made her laugh. None of his business: and that day again he had felt himself to be old and grey, carrying winter around with him.

He walked behind everyone else, in no hurry, to class. He chose his seat simply because no one else was sitting in it. The teacher, Mr Watkins, shuffled papers on his desk and made ominous marks with a blue pencil. Play acting, Jim thought. The second bell rang. Like light fading, the class dimmed, slouched into as comfortable positions as were possible on the straight chairs, leaned their heads on their hands, crossed their knees, their eyes mute and dazed. Mr Watkins came into his own; but without gladness, from habit. As if speaking to stone, he asked questions and usually led the pupil until he got something resembling an answer. He had done this for years. He has a family, Jim thought, and they're not rich enough to keep up a good front. He has to do this. Jim, too, slumped in his chair, a feeling of horrible weariness over him. Mr Watkins' voice went on: the dead talking to the sleeping, Jim decided. Would anything excite them; would anything make them uncross their knees and jerk up in their chairs. Now, if Mr Watkins just said, suddenly, 'Anybody who plays football is a fairy ...' He grinned.

'Share your joke, Barr.' Mr Watkins' voice was cold. There were limits to everything. He was used to talking to those glaucous eyes which the young turned on him. He was used to the awful parrotry of their replies or the uneasy shuffling when memory failed them. He was used to saying to himself: I am a fourth-rate teacher in a sixth-rate high-school in a small western town. But he wasn't going to be laughed at. He was too old now; there was nothing he could do to change this.

Jim sat up, he wasn't aware that he had smiled, but he knew he couldn't tell that joke, even if it was one ...

'I was thinking about something.'

'Remarkable,' Mr Watkins said, knowing, with disgust, that this was the easiest, the cheapest, reply.

The class tittered.

Suddenly Jim was angry, angry because the room was hot and thick with much-breathed air; angry at the lumpishness of the class and Mr Watkins feebly protecting his dignity, and at himself.

'I think, once in a while, to keep from going nuts.'

'You find it so dull here?'

'Worse than that. Dead.'

'You are not forced to attend school, I believe – you have passed the age limit.' Mr Watkins knew he would feel sick, flushing and weak with shame for this, later. But now, it was Watkins or Barr. I can't be laughed at, he thought, if I am, I'm finished, and I've got to keep my job.

'I wanted to look like somebody who's been to school, so I'd get a decent job,' Jim said. 'But I don't learn and I can't take it.'

He rose, sweeping notebooks and pencils off the chair arm.

'Don't be ridiculous, Jim,' Mr Watkins said. 'It's the end of the day, we're all tired.'

'Listen,' Jim said. 'I know about jobs. How you gotta get them and then you gotta keep them because of grocery bills. I know about that. I'm sorry for you, too.'

The door closed behind him noiselessly on automatic springs.

Mr Watkins was aware of a small chirping noise, smothered: Clara was crying.

* * *

For a while he enjoyed simply being able to yawn out loud; being able to dawdle around the house, looking for a comfortable or fairly quiet place to sit, reading the papers or books chosen with care and excitement at the public library. For a week, perhaps more, it was a satisfaction in itself to know that he didn't have to go to school. He stopped shaving and abandoned the mustard-coloured jacket for a torn, soft sweater. When sufficiently pressed he helped his mother, sweeping or wiping dishes or collecting wood outside. He tried not to see his father. He had reasons for this. He had loved his father and thought there was nobody like Luke Barr in Harriston. He used to watch his father at work, building neatly with his hands, neatly and carefully; making the furniture that they sold at C. D. Magnus' furniture store, or making handsome pieces to order for Dr Swivelton and Mrs Maxwell, who was the town's great lady, and for others who wanted good work done and could pay.

His father worked very slowly: he liked the special orders best, because he could then buy finer quality wood, and he used to explain woods to Jim, talking to him about seasoning, and staining, and polishing, and the rich real colour you could get. Being a hand cabinetmaker he never made much money: there were machines, and who in Harriston knew or really cared about the pride and love Luke Barr lavished on each drawer and panel and chair-back and bed-post. Who knew about the feel of wood and the way its colours rippled in a good light. Still, he had made enough money to keep his family decently, and there had been pieces of furniture in their own home, a home long before this one, which Luke used to stand and look at, saying nothing. He had taught Jim the word 'skill' when the boy was little. His own father had made great chests high as a man, Luke Barr said, and he also knew how to carve, but he was a finer craftsman: that was in England. He himself read only about cabinet making: but he took Jim to the public library in Harriston when he was twelve years old and said: 'Don't come home till dark.'

Six years ago C. D. Magnus decided to buy only factory furniture. Slowly the people who lived on Oakdale Road and Harriston Drive stopped ordering furniture since they already had furniture, and you had to make a choice, now that there was a depression. One day, without saying anything,

Luke Barr had gone out and gotten a pick and shovel job on the roads. But he was not young and he hated the work, and finally he couldn't even find work that needed no skill whatever.

He had sold the furniture in his home and at last, in a rage that no words would fit, he had taken an axe to his dining-room table, chopped the fine polished walnut into kindling and carried it to the lake and thrown it away. For the last two years he had avoided his family, hating to see his own failure in them. Clara was too young to remember clearly the other house, the other life: but Jim knew. For years he had been too sorry for his father to speak; and now he was too absorbed in his own problems to care about the older man. Mr Barr was glad of this. He had a habit of disappearing all day. No one knew where he went and no one asked. He would eat breakfast in silence and leave the house quickly, walking towards the woods as if he had a meeting planned or even, wonderfully, a job to do.

The days were very quiet. Mrs Barr talked to herself at times, in a soft whining voice. Occasionally Jim heard her making conversation with unknown neighbours about new things she had in the house, her new curtains, the lovely new bed Luke had made. He managed to get away, when that started: we're all lying to ourselves, he thought; we can't any of us, except Clara perhaps, admit that our lives are really like this.

Clara came home some evenings, or late in the afternoon. She was always hurried; the Carters ate, changed their clothes, mussed their rooms, slept in their beds. All of this was Clara's concern. 'Dirty and lazy,' Clara would say in her brief passage. 'I gotta hurry back: there's always more work than I can do, anyhow, in the day.'

'How's school?' Jim would ask.

'Oh, fine.' But she didn't want to talk about it. Jim had been a wash-out at school. She thought it was better to be nice to him and not talk about it. He was a sweet kid, anyhow: perhaps it wasn't his fault … With quick hatred she would stare at the clogged kitchen where they all lived, ate, read, quarrelled, and hurry back to the Carters.

Jim got up later and later in the mornings. He used as much of the day as he could sleeping: and for hours, silent, frowning in concentration, he read. As it grew colder he chose books about warm countries. About travel: men who were surprised by things happening in far off places which bore no resemblance to the civilisation they knew. He didn't have a wide choice in the public library but he managed to lose himself almost steadily in books about Tahiti and Borneo, Java, Bali, India. He began to build stories from these books with himself as hero: himself discovering incredible plants which cured cancer; finding a flower dust that stopped tuberculosis – but none of this with agony, working too hard; feeling any of the heat he imagined around him as a blessing. It just happened: Jim Barr in white shorts, an open necked shirt and a sun helmet: still young …

One day he rose very late and told himself simply: this morning I have tropical fever and can't go out in the jungle. Unaware of his mother, the silence that was his father's and Clara's absence, he fumbled for soap at the sink, washing himself, thinking about what he would work over in his laboratory today. He had almost decided on a small vermilion berry, properties as well as name unknown, when he looked into the mirror above the sink. He saw there, as amazingly as if he were looking at a stranger's face, a yellowish mask, unevenly grown with beard. The face looked old and, in some disgusting way, slipped, smeared, like rotten fruit, he thought, or something that's been dug up. He stood before his own face in silence; not touching himself, not moving. Finally it became clear to him that this was Jim Barr: this was the way he looked for everyone to see and probably he himself was like this face. He tore his jacket from a peg and ran out into the morning, with a wilted dandruffy snow falling.

\* \* \*

He went to the pool-room: it took what may have been hours, running through the thin snow. He went without noticing directions and without plan. He stopped from time to time, stood still and passed his hand over his face. He could feel the stubble of beard and the flesh felt loose. Anyone who saw him, bent a little with the cold, stroking his face, thought: that boy is drunk. He had no reason for going to the pool-room except that he saw it before him suddenly, lighted up against the grey morning, and it looked warm inside.

'Lo, Jim.' … 'Got two bits?' … 'Wanna drink?' …

He heard that. He wanted a drink badly. Presently, he found that he was something of an authority on billiards, standing over the green tables, urging and advising, groaning at a stupid or failed play, slapping people on the back. Later, he even thought what a fine thing it was to live in a town where you knew everyone and there were such swell guys around in the morning to talk to. Friends. That was what, people you could talk to. People just like you. Finally, he remembered vaguely that something had shocked him that morning, something disgusting. His own face, by God. He wandered to a mirror and looked at himself until he could see what he was looking at. Then he thought it was a pretty good face, like everybody else's, like his friends' faces. That was just a nut idea – the kind of thing you thought when you were alone, and no swell guys to talk to. He fell asleep on one of the benches along the wall, but the proprietor didn't put him out, he liked Jim all right and it was still snowing.

Mr Barr spoke frequently now about the way his son was a bum, and what was the use in having a son if he only grew up to be a drunk and it was a funny thing that a boy couldn't get any decent work, but he could loaf around and get free drinks easy. Mr Barr lived bitterly with his idleness and Mrs Barr lived with her ailments and her sense of being cheated by the Relief. Jim, between bouts of drinking and queasy hangovers, paid no attention to either of them.

He had found it was hard to talk to the men at the pool-room unless he was tight. Perhaps he was shy, he thought, or too young. But there was Dick Manfred, who came home for Sundays and started getting drunk Saturday night and rolled back to Ferguson, where the mines were, Monday morning, shaken, but sober enough to work.

In the short period before they were both too happy or too sodden to talk, Dick told him about the mines.

'The first day I was scared outa my pants, I thought sure everything was gonna fall in; I was at the eighteen-hundred level just shoving slush around on the wagons. I went up the ladders to watch the guys drilling, and I was so scared and excited I almost passed out. I thought: By God, this is some work! None of your old desk jobs for me, I thought. And then I figured I'd take a correspondence course in mining and engineering, and get to be one of the guys in high boots who go around inspecting and then I'd be the manager.'

Jim listened: he knew about this: he had told himself these stories too. An intern whom nobody noticed: just standing around, holding things or maybe putting iodine on cuts. But one day he'd have to do a major operation because nobody else was there, and save a life, and everybody would swat him on the back, and he'd be resident surgeon. And then he'd discover cures. And then and then …

'Well, what about it,' he said.

'Oh,' Dick Manfred was looking around in his mind for the right words. He wasn't drunk yet and he felt too tired, too disgusted, it was hard telling Jim about this. He could talk to lots of the young guys in the mines and they'd know. 'Listen,' he said. 'I can't quit on account of my mother, and my father was a miner and she don't seem to know what it's like. She's so used to all that, she thinks it's the way people live. I gotta take care of her. But don't you do it. Don't you do it, boy. Jesus,' he said. 'Hey Sam, where's that whisky.'

'But work,' Jim said, still sober. 'There's times I think anything would be swell. Anything; not just hanging around, waiting for the time to pass.'

'That's the bunk. The kinda world we live in, people like us only got a choice between how they wanta conk out. Me, I'd a damn sight rather go at it easy and slow. If I was free, boy, I'd grab rides on the freights and see the world.'

'You would, wouldja? I've done it. The freight bulls are pretty boys, I wanna tell you. And people take a look at you and say "Bums" and slam the door or call a cop. You can't sit anywhere or lie anywhere. Every time you look around you get run in for vagrancy. See the world is right, running like hell with some guy running after you. You know a lot.'

'Well, what can we do then?'

'I dunno. Get an education I guess; get so you can be an engineer or a doctor or something like that. Then you can work like a real guy and make money and people think something of you. As long as you're just common labour you can't do a thing.'

'And I guess you're gonna pay for the education with smiles and many thanks. That's a good one too.'

There was a silence. 'Sam, how about the whisky,' Jim said.

Finally, while he was still shaping his words clearly, Jim said: 'There's nothing for us. We're the guys who don't count.'

'Take some whisky,' Dick said, 'I got some money left. Go ahead and drink. It'll be Monday soon enough.'

The pool-room closed at one on Saturday nights. Dick Manfred, having finally realised that it was necessary to leave, arose, draped his coat around him with a large if imprecise gesture and rocketed through the door and across the street. Calling for him to wait, Jim followed. A truck, doing night hauling between Spokane and Lewiston, rumbled around the corner, swung out a little, righted itself and drove towards Jim. There were no street lights at this hour: Jim's dark wavering figure appeared like a sudden shadow, before the square high nose of the truck closed him out. The brakes howled and the truck, with the sudden stopping, lurched sharply sidewise and hit a lamp-post. The driver dropped from his seat to find what he had killed, shouting curses, terrified. They picked Jim up across the street against the kerb, limp, his hair wet and dark with blood. Dick Manfred leaned against a store and watched all this: his mind said soberly, Jim's dead, but he could not move, only the wall behind him kept his legs from melting under the weight of his body. The truck driver got Sam to shut the pool-room at once and drive his car to the hospital. The truck driver held Jim on the back seat, swearing the boy had run under the truck, how could a guy see on a dark street and Sam said don't you worry he was drunk, but it's too bad, he was a good kid that one.

At the hospital a sleepy but pleased intern (something important to do at last) examined Jim on the operating table. The whole thing disgusted him beyond reason: aside from a dinky cut on the head, probably from the kerbstone, there was nothing the matter with this guy. Perhaps shock. Damn good thing too; teach him not to run under trucks. He deserved at least a double fracture of the arm, or an amputated leg. But nothing. Stinking drunk and limp; got brushed by the far wheel and thrown; just folded up soft like a handkerchief. The intern took eight stitches in Jim's head, cursing everybody with soft regularity and told the truck driver and Sam to get the hell out so he could sleep.

In the morning, the intern explained the accident to Jim angrily. The next time he said we'll let you bleed to death: you don't deserve much more. You kids can't hold your liquor: there ought to be jail sentences for goddam mugs walking under trucks.

Jim watched the life of the hospital: the nurse carrying things to him on glass trays, such clean orderly things and the way she handled them, as if she could see germs and was politely avoiding contact with them. His fever chart. The intern who relented after a day and told him stories about operations. He thought: It's a funny way to get into this kind of place where I've always wanted to be, but it's worth being hit by ten trucks, at least.

He asked questions until the intern said listen I've got some books you can have but for God's sake fella they're other people in here. He lay on his bed with his head hanging down towards the floor, to get flushed and hot, praying for fever, a slight infection, anything that would keep him here longer. He opened every closet, when he was allowed to get up, and hung around the operating room door white with excitement. They let him watch an appendectomy, against all the rules, but because his eyes were there outside the door, enormous, desperately pleading. He had a fever that day from joy, feeling that he had at last come where he belonged. And in his mind he placed every detail of the operating room, to hold it sharply forever. The silence, the precision, the white-clothed people working: instruments passed without orders, without words, according to ritual: the quick deft hands of the surgeon, the feeling of absolute safety: this thing could not fail now or ever; these men were skilled, were above other men, any kind of men. He lay in his bed that afternoon and stared at his hands, smiling, released of doubt about the future. When the nurse came in at night he said: 'Are my hands all right, have I got hands to be a surgeon?' She took them in hers and stroked his hair: he's good-looking enough to get in the movies she thought, what a mutt to want to be a doctor. 'Sure you have, fine hands,' she said. And took his temperature. He slept happily. He had seen again clearly where he wanted to go: and now he had only to get there.

* * *

They had turned him down pleasantly in Harriston: the bakery, the garage, the Horny-Hand Café, Schultz's grocery, the Mammoth Construction

Company, the Beaver Saw Mills, the Apex Drug Store. In Ferguson they were less chatty about it and just said, sorry nothing doing. By the time he got to Newberry Forks, he looked like a tramp and was hungry. They didn't know him there, and strangers were just more labour unwanted, or else guys bumming a meal. The constable told him to get a move on. He knew that phrase; he knew a lot about vagrancy charges. In all it took him a week to prove to himself again that there wasn't any work for people like him: though no doubt interns were besieged with offers of fine positions in hospitals. When his mother asked him about his luck, he said: 'Oh, I had a fine walk. Nothing like exercise to keep a man healthy.' His stomach was so shrunken, he could scarcely eat. He told his mother not to worry, he was fine. Didn't she know that he was twenty-one, the finest years of a man's life: and he could probably always get a job in the army unless his arches had fallen somewhere on the state highway.

He was too tired the first night to notice that something was more wrong than usual.

He finally wondered what they were keeping so quiet about. Mr Barr appeared only at breakfast and dinner. Mrs Barr went about the house complaining softly. But there was something more. She would pick up a plate to dry it and stand with it in her hand staring at the floor, aimless and uncertain. He would see her sitting on the side of the bed in her room, holding a mop, her eyes blank, weeping without knowing it.

Clara came to dinner on her night off: only because food was free, at home. Jim knew that: but he watched his father, feeling everyone's silence, these people who usually shouted at each other in anger. Finally he asked: 'What's biting you? What's wrong Dad? Anything worse than it always is. And Clara for Christ's sake stop sitting there looking like you had a mouth full of worms.'

She stared at him.

Mr Barr said nothing.

'What is it?' Jim said. 'For God's sake let me in on your fun.'

Mr Barr stopped eating. He put his knife and fork down, carefully crossed on his plate.

'All right,' he said, 'I'll tell you. That girl is no good. She's a whore.'

For a moment no one spoke. Then Clara stood up, very quietly, and said: 'Shut your dirty mouth.'

'You see she don't deny it,' Mr Barr said, with grim pleasure. 'Because she can't. I know all right. All the neighbours are talking; if you weren't always drunk or away somewheres you'd have heard it too. Maybe they make jokes about her at the pool-room.'

'I'll kill you,' Clara said. 'Keep your dirty mouth shut.'

Mrs Barr silently, without moving, wept; she watched them with stupid eyes, and the tears ran down her face.

'What are you talking about?' Jim said.

'What beats me is how they do it,' Mr Barr's voice had gone high and false. 'In the back of the grocery truck, maybe. It's too cold outa doors, and they can't go to a hotel. Unless they take one of them rooms with bedbugs down at the Lone Star for fifty cents. It must be swell isn't it Clara, rolling around with the bedbugs.'

The plate she threw sailed over his head and smashed against the wall. Jim turned to his father fiercely and said: 'Shut up.'

'Clara,' he said. 'Listen kid. What is all this. Go ahead and tell me.'

'He's talking about me and Joe Bartlett. Sure it's true. What about it? What else can we do. Get married I guess. That's a hot one. What would we be getting married on. On the Relief I guess. Not me. Besides,' she turned towards her father, 'who're you to talk? What do you do for me? You pulling this my daughter stuff and fallen woman and such crap. What're you? You're nothing but a man who can't get a job. I'm free, get that. I don't owe nothing to nobody: I'll do what I want.'

She was standing above them, white-faced, with the black rings around her eyes looking painted on. Thin and sharp: seventeen, Jim thought, seventeen and bitter and tired.

'And it's the only thing I know that don't cost money,' Clara said, and suddenly crazily laughed.

He got up and put his arm around her. He took her to the only chair in the room that wasn't unsteady, and sat down and held her on his lap. She leaned against his shoulder and wept, saying: 'What else can we do, what else can we do? I love him; I gotta have something in my life. What fun do they think it is for me to live? I'm working all the time and I ain't got anything I want or need and he's the only person makes me forget what it's like all day.'

Jim stroked her hair, and said quietly: 'Sure, honey, it's all right.'

'Oh, it's all right, is it?' Mr Barr said. 'It's fine; it's a fine thing to do, is it? Who do you think will marry her now? Just a little cheap whore you can have for nothing. Why don't she act like other girls her age?'

Over Clara's head Jim said to his father: 'Keep quiet. How can she act like other girls: do you want her to be like Nancy Tredway that's got a Chrysler maybe, or Sally Allison that goes to Seattle for Christmas vacation and the winter sports? Can't you see the kid's tired to death and there isn't anything for her that's fun. Do you think she'd be doing this if she had a good home, and clothes, and could go to the movies sometimes, and have boys in to supper and things like that?'

'I love him,' Clara said.

'Sure you do. Sure you do. I'm sorry as hell for you, kid.'

'She's a whore, that's all,' Mr Barr said. 'And she can just get outa here and go back to her grocery truck.'

'Listen,' Jim said. 'You shut up or I'll knock you out. Just being my father isn't so much. She can stay here as long as she wants. She belongs here. And if she has fun with Joe, you leave her alone. She's got a right to something. She's got a right to whatever she can get.'

He held Clara tightly in his arms. 'Don't cry, kid. Don't cry. It's all right. We don't care. It's all right.'

Suddenly Mrs Barr got up and came towards Clara. 'It's time for bed, dear,' she said, her voice a soft whisper in the room. 'Come along, mother'll undress you and you can say your prayers. I'll fix you a nice picnic to-morrow and you can go swimming with Jimmy. Don't cry: that old tooth won't be hurting for long.'

All three of them, silent, stared at her. Clara shrank back against Jim. Mrs Barr's eyes saw nothing, settled nowhere, and her hand stretched out towards Clara. The room seemed to have grown cold.

\* \* \*

The doctor kept saying it's nothing at all, nothing at all. Happens all the time, these days. Just a breakdown from worry, you know, nerve strain. Fix her up in a few weeks, just needs a rest. The family sat and listened to him with wooden faces. Even if he could fix it up in a few weeks it shouldn't have happened, ever. They were all ashamed, realising they had left this complaining bewildered woman entirely alone with whatever thoughts haunted her. The social worker in charge of their family came and was gentle and took Mrs Barr away; Mrs Barr was very sweet about going. She said she'd be back in the afternoon and for the children to be careful not to get their feet wet. She said the spring weather is so dangerous; you never know when colds will turn into pneumonia. They stood and waved at her, and as she left they could hear her saying to Mrs Meredith, the social worker: doesn't Clara look lovely with that pink hair-ribbon, she's going to grow up to be a beautiful woman.

Clara came home: they needed her and she didn't question this. The house ran very quietly, probably better than when Mrs Barr's patient but ineffectual hands cared for it. Mr Barr, shocked into deeper silence, spoke not at all; didn't seem to know Clara was there, and even ignored Joe Bartlett when he came some nights in the grocery truck to fetch Clara.

Clara, Jim thought, is lucky. At least she's needed: we need her here. I could die and nobody would notice it. Clara had school, too: she would finish, she was younger, younger, there was time for Clara. And he sat in the kitchen and looked at his hands and felt his thoughts slipping and skidding, in terror. But he was very quiet, speaking to no one of this.

\* \* \*

He thought when Mr Peck hired him that it could only be from pity. Why else would he get a job? He was used now to being refused and it seemed to him that the reason had to be himself, this unemployment was a personal thing based on his own unfitness. To be ashamed of, as you'd be ashamed of a club foot or ranking last at school. He was apart from other men and felt himself marked and degraded. And he was terribly frightened. I'll be fired, he thought, I'll be fired right away. And this will be the last chance I ever have.

He drove the J. P. Peck's General Clothing Emporium truck as slowly as it would go, without rattling to a halt. His hands on the wheel were cold and trembled. He never rang door-bells more than once, for fear the customers would complain of impoliteness on the part of the driver-delivery boy. He said nothing when Saturday rush meant driving until ten at night through a sticky swirling snow. He stayed awake at night thinking about the roads, the tyres on the truck, should he say good morning when he handed the package to the lady at the door, or just give it to her without saying anything. It was more than a job now. It was something he had to prove to himself: the last thing in the world to hold, his feeling that he was a worker, he was capable of work and meant to work. He earned five dollars a week.

He had worked a month before he realised what his work was, how the days passed. He began to notice more than the backfiring of the truck, the way the brakes screamed and the grinding of the gears. Or the fact that some ladies smiled and some just grabbed the parcels that he delivered. He began to think about his hours and the pay. But mostly he thought of being a doctor, of the hospital and the operating-room. He looked at his hands, raw and chapped, and wondered what sense there was in living. In the spring he would be twenty-two and the only job he could get was driving a truck for five dollars a week. He learned nothing. He could also have driven a truck when he was sixteen.

He gave Clara his five dollars and she took it without looking at him or saying anything. But he knew that she wanted to give it back and say to him, go away, get out, let's both get out somehow. If only there was some place to go where it would be any different, if only they could kid themselves about that …

He didn't know quite what it was: but probably it was Dick Manfred. One night, when Jim had finished his deliveries, Dick tied a sled on behind the truck and picked up a girl named Susy and hugged her as the sled skidded across the road. Then he told Jim to go out and hang on to the girl, who was a pleasure to hang on to, and drove the truck himself. The snow was icy and stinging on Jim's face and the sled rocketed in a straight line and then swung wide like a deranged pendulum and Susy screamed and held his arms very tight around her, so that above the noise and speed and the fine feeling of wind down his throat he knew she had good breasts. He went home that night singing Jingle Bells at the top of his lungs and his father looked at him darkly, thinking him drunk again. He decided that it was possible to have a swell time now and again if you stopped worrying about tomorrow and all the things you never would have. He told Clara defiantly: 'I'm going to have some fun.' She smiled at him and said: 'Good for you.' He also said to her: 'I got to keep a little of my own money, Clara. I got to.'

'Keep it all. You got a right to it. I can fix it up with Mrs Meredith. She's all right; she knows it's tough the way we gotta live. My God, if a man hasn't a right to five dollars he makes, it's a lousy world.'

'I'll only keep a little.'

'You keep it all unless we run outa groceries.'

Five dollars, he thought: five dollars to spend. Not for something he needed. What he needed couldn't be bought with five dollars. He needed ten years to study, or almost that, and he needed clothes, and a home, and food, and warmth, and safety for his family. If he thought about his needs five dollars was an insult, a piece of paper to burn in disgust. But if he was thinking only of his happiness … he sat near the stove that night and turned over ideas in his mind. He scarcely knew where to begin. Automatically he thought of clothes: he could get a sheep-skin at the miners' store in Ferguson for five dollars, at least a worn one. And he was cold all the time. He threw that out: no, it was five dollars as a luxury, for something to enjoy. He thought of books, but he hadn't read everything in the public library yet and it was a waste to buy something he could get free. After work at night he walked along the main street of Harriston looking in the store windows and thinking. He was waiting for Friday, and his five dollars, but he had to be ready. If he didn't know what he wanted he might spend the money in a silly trickle on pool and movies and drinks. It couldn't be that way, he would have to get something to keep, to look at every day and be sure that he had bought it himself because he'd earned it and wanted it.

He had to leave the truck one night at a garage to get the brakes tightened. There was a bedraggled second-hand store next to the garage. He never looked at it: the windows were clogged with old china and flat irons, broken porcelain lamps, ragged shawls. But tonight he saw something red and bright, and stopped. It was a small accordion, with some roses painted on as decoration, and the keyboard was very neat, and it sat jauntily on its side, a little pulled out, gay among the broken oddments of the window display. He stood before it shivering and wondered how long it took to learn to play it. And he saw himself at home at night playing grand music sounding like an organ, and being happy, and far away from the kitchen. He went in and asked the little grey man who ran the store, how much it cost.

'Six dollars.'

'It's not worth it,' he said and hoped his voice didn't tremble.

'It's not worth it? Are you crazy? You couldn't get this accordion in Spokane for twenty dollars. I wouldn't have such a fine instrument here, only a crazy miner came down and got drunk and sold it for whisky. And I'm letting it go cheap because folks around here don't know nothing about music and fine instruments like that. I'm giving it away for six.'

'It's not worth it, but I'll give you five for it, and you can take it or leave it and see if I care.'

There was a silence; casually he fingered a broken china shepherdess and studied a fork with one prong missing. He tried to look careless, and he thought, I'll break his nose if he doesn't take five. I've got to have it, I've got to have it. He could hear the music already: the Blue Danube and the Volga boat song. He knew he would be able to play the accordion at once, because he wanted to. He saw himself playing it under the trees by the lake, in spring, with a beautiful girl listening. It was reason enough to live until spring. The great surgeon Dr James Barr who is also a talented performer on the accordion …

'All right,' the little man said. 'Cash.'

'I'll come for it tomorrow night at six.' He walked out. When he was out of sight he began running. He wouldn't tell anyone until he had it, but he wanted to run to keep from shouting to the whole town that he, Jim Barr, was a musician not a truck driver.

\* \* \*

He put it on a shelf by itself, in the kitchen. Clara said it was beautiful, she had never seen anything so pretty and what could he play on it. He said that he didn't know yet and it might take a little while to figure it out, but he thought he would play wonderful things. Mr Barr didn't see it at first. Then he said: 'What's that thing?'

'It's my new accordion.'

'Where'd you get it?'

'I bought it at Raphaelson's junk shop; it was a bargain. Only five dollars. It's a fine expensive instrument.'

Clara watched her father. She could see the muscles in his face tightening.

'You mean to say you went and spent five dollars on that thing when you know we need clothes and coal and food. Are you crazy,' he shouted, 'or what kinda hog are you?'

Clara got up from the table. 'He's got a right,' she began.

'Keep quiet, Clara,' Jim said, and turning to his father: 'You listen to me. I've given my money to the family for months. I never bought anything I wanted just for fun, just because it was nice and I wanted it. I make that money. And, besides, who in hell are you to squawk? If anybody has a right to kick it's the Relief. They're keeping this family, them and me. You just board here, free.'

'This is still my house.'

'And how do you figure that? We pay rent on it, or we're supposed to. Where does the money come from, I wanta know? I guess you'll say you pay the rent on the quiet without telling us, out of all the money you earn when you're not sitting here in the kitchen doing nothing.'

'I'm your father anyhow, I'm older than you. You haven't got a right to throw away money.'

'I got a right to be happy if I can sometimes. If I don't think of myself I wanta know who will. You leave us alone, Clara and me. We'll do what we gotta do for ourselves, and we'll get some fun any old way we know. We don't say anything to you so you keep your mouth shut about us.'

'I'm older,' Luke Barr said, and stood up. He wandered around the room, pushing the chairs out of his way, his eyes dark and bewildered. 'I'm older. He's my son. I'm the one who ought to give orders.'

Clara put some more potatoes on her father's plate. She didn't look at Jim. Jim was thinking, he used to work with his hands and he loved the things he made. He used to play spelling games with me so I'd learn words and how to write them. He isn't like this. Everything has gone wrong for him, but he isn't really like this.

'Dad,' he said. 'I take it all back. Only I want that accordion and it's mine. I'm sorry I said what I did.'

'If I could get some work,' Luke Barr said, as if he were talking to himself. 'If I could get anything. We wouldn't need their money; they could spend it the way they wanted and go ahead and live for themselves and have their own things. I'm too old.'

'Dad,' Clara said. 'Your potatoes are getting cold. I got some butter to put on them from the Relief commodities today and they're real good. Come and eat your dinner.'

Jim said: 'You had a fiddle when I was a kid, I remember it. Maybe you could play the accordion right off.'

'My hands aren't any good now,' Mr Barr said.


## II. JIM AND LOU

It made an interesting noise, but it was definitely a noise. He had waited until Sunday morning before he gave himself up to the luxury of being a musician. It was now Sunday afternoon and Clara was worn-out.

'I don't want to be mean, Jim, but it's not awful cold today, and you could borrow Dad's coat. Would you mind taking it outside to practise for a while. When you're playing pieces it'll be different.'

He put on whatever warm clothes he could find around the house, finishing off with a bright wool scarf of Clara's, known as her 'sports outfit'. He walked fast to store up heat for sitting still later. In a pine clearing in the woods, he found a log which would do as a chair. He thought it was a wonderful day, and this was really a nicer place to practise. He whistled busily and tried everything the accordion would do. It was exciting and full of surprises: sometimes it sounded like a piano and sometimes like an organ and sometimes it was just sound. He was very happy.

The girl had come up behind him, but he wouldn't have noticed her anyhow. She said: 'It's music, isn't it?'

He looked up at her. She had a market basket over her arm and it was almost full of wood. She was hatless, and her hair rumpled darkly over her head. She was very small.

'Do you like music?' Jim asked.

'Sure. I been listening to you for a long time. I heard you about five miles away and I been running all over the woods to see what it was. I didn't think it was a man,' she said doubtfully. She looked a little disappointed.

'It's an accordion.'

'Oh,' she said. Then she sat down beside him on the log, and put her basket on the ground. 'I'll just sit here and listen till I have to take this wood home.'

'Where do you live?'

'About three miles up the Ferguson road. I gotta pick up wood. We don't have any coal. Till Thursday.'

He looked at her. He thought she was lovely; she had a face for the woods, for the woods in spring. She was so much smaller and neater than most girls, with a tiny nose as if she were sniffing cookies baking; and brown eyes.

'What's your name,' he said.

'Lou.'

'Mine's Jim. Pleased to meetcha. I guess I'll go on practising.'

He bent over the accordion, pulling it out and in fast and slow, moving his fingers over the keys, waiting to see what would come forth. She was as quiet as the trees. He felt sure she was watching him, her eyes bright and intent like a squirrel. And he kept thinking isn't it fine that she can sit still and not jerk around the way everybody does. It grew colder, and the sun was brushed out behind the pines. Once or twice he felt her shiver.

At last he said: 'It's getting dark. I gotta be going.'

'I had a swell time,' Lou said. 'Thanks for the music.'

They stood up.

'How old're you?'

'Seventeen,' she said.

'Do you go to school?' he said.

She looked at him.

'You ask a lotta questions don't you. I'll tell you all about me if you wanta know. I don't do anything. We're on Relief. We been on Relief a year and sometimes I think we were always on it. We moved here six months ago because Dad thought they'd get him on farming, there's Relief farms you know. He's nutty: he never had experience farming. He was a book-keeper, he did the work for a hotel in San Francisco and they laid him off cause he's old now. So we moved to Chipsaw, that's north of here, where he was born, but there wasn't anything there either. We live in a bum house, and there's no money for me to get clothes and go to school and I hate it all. I hate the people who fired him and I hate this town and everything about it. Now you know.'

'Lou,' he said, 'we'll have fun with the accordion and with Dick's sled. Honest we will. If you don't think about it too much you can have a swell time.'

'I went to high school in San Francisco and had clothes like everybody else. And here I wash dishes and make beds and I wish I was dead most of the time.'

'I know about that,' he said.

'Well, if you want to come to see me, my last name's Weylin. I live out towards Ferguson, about three miles, there's a side road with a gas station where they cross. I live just up the hill.'

'Lou.' He slung his accordion on his back like a knapsack and took her basket of wood from her hands and set it on the ground.

'Lou, kiss me.'

'Yes,' she said. 'Oh, sure. It don't cost a thing. We're giving them away for samples.'

* * *

'Lou,' he said, 'I'm crazy about you.'

She leaned against him. 'That's fine,' she said. 'I'm cold. How about you.'

'Oh, sure.'

'Never mind, it'll soon be spring. And then it'll be summer and we can be hot for a change. But I guess we better start walking now Jim.'

Brown like an acorn, and little and quick like a squirrel, he thought. He took her hand and pirouetted her, elegantly, as if they were dancing the minuet. Then pulling her after him, stumbling and laughing, they ran out of the woods. 'Hurry Lou, Hurry Lou, the icicles are after you.'

'Hey, stop. Gosh how I'd like to sit down and get warm.'

'If I could make a dollar saving a millionaire's life, we could go to a hotel.'

'I won't go to hotels.'

'I know you won't honey. You're shy.'

'I am not shy: don't be a fool Jim Barr.'

'Tough as hell.'

'Come on you sap.'

'Stop dead in your tracks so I can kiss you.'

He took her in his arms: it's like holding a bird, he thought. Little and soft and cold; I must be very careful of her. I'm going to get a fine job soon, and have things to give her, and a place for her to live … 'Let's pick us a house today,' he said.

They had done this before, but there were endless possibilities. Lou started it one day when they were very cold: the woods she said are fine, but me, I want a house with a furnace, so let's go and pick one and have it sent to us next week. They had walked around Harriston, up the rich streets, looking at the houses: it was dusk and the snow made everything distant and more graceful than it really was. Lou said: 'I think that one will be fine.' Jim stood considering it, and then he said: 'No, it would be awful when there's no snow on it; besides we have to have a house with a side door and a drive up to it, so I can have my office in the house and my patients won't be embarrassed, and of course so the children won't get in the way.' Lou thought about that: 'The children,' she said. 'I forgot.'

'A fine kind of mother you are.'

Now they walked up Harriston Drive, holding hands. Lou was not very well dressed for winter: she had a thin serge coat, obviously taken in for her, and shiny. They had never mentioned their clothes to each other. Jim thought about her coat steadily, he had a feeling of guilt and anger against its ugliness and thinness. He wanted to see her wearing warm soft clothes, brown he decided, like fur or fine wood. He told himself stories about the dresses and coats and shoes he'd give her, when he was driving the truck: and every once in a while, waiting in J. P. Peck's for the parcels he had to deliver, he would loaf over towards the ladies' department and watch the girls selling. He almost never saw anything he thought was beautiful enough for Lou.

Now they walked fast, and Jim said: 'We could hopscotch, it makes you plenty hot, I remember from when I was a child ...'

Suddenly she saw a house. It was set back from the street with pine trees neat around it. It was low and wandered over the snowy lawn, as if it were comfortable sprawling that way. It was made of white slats and the curtains behind the windows were white and soft, and 'Look,' she said, 'the curtains look like beat-up egg whites. I bet it's a clean, pretty house inside.'

Jim studied it carefully, there was a carriage drive with white gravel on it, between the pines: and a low step led up to the side door. 'We'd have to build on some rooms,' he said. 'But it's all right for a start.'

'Jimmy, it's a wonderful house. It'll do us for ten years, anyhow.'

'It's all right.'

'It's wonderful.'

She stood in the street, rubbing her hands together, and shifting from foot to foot. 'We can build a play-house in back for the children so's they won't make any noise for your patients.'

'Dad could make up the plans for that.'

'All right. Only a little playhouse, though. We don't want to spoil them.'

'No, we got to be careful about that. I'll tell them "Your Dad got everything he has, for himself, you got to learn to make your own way."'

'All right, Jimmy, but don't sound mean will you?'

'You're spoiling them already.'

'I know, I know ...'

'I wonder whose house it is?'

'I think it's the MacIntyres'. I never met Mrs MacIntyre at any of the parties I go to.'

'You mean that old MacIntyre who owns the Drug Store?'

'That's the gent.'

'Oh; Lou, that old man, that old man and an old woman, living there, and us standing in the street.'

'Now,' she said. 'Don't act silly. We're just standing here deciding if we'll buy the house. Just because our own house is too little ...'

He put his arm around her. 'Lou, I love you better than anything in the world.'

The lights on the second floor went on. Lou looked at the sky.

'My God, it's late,' she said, 'I got to get home.'

'Not yet.'

'Yes, honey. I got to make dinner, and put the kid to bed and see that Mother and Dad don't fight, and listen to Mother crying if I wake up and hear her because Jack didn't write for a month and Frank's in jail for being a hobo in New Mexico. Oh, sure, I got to get home.'

'Lou, it won't be long now. We'll have our own place in the spring and you won't have to work like a nigger and everything. I'm gonna get a fine house for you and take care of you, sweetheart. It's only a little while longer now.'

She took his hand and held it. He couldn't see her face in the darkness. She was looking at him tenderly, smiling, the way a woman would look at a little boy wearing a cocked hat made of newspaper, playing Napoleon with a broom for a horse ...

\* \* \*

Clara got a letter. Nobody in their house ever got a letter. Jim waited before going to work to see what it was about; even Mr Barr, instead of disappearing right after breakfast, lingered with his hand on the door-knob. Clara sat on a chair by the stove and opened it. It took her a long time to read, but Jim could see that it was only a few lines. She didn't say anything: but her body stiffened, and the muscles in her cheeks moved as if she were keeping her teeth closed on any sound she might make.

Mr Barr looked at her and quietly opened the door and went away.

'Clara,' Jim said. He went to her and put his hand gently on her hair. 'Clara dear.'

She turned to him; he was afraid of her eyes.

'Look at it,' she handed him the letter.

It was written in purple ink on ruled paper: 'Clara, we don't get anywheres, and we can go on like this till we go crazy. I'll never get any money. It isn't that I don't love you. I'm going away. Some guy told me that in Florida ...'

'As if,' Clara said, 'the name of the State makes any difference if you're outa work.'

'The bum,' Jim said. 'The goddam lousy bum. Walking out on you. He could of stayed and gone on anyhow, or at least taken you.'

'Sure,' Clara said. 'It's fun being hungry together. He's not a bum. He's right. Now,' she said, 'I can go on getting up every morning and going to bed every night.'

'Oh, Clara.'

'Listen Jim, you marry Lou. Don't wait for anything, and don't think you'll get anything. Just marry her. Jobs,' she said, her voice rising. 'Jobs. And enough money and a decent place to live and clothes and food. Oh, Christ, if I knew how I'd laugh my head off ...'

'You poor little kid.'

'Don't worry.' She got up. She took the letter and put it in the stove. Her eyes when she turned to him were like pebbles, smooth and hard. 'Don't worry. I don't give a damn now, and it'll maybe be a lot easier for me. There are lots of men for a girl like me, and maybe I can get myself a fake fur coat if I work hard enough.'

He put his hands on her shoulders. 'Come with me today, in the truck. I got to go now kiddo, but come on with me. I'd just like to have you around.'

'No. But thanks. And don't you worry.'

He thought about Clara all day. But he kept saying 'Lou' to himself, whenever he could, stealing back to her for comfort. It wouldn't be that way with him and Lou: everything was wrong but not Lou. Lou would never leave, and he'd be able to put his hand out and touch her and be safe. Nothing would ever be entirely ugly or destroyed for him, because there was that little brown girl wrinkling her nose and smiling ... Clara, he thought, God what can we do for you: we have nothing to give you.

'This is the last delivery today, Jim,' Mr Smithers said. 'And here's your money for four days' work. I'm sorry kid, but one of the sales-clerks can do what delivering we need: March is a slack month. We'll be getting you back around Easter when it picks up again.'

Jim held out his hand as if he weren't sure whose hand it was. His mind lay numb: not a job, not even this job, and how about him and Lou, didn't they know about him and Lou and what they were planning, and how hurried they were because they had no place to be together, and how they couldn't wait ... 'But,' he said.

'I know, Jim, it's tough. You're a fine kid and we don't get any complaints about you. We all like you fine. But March's a lousy month. The store's losing money you know. Around Easter. And' – Mr Smithers looked at the empty store: he felt uneasy about this. Was the boy going to cry. 'Here's a pair of gloves for you, Jim. Just keep your hands warm till Easter.' He patted Jim on the back. And thrust the gloves into that still outstretched hand. They were bargain gloves, on sale as odd lots for forty-nine cents a pair. Jim walked to Lou's house with them in his hand, out in front of him as if they were made of glass or dynamite.

'I hate those people,' Lou said. 'Smithers and Peck and the bums at Dad's hotel. I'm coming over to your house tonight soon's the dishes are done. But don't look like that. It wasn't such a good job. Anyhow, damn them,' she said quietly. 'Damn them. Damn them. Don't let them make you look that way. I'm coming over later. How's Clara?'

He told her about the letter, Joe heading for Florida believing in the sun probably or that a man could live on oranges …

'Go home and be good to her,' Lou said. 'She's got real trouble. Your job doesn't matter. We'll get something better, soon. Honey boy.' She took his head in her hands and kissed his eyes softly. 'I'll eat awful fast and wash everything in a minute. I'll be there before you will.'

Clara was not home. Mr Barr had made some supper. 'I don't know where she is,' Luke Barr said, and Jim thought this is the last thing he can stand; his voice sounds as if he were never going to try again. 'I don't know what to do, Jim.'

'We can't do anything about her. We haven't got anything to give her.'

He told his father about being laid off while he ate. He said: 'Look at the swell gloves they gave me. We can pawn them and live for two years on what we get.'

'Yes,' Mr Barr said. He got up and went to the bedroom. 'I'll sleep in here,' he said, 'since Clara's gone.'

'She'll come back later. Don't you worry, Dad.'

Lou stood in the doorway and watched him go. 'Where's Clara?'

'We don't know.'

'I'll wait with you, Jimmy. And we got to get married soon, sweetheart. Your house and my house and sometimes I think I'll go crazy with it all.'

'We'll get married on what?'

'On Relief.'

'Are you nuts, Lou? What do you think I am? Do you think I'm going to start off that way? We're going to get married like real people, and we're going to have a decent home, and we're not going to be beggars all our lives. We're going to be a man and his wife and not two Relief clients.'

'All right, Jim.'

He put his arm around her. 'Come and sit on my lap. You're such a skinny little thing I guess we can both sit on this chair.'

She put her head against his cheek; her hair was soft, and smelled of wood smoke.

'I wish we could sleep together, Lou.'

Her arms were around his neck. 'All right, Jimmy. Any time. I don't care where or anything. We got to take whatever we can.'

'When it's spring,' he said.

'Sure. That spring. I forgot about it.'

He rocked gently. 'If Dad wasn't sleeping I'd play the accordion for you.'

She mussed his hair. He could now play the Blue Danube definitely, or almost the Blue Danube. She knew every note by heart, she even knew the notes he missed.

The dollar alarm clock ticked with a sound of clattering tinware and they dozed.

The door opened so hard that it slammed against the inside wall of the kitchen. Clara swayed in the doorway, dusting snow from her shoulders. She was drunk. She looked at them for a while and then recognised them. 'Lo, kids. How's everything? How's every little thing?' She pulled the door and it slammed heavily behind her. She walked over to the table and leaned on it. She opened her coat and from the neck of her sweater she pulled out a crushed five-dollar bill.

'Easy money,' she said. 'And there's a lot more where that came from, or from two other guys. It's a fine thing to be a working girl.'

Lou buried her head against Jim's shoulder and neither of them spoke.

* * *

'If this damn slush ever melts I bet you a violet or something would come up.'

'Walk over here,' Lou said. 'My shoe's got a big hole.'

'I was thinking: I can maybe get a job at the Jenkins again in the

161

summer; they know me now. If I go early maybe I can follow the harvest. Three months, if I was lucky. I can save the money and that'd be a little for us to get married on.'

'But, Jimmy, you said the spring.'

'I know, honey, but I won't have the money. If I start at Peck's around the middle of April and spring is May first about, isn't it?'

'There's the Relief,' she said stubbornly.

'Lou.'

'I won't wait all our lives. I won't do it. You said spring.'

'But, sweetheart, I won't have money to buy you a dress to get married in.'

'Do you think I'm worrying about dresses? Do you love me? Do you want to get married to me or don't you?'

'Lou,' he said, with horror. 'Lou, how could you say that even if you're sore. It isn't that way with us. We're always going to love each other.'

'Put your arms around me, Jimmy and marry me quick. The winter's been long enough.'

He picked her up and snuggled his face against her throat. 'Spring is here,' he sang off key, noisily. 'Spring is here.'

She laughed at him. 'You're tickling me.'

'All right, walk on your own feet, pee wee.'

She put her hand in his and smiled at him. 'Let's go and sit on our log.' They found a fallen tree which had served them all winter, when it wasn't too cold to sit down.

'How's Clara?' she said suddenly.

'She comes home sometimes. She has money.'

They sat and watched some clouds like white rabbits, jumping before the wind.

'Dad's funny, too. He's getting so quiet. He always was quiet, but it was different. Like he'd bite you if you talked to him. Now he's quiet, like a blind man, some way.'

'It's better your mother's away.'

'Yes,' Jim said. 'But it's pretty funny when you're glad your own mother is shut away somewheres. It's pretty funny thinking she's better off like that.'

'I hate where we live,' Lou said, beating with a small fist on the log. 'I'm sorry for our families, it isn't their fault. My father isn't a mean man and my mother didn't used to be crying all the time, and we had a good house and clothes, and went to school and parties and everything. Your family's all right, too. But it's awful now and even us, when we're together we got to be careful a lot of the time, not to argue about getting married and things. I hate it. I won't stay in it any more. We got to get married.'

'Lou, baby. Come here.' He held her head against his shoulder and rumpled the short brown hair. 'You can cry if you want to. I guess I know how you feel. But you're wrong about us. We don't have to be careful about arguing. I'll do anything you want.'

'Will you marry me the next day after we see the first crocus?'

'Yes.'

She sighed. 'Everything's all right then. I don't want to cry.'

'Well then, come on and walk, my seat's getting wet from this log.'

'All right. But I got to get home soon. The kid's got a cold and mother's sure it'll be pneumonia, so she can't do anything except cry, thinking he's going to die. Oh, hell,' she said very slowly, very carefully. 'Oh, hell.'

'You tell me what you did today and then I'll tell you.'

It was a game Jim had invented since he no longer drove the truck, and his days were empty and marked only by the dishes he washed, or the wood he cut.

'Well,' Lou said, taking a deep breath, 'this morning I thought what a fine day it was, so I put on my riding clothes and I rode Black Beauty out to Narrow Lake and back, and galloped.'

'You did?'

'You bet I did.'

'I didn't know you could ride like that.'

'I'm good.'

'And then what?'

'Then I got dressed in a nifty sports outfit and got into my Chrysler ...'

'Did I see that car?'

'No, it's my new one. It's a black sports roadster with red wheels. Then I drove out to the Country Club and I had a swell lunch.'

'What did you eat?'

'Creamed chicken and peas.'

'God,' he said reverently.

'I knew you'd be jealous about that.'

'Hell, no. I ate at my men's club downtown and I had lobster.'

'I bet you don't even know what it looks like.'

'I had steak then.'

'I bet it was horse meat.'

'Meanie.'

'No, but if you don't want to know about the rest of the day ...'

'Go ahead.'

'Well, I talked to Mrs Drayton about the kids. We figured it was about time to send little Jimmy to school in San Francisco so he could begin studying for college.'

'Oh, Lou.'

'What?'

'That's not fair. He isn't ready for school yet; he's only about three.'

'All right.'

'And, anyhow, he's going to Andover.'

'What's Andover?'

'I don't know. It's a school somewheres, I read some boys books about it. It sounded like lotsa fun for the kids.'

'All right, but I'm going to pick little Lou's school.'

'Hey,' Jim said, 'isn't that smoke? Don't you smell it? It looks like smoke.'

'Can't be a forest fire, everything's too wet.'

'Come on.' He took her hand and pulled her after him, jumping fallen logs and scratching their legs against stiff bare bushes.

'It's over this way,' Jim said. 'Of all the crazy things, a forest fire when everything's soaking …'

It was hard running and they walked: from habit and practice they made very little noise and they were too out of breath to talk.

They came into a clearing: a bonfire burned in the middle of it and sitting beside the fire, turned sidewise to them was a man. He was sitting on a three-legged hand-made stool. A little shack of the lean-to variety was behind him, roofed with twigs, lurching unsteadily towards the trees. He was making something, and around him on the ground were other things he had made. Chairs and tables, suitable for a big doll or a very small baby: a bed, a bookshelf. He was at work now weaving some split twigs together to make a rush seat for an armchair. He had few tools: a small cheap hammer, a little saw, a hatchet, a plane, and a matchbox beside him full of nails. He was working steadily with clumsy intent hands. It was Luke Barr.

They stood watching him: Jim could not even feel himself breathing.

Mr Barr finished what he was doing: he nailed the woven twigs over the framework of the chair, stood it beside him on the ground and stared at it. Then he frowned. He picked it up and carefully pulled out as many nails as he could and began all over again, trying to make the chair better.

'He's been coming here then,' Jim whispered. 'All the days he went away right after breakfast and came back after dark. Every day he's been coming here, making things to keep from going nuts.'

He felt Lou's hand gripping his, her fingers like cold wire.

'God,' Jim said. 'Oh, my God.'

Lou pulled him back silently and still pulling, led him quickly and noiselessly away.

'You can't look at things like that,' she said.

'He never said anything. He never told us and we treated him like dirt.'

'Jimmy,' she said, 'for God's sake let's get out before we get like that too.'

'He used to make fine furniture,' Jim said. 'He even knew how to carve some.'

* * *

He had been driving the truck again for a week. He was tired. Where the hell do all these people get money to buy clothes, he thought. Easter. An Easter bonnet. Myself, I would like some Easter b.v.d.'s and my girl could do with some shoes that had more on them than the shoe laces. Five dollars. You're just starting life, young man. If you save that five dollars in fifty years it will be ten dollars and you can go out and get stinking drunk on rubbing alcohol.

'How's things, boy?' It was Dick Manfred. These last months Jim had not seen him. Lou wouldn't want him to hang around the pool-room and besides ... two bits to waste. Two bits: five cans of soup by God; the things you had to have, not the things you wanted.

'Well, this truck now,' Jim said, 'named Man o' War. I'm still driving it. That's how things is, my man. And how're the mines?'

'Fun. Lotsa fun.' Dick's face was yellowish in the morning light. He looked thin but principally his eyes looked desperate and lonely. 'Wanta drink?' Dick said.

'Can't, Dick. Gotta deliver parcels to Mrs Whoosis with the fat behind who just bought a new corset for Easter.'

'It's better than working in the cellar.'

'Sure.'

'I'll see you in ten years,' Dick Manfred said.

'And we can say just the same things. So now I'm gonna get drunk.'

No, Jim thought. No, by God. Not me. Lou, my darling, in ten years we'll be wondering if it was really true, all this winter, all this long hell winter. Lou, darling, darling …

The days were longer and the sun spread after it was behind the mountains and the sky turned gold high up and green along the horizon.

Spring. And spring, like winter, meant five dollars a week, if he was lucky. There would certainly be a slack season after Easter – they can't buy clothes for ever, the bastards – and five dollars would be a fabulous memory. So living was that: spring and summer, the harvest and the winter and snow and waiting. Lou, darling, what can we do? We've got to hurry, there's so little time and I have nothing to hope for, but it's spring now …

He was very tired. 'It'll smell good in the woods,' Lou said. 'Let's take a little walk and then you go to bed.'

She held his hand. She thought: he must marry me now, soon. He said we would in the spring. And if he won't do that because he's afraid to think of us starting all over just like our parents, then we've got to be lovers. We must have something, we must have something.

She was watching her feet, her head lowered against the golden sky. Oppressed with the soft air and the rich warmth of the earth and the smell of rotting wood and new leaves. She almost crushed it with her foot and jumped as if it were a snake.

'What is it?' Jim grabbed her arm. 'What's the matter, Lou?'

Her face was very pale. She stooped and gently uprooted it.

'It's a crocus,' she said.

He passed his hand over his eyes, his forehead: too tired to think. What was there to do now? What could he offer her? Could he bear to look at his wife and know that she wasn't his at all, that something as remote as the Government and as immediate as a social worker was providing for her?

'Jimmy, if you don't want to get married, all right. But let's show it's spring, anyhow, and we did get through the winter. I'll be proud to be lovers with you.'

'I can't give you anything, Lou.'

'I want you, Jimmy. I don't want anything else at all. I don't care how I live or anything if I have you.'

'You're so beautiful, Lou. What if a rich man came along …?'

She put her hand over his mouth quickly. 'Jimmy. You can't say things like that.'

'It is a crocus,' he said and took it from her, holding it carefully, the white flower bright against the stained palm of his hand. 'It's spring, Lou.'

He looked at her as if he wanted to remember her when she wouldn't be there. She thought swiftly, this is the best, this is the best, anyhow, no matter what happens later. The woods are ours and there would be nothing as fine as this anywhere even for the people with money. And we're young and this is love, no matter what things ever happen to us.

'I love you, Jim.'

He picked her up in his arms tenderly; he felt that he was walking under water, everything swayed around him, he had a feeling of being carried on the air, only touching the ground lightly as someone who dances, flies, floats in green clear water. He walked with her towards a place where the pines grew close together, and behind them the narrow clean trunks of the birches rose with little leaves like green smoke high against the high gold sky. There was moss on the ground, and a tiny unceasing noise as of things moving faintly, insects, buds opening, the air sliding among the leaves and curling under the moss. It was in his eyes and his throat, this small steady pulse of the woods, and his body was shaken and warm with it. He could not feel her weight in his arms, and he knelt to ease her on the moss. She looked up at him with clear welcoming eyes and the crocus fell from his hand and was crushed between them.

\* \* \*

Every day he waited for Mr Smithers' voice to rise at him cordially saying: 'It's slack now, Jim, we don't need you any more.' I wonder what he'll give me this time: a pair of ear muffs or a purple tie? He watched Mr Smithers with fear and hatred and was surprised each day when Mr Smithers only said good night.

He lived now for the end of the day, after supper, meeting Lou in the woods, with the sky still golden and staying until the sky was blue like not too deep water and then, later, like black fur. They had different places where they met, sometimes under the pines, with the fallen needles a little damp, but slippery and smelling a cool male smell. Sometimes on the moss, the moss sagging softly under them and green and staining their clothes. They watched the birch leaves uncurl and grow until they were like close-woven gauze across the sky; they picked out different trees and each day waited for them to hasten ahead to summer. They spoke very little because there was nothing to say; there was only the moment, the hour, to live and to be glad of. And they were afraid to think for fear thinking would mean planning. They could make no plans. Five dollars was five dollars.

'Lou,' he said. 'Are you happy?'

'I think I'm dreaming.'

'If you ever left me or got tired or didn't love me, I wouldn't want to live.'

'Yes,' she said. 'Don't be a sap.'

One night he had just said: 'You know what? I think you're more beautiful than Marlene Dietrich.'

She said: 'Jim, I got to talk to you.'

'Do you want to be introduced, Miss Weylin?'

'No, it's serious.'

'All right.' He tightened his arm around her shoulder and watched his cigarette, like an anchored glow-worm before him.

'We have to get married, at least I think so,' she said.

He said nothing.

'You got to say something, Jim.'

'I don't know how to say it. I'm sorry as hell because it's my fault, and it isn't fair on you. And the other thing is, I don't want to do anything except marry you. That's all I got to say.'

She was crying now, as softly as the air moving in the leaves. Her body felt limp beside him. 'I was afraid you wouldn't want me. I was afraid you'd do it because you'd have to.'

'Oh, Lou, are you crazy, sweetheart, don't you know anything, don't you know anything at all?'

'And it isn't any different now from what it was.' She drew in her breath and said it: 'We'll still have to go on Relief, specially with a baby.'

'Little Jimmy,' he said, 'who's going to Andover.'

He felt her turning her head away from him, against the moss.

'I didn't mean it like that, Lou.'

'Yes, you did.'

'He'll be a fine baby.'

They lay there quietly and a star perched like a bird on the top of a tall pine.

Suddenly, Lou sat up. 'Listen Jim. Listen to me. This is the last time I'm going to say any of this to you and either you got to understand or we won't have that baby and we don't have to get married. I'll go on being lovers anyhow. But, if we're going to get married, you got to get this straight.' He was sitting up too, leaning against a tree trunk, seeing her profile in the darkness, the little chin hard and her voice quiet, an older voice than hers had ever been, and sure.

'We will have to go on Relief. That's not our fault. You work when you can and you work as hard as any man could. You'd do anything you got a chance to. It isn't your fault if we have to go on Relief. It's their fault. It's the fault of the rich people who run things, it's not the fault of people like us. We'll take what we can get from the Relief and not go around thanking them either. If we can work and want to work, we're not beggars, no matter what anybody says. If we get married, Jim, and have to get help because they messed up everything, we will. But we *can't* be ashamed Jim. We *can't* be ashamed. We may as well go ahead and die if we're ashamed.'

Her body was bent with sobs. The words came out in jerks, but her voice was clear, and rang in the woods, with anger and with passion. He sat watching her, he hadn't known she was able to talk this way, and he knew, suddenly, that she was right. A man without two bits in his pocket was a bum, a man without a job was unemployed, the same thing as saying unfit, a loafer, a drain on society. But that was what they thought, and they were the ones who had let this mess happen. She was right. He knew it, and she did. No matter what the other people, with jobs and money in the bank and taxes to pay, might think. He and Lou could stand together and take it. They were all right. He had his goddam hands and his goddam muscles and anybody could hire them. If nobody wanted them, that wasn't his fault. It might make his life hell and hers too, and it was nothing to bring a baby to, but anyhow it wasn't shameful. They could stand together …

'Lou,' he said, 'we'll get married and we'll maybe manage to live on what I can get. And maybe we'll have to go on Relief sometimes. But anyhow we won't be licked.'

'Then it's all right,' she said.

'It's all right now.'

She slept on his shoulder thinking, until winter anyhow we won't need any money for rent, and I read a story once about shipwrecked people living on berries …

\* \* \*

They were going to be married tomorrow, Sunday. He had lain awake all night thinking of it. He kept saying to himself: 'We can't be ashamed. We aren't beggars if we can work and want to work.' And all the time he was thinking: we're young and we'll only get married once. We're young. She's so lovely that little girl with her brown face and her brown hair and her hard, smooth legs. And we'll only get married once. It ought to be grand and fine and happy and everything like the spring; I ought to be able to give her … We can't be ashamed … But we ought to be fine and good-looking and well dressed and everything if only once, if only now, when this is happening to us. Only tomorrow, only once will anyone say, 'And I pronounce you man and wife.' Man and wife. Jim Barr and the little brown-skinned girl; I won't be a truck driver waiting to be unemployed; my wife is not going to be married in a dingy dress she got handed out to her by the Red Cross or the Relief or somebody. My wife, my beautiful little wife. We are not ashamed. We are young and it's only going to happen once …

He could hardly see the turns on the road all day; he sweated at the wheel and his hands trembled, and all day he refused to tell himself what he knew he was going to do. He had it planned in his mind, but he wouldn't give it a name. He kept saying to himself, 'Supposing a guy …' But he knew he would do it. His stomach churned and writhed with the fear of it, and he knew he'd do it anyhow. His head began to ache thinking all around it, but never giving it a name, and he kept wondering isn't it almost time.

Mr Smithers gave him the last parcels, and Jim said, 'I'll turn out the lights. I'll just be a second, gotta go upstairs,' he said, pointing to where the toilet was.

'Okay,' Mr Smithers said. 'See you Monday.'

'Yes sir, good night.' The doors locked automatically. The clothes were stacked on tables under sheets, put in drawers, hung behind glass. He went upstairs and vomited into the toilet.

The shades were all pulled down in the show windows and he heard no steps on the concrete outside the door. Swiftly, but with his eyes stinging and his hands frozen and clumsy, he grabbed what he wanted. A little red dress of heavy, good crêpe, cut plainly; a pair of slippers. He tore a white shirt from a box, hoping to God it was the right size, a tie, a pair of shoes from the show-case, thinking, if they're too small it's only once, it's only once. Then he went to the glass case where the good suits hung. He saw one of rich brown tweed and he could even read the price-tag on the sleeve. Thirty-five bucks he whispered to himself and his courage almost failed. For a tormented instant he thought the glass door was locked: it stuck and squeaked as it opened, and he choked for breath. A hat for Lou, a hat for Lou, but by now there was blood before his eyes and his terror rode him. He seized the first thing he saw on a counter, a bargain counter, in his hands it felt like velvet, a little velvet beret, marked down because it was winter wear …

He bundled them all together inside the suit, turned out the lights and holding himself so stiffly that he walked like a soldier on parade, to keep from running, to keep from screaming in blind panic and running down the street, he got into the truck. He drove it out near his house, left the clothes in a dry ditch, and took the truck back to the garage.

He did not sleep. The clothes were in the house; every noise was the police, and when, for an instant, he dozed he started awake sure that a flash-light had gone on in his face, sure he had heard a voice saying: 'Here he is.'

And all night he said to himself: 'Dearest Lou, we're only going to do this once; it's the only thing we're sure we'll have, it must be fine, it's going to be hard and ugly and poor afterwards, but this has to be fine. Lou, Lou…'

Oh, God, he thought, I hope she likes the dress.

He got up at sunrise and dressed and left the house. He walked in the woods and had to lie down, feeling weak and dizzy. He got to Lou's house, having skirted the town so that no one would see him. They were going to be married in a little church on the Ferguson Road, early, before the regular service. He wouldn't have to go through town again. Clara and Mrs Weylin were the only people who were coming, as witnesses. He waked Lou; the Weylins had no reason to lock their door.

'Jimmy,' she said. 'I'm going to be a bride.'

'I got a wedding dress for you.'

She sat up fully awake and looked at him. 'Jim,' she said, and asked no questions.

She took the red dress and held it up before her and said, 'I never saw anything so beautiful.'

'Mr Smithers loaned me the things for us to get married in,' he said.

'Oh.'

She gave him some black coffee but he was sick again, running outside. When he came back she was dressed, and Mrs Weylin was walking ahead of them, down the road towards the church.

He took Lou's hand and said: 'You love me, don't you. You'll always love me.'

'I love you better than anything in the world,' she said. 'For always.'

When they were almost at the church, she said: 'We're swell looking people, we're a swell looking couple getting married. I'm proud of us, and I'm so happy I could sing.'

That made it all right. She was glad to be lovely; the dress fitted her, the little beret sat gaily on her brown hair, and he stood beside her at the church door, thinking it was worth it, no matter what happens, it was worth it. For just this once. For just this once to have something good, to have enough, not to look and feel like people who never have anything they want.

The minister wanted to be sure to get finished before the congregation arrived, and he cut sections out of the marriage service, and there was no music. Clara looked at their clothes questioningly and said nothing, and fortunately the minister was not a worldly man, and he would never have noticed unless they had been inadequately covered. Jim held Lou's hand, and she smiled at him, and he thought there's no one in the world so beautiful, no rich girl in Seattle or Spokane is as beautiful as she is. He heard nothing except the minister's voice saying: 'I pronounce you man and wife.' Her lips were trembling as he bent to kiss her. Clara's face, gaunt in the morning and tired and hurt, smiled at him as if she had lived longer than any of them, understood everything, and Mrs Weylin said: 'I hope you'll be happy. Be good to her Jimmy. God bless you.'

They shook hands with the minister, and walked out into the sunlight. Lou stood for a minute on the church steps, preening herself, with her hand on Jim's arm. 'Mrs James Barr,' she said. 'Oh, Jimmy! Oh, Jimmy!'

I should have stolen a ring, Jim thought. I should at least. Mrs Weylin had lent hers, and now Lou gave it back but gaily, not as if she minded.

'Good luck to you kids,' Clara said. 'See you later. I guess I'll go home and get Dad his lunch.'

Mrs Weylin kissed Lou.

I pronounce you man and wife, Jim thought; and for once we are as good as anybody, married in a church and looking fine, looking like people who have a home to go to and a job ...

'Well, good morning.'

He noticed then that old Mrs Sankey from Harriston was walking up the path to the church; she would get there early. Wanting a front row seat and a chance to look at everybody as they came in.

'What're you kids doing here? Didn't know you belonged to this congregation.'

'We don't,' Lou said, and her voice sang, and the sun flashed off her.

'We just got married. This is my husband. I'm his wife.'

'Well, congratulations. It's a fine day to be getting married.' She was closer now. She stopped and stared at them curiously. 'And my heavens if you aren't swell, you're sure dressed up for your wedding all right. Where'd you get those fine clothes; I haven't seen anything so pretty for a month of Sundays, not up here in a poor congregation, though you might see such things down to the Reverend Johnstone's church.'

'We …' Lou started and Jim tightened his hold on her arm until she bent a little towards him, silenced, startled, her face responding to the pain.

'Santa Claus,' Jim said. 'He takes care of good little children. We got to hurry. We're taking the day off for our honeymoon.' He waved to her and walked Lou swiftly down the path to the road.

'I stole them,' he said. 'The clothes. I had to. We couldn't get married as if it was any old day.'

She pressed his hand against her cheek, but they did not stop.

'I loved our wedding, Jimmy. I'm glad you did it. And it's all right. We'll go away quick to another state, Washington or something, and have the baby, and they'll forget all about us.'

'It's a fine thing to ask your wife to run away like you're a murderer.' He was whispering to her, but he didn't know it.

'If you were a murderer, I wouldn't care.'

'You can't come; they'll find us, I know they will, they always get you, I'm not going to let them get you in prison, Lou. Oh Lou, I love you, you know how it was.'

'I don't care at all,' she said. 'I'm glad you did it. And it's not running away. It's just our honeymoon.'

He stared at her: was it true, was it possible anyone could be so serene and not frightened by anything, not by the police or hiding or all the things they didn't even know about that lay ahead. Could anyone love him like this?

'It'll be swell having the accordion,' she said in a clear voice.

He stopped then and kissed her. There were things he couldn't say, he didn't know how to thank her. Suddenly he heard voices behind them, coming towards them. Whose voices, what were they saying, whose voices? His hand clamped on her arm, and he pulled her with him, down the road, away from the voices, faster, faster, the dust streaking over their new stolen shoes. Don't run, he said to himself, oh for God's sake don't run, don't run!

# *Ruby*

RUBY LET THE wind push her head back. Her coat, made from her father's old one, flapped out behind, and one of her stockings tore loose from its safety pin fastener and rumpled around her ankle. 'Hoo-wee', Ruby shouted. The coaster bounced every time it went over a crack in the pavement and Ruby hung on tight and shrieked with fear and joy. 'Lookit, lookit!' she screamed seeing Myra standing on the corner down the street. 'Lookit me! Lookit how fast I'm going.' The coaster all but flew across a crack, and Ruby bent over the wooden handle and prayed that it wouldn't break.

'Hey Ruby, you be careful,' Johnny yelled from up the block, cupping his hands around his mouth to make the words carry. 'You be careful of my coaster.' Ruby didn't answer. Her hair lifted from her head in brown wisps and floated like water weed; her hands were cracked and chapped with cold, but she didn't notice. She gripped the wooden handle bar until her knuckles stood out white, and sang to herself not opening her lips. Lookit me, lookit me, I'm flying! … Finally it had to end. She bumped off the kerb at the end of the street, and Johnny screamed with fury, saying: 'Damn you, Ruby, you'll go and break my coaster; what do you think it's made of anyhow, iron? I'll never never let you ride on my coaster again.'

She turned and pushed it up the street. 'I didn't mean to, Johnny; it just wouldn't stop, it was flying. But it's all right,' she said, and slowly, lovingly, ran her stiff hands over the coaster. Johnny had made it himself. Johnny was twelve: Ruby thought he was the smartest man alive.

'Come here,' Johnny said, 'gimme that coaster. You don't deserve getting a ride the way you do with it, bumping it. Looks like you're just trying to break it.'

'I wasn't, Johnny. I wouldn't break it. Please, Johnny,' Ruby said very sweetly, blinking up at him, 'please, Johnny, can I ride it again?'

'No, I gotta go somewheres on it. I got work to do today.' Johnny pushed off, going very fast, grating down the hill. Myra came up and sat on the front steps with Ruby.

'It's cold,' she said, rubbing her hands together. 'I wish I had gloves.'

'Me too.'

'You got any coal at your house?'

'Yes, some. The Relief lady come to us Tuesday. You wanna come in and get warm?'

'Yes. We ain't got none. We ain't had none for four days. My Pa sez he's gonna steal some off the railroad tracks tonight, but Ma sez no, he oughtn't, because Miz Hammerstein's husband got arrested for stealing coal off the tracks.'

'Oh,' Ruby said, not hearing or remembering, 'well my seat is cold, too, come on in. Listen, Myra, d'ju think we could make a coaster, d'ju think we could find that lumber place and all?'

'Where'd we get the wheels from?'

'Maybe they got old wheels in garbage cans; I saw ole Maria down by the river poking in garbage cans and she gets a lotta junk.'

'Well,' Myra said, settling the matter judicially.

They went into the house. All the houses in that block, and in the blocks around it, were brick, two and three storeys high. Most of them seemed empty; dirty windows or none at all, and cold and barren with no one moving around them or in them. Being winter still, or the bleak beginning of spring, the street was quiet. No one could afford to go outside and get cold.

Six families lived in the house. Ruby lived with her mother in one room. There was a stove and a streaked sink in it for washing dishes and bodies and clothes. In the hall on the second floor the bathroom, grey and unlighted, boasted a choked-up tub and a toilet with a broken seat.

Ruby said hullo casually to a little boy who peeked out of a door on the first floor. 'Hullo, Tim,' Myra said. Tim was Johnny's littlest brother, he was three years old; there were four others and then Johnny: the Durkins lived in three rooms, the biggest apartment in the house.

Ruby knew her way up the steps: the gloom of the stair well was something she could remember always, from all the other houses, ever since she could walk. Steps were something you felt but didn't see.

'Hey,' Myra said, 'where's the bad step?'

'Up here, come on. I'll show you.' Ruby waited. 'There, better step up two, the other one's about gone too.'

They opened a door on the third floor. Mrs Mayer was washing clothes in the sink.

'Hullo Miz Mayer,' Myra said. 'S'nice and warm here. We ain't got no coal at our house.'

'Oh,' Mrs Mayer said. 'Well, sit down by the stove and get your hands froze out. Ruby,' she said suddenly, 'what have you done to your stockings; you know you ain't got any others, and now you've gone and tore off most all the top. I've a mind to spank you.'

'I didn't mean to, only I was flying,' Ruby said, her face cloudy and dazed with the lovely memory, 'flying through the air with the wind yelling at me.'

'She means she was coasting on Johnny's coaster,' Myra said.

Myra pulled out a handful of something – it might have been a cushion, or a wad of blanket or just rags, and sat down on the floor by the stove. Her mother had said that the Mayers were even worse off than some; there was a kitchen table and two uncertain chairs in the room, and against the wall, heaped-up, a mass of greyish-brownish something; old clothes and rags and rests of blankets. Mrs Mayer and her daughter slept on this; pulling it under them for softness, and over them for warmth. Mrs Mayer was nice, Myra thought to herself, but her house was awful. Still it was warm; they were good and lucky to have got their coal this week.

'Our Relief lady didn't come this week,' Myra said chattily, realising it was her duty as guest to keep the conversation going.

'Who is she now?'

'Mizz McAdams. She's purty and young, but she don't know nuthin' Ma sez.'

'Well, if she's good to you that all that counts,' Mrs Mayer said. 'Ours is purty good, Mizz Sanders. About coal anyhow, and she sez she's gonna get Ruby some shoes. But my, we do have to scrounge on food. She's only giving us $3.50 a week, and that child likes to eat.'

Ruby sat on one of the uncertain chairs and dangled her legs, thinking about the coaster. Of course, Johnny was twelve and she was only ten, and he was a boy and they could do more than girls, and they were smarter; but still she didn't see why she couldn't find wood and wheels and things, and then if she couldn't *make* the coaster Myra would help, and Myra was as old as Johnny so she ought to know how to do things.

Myra's hands were a normal colour now, and she felt warm enough to leave. 'Guess I'll go,' she said. 'Thanks, Miz Mayer.'

'I'm coming too,' Ruby said. 'G'bye Ma, I'll be back for supper.'

'Yes,' Mrs Mayer said, bending her back over the sink. The door slammed and she could hear Ruby saying: 'Lookout, that's the bad step'; and she scrubbed the thin remains of Ruby's night-gown and her own and her one pair of underpants and Ruby's other dress and two towels. God, she thought, she sure will be here for supper and breakfast and lunch. If only people could get along without food, Mrs Mayer thought, it would be easier for all of us. And she thought with almost horror of bread soaked in soup again another night; thinking to herself it would be a lovely thing now to have a nice hamburger steak and some canned peaches … She kicked the rags back against the wall and hung the family wardrobe on the line to dry. And then sat down on a chair and looked at her idle, ugly hands, without seeing them.

Myra went home, and Ruby, saying nothing about her plans, drifted down the street. When she was out of sight of her block she walked fast and surely towards the river. Presently she stopped and, looking behind to be sure she knew no one in this neighbourhood, she walked into an alley. When she began on the first garbage-pail it seemed to her a hard thing she had decided to do. She found a stick and prodded around, wrinkling her nose and trying to hold her breath. She couldn't find anything. She stood off and looked at the pail and her heart went out of her work. 'Stinking,' she said to herself. 'What awful smells there are.' She turned and started back but remembered suddenly, with passion, the wind flying down the hill and how her heart thudded with the speed and the dangerous exciting way the coaster leapt the cracks.

'No,' she said aloud. 'No, I'm gonna find wheels.'

The alley was long. Every other house had a garbage-pail, and a few houses had regular ash-pits, twice as tall as Ruby. Her stocking furled around her ankle, and the brown weedy hair fell over her eyes. Her hands were cold and slowly dirtier, stained and evil, with coffee grounds under the nails and grease from other people's waste food. She dug in with her hands now furiously, tearing out egg-shells and old cans, and once she cut her hand and stopped, not hurt but disgusted to see her blood running on to the clammy rests of food. For over an hour Ruby zigzagged down the alley from one garbage-pail to another, stirring the tops of the ash-pits, when she could reach them, wearily. She found a broken comb and in an ash-pit an old sewing-basket that had once been green raffia trimmed with red. She kept these. But there were no roller skates. Night came down, and she couldn't see what her hands were getting into, but only feel the slime of food over them. A cat scraped against her bare leg and she screamed softly. It was cold. Her hands and her legs and the foot which had only half a sole to keep it from the ground, tingled and ached with the cold. There weren't any roller skates; not even just old wheels, any kind of wheels at all.

She put the basket under her coat and got both her hands inside the sleeves to warm them, and limping a little, to try to keep the almost bare foot off the alley cobbles, she walked home.

Mrs Mayer was angry, because she had had to keep the soup on longer, waiting for Ruby. Some had boiled away, and that made less to eat when already there was so little. She shook Ruby and said what are you doing out so late, don't you know, and how about dinner, you're a naughty girl, and what have you got there?

Ruby gave her the basket and Mrs Mayer looked at it not knowing what to do with it: it wasn't pretty or useful, but the child had brought it. 'Where did you get it, Ruby?'

'I found it,' she said, her voice heavy and toneless with fatigue and disappointment.

'Thank you, Ruby, it was nice of you.'

'All right.'

Ruby sat opposite her mother at the kitchen table and soaked her bread in the soup and swallowed it without tasting it or thinking that she was hungry and it was good to eat. No wheels anywhere. Lucky there was only the oil lamp and her mother not a very noticing woman anyhow. She'd wiped her hands on a piece of paper, blowing down the street, and then on her coat. But still there were coffee grounds under the nails and they smelled. 'Can I wash after supper?' she said.

'Sure, but whatever for, in this cold weather?'

'Well,' Ruby said.

They slopped up the damp bread.

Ruby thought, with misery, of the afternoon; there was no use in anything. Even if she could go to every garbage-pail in the whole city she wouldn't find the wheels. Inside her eyelids, tears filmed and blurred the soup plate.

'Ma,' she said, 'what do you do when you got to have something?'

'Oh, got to have something.' Mrs Mayer laughed. 'You don't got to have something. You just don't get it, so I guess you don't got to have it.'

'But I mean got to have, got to have, can't not have,' Ruby insisted.

'Well, there's two kinda things I guess,' Mrs Mayer said, and her voice sounded remote and gentle. 'Some things you ask God for, Ruby, and some things you ask the Relief lady, and sometimes you get them.'

Presently Mrs Mayer said: 'All right, Ruby'; and Ruby said: 'Yes, g'night Ma,' and Mrs Mayer blew out the oil lamp.

Ruby lay under her share of the rags and whispered softly, so that only God could hear and not her mother: 'God, if you got time, please put a garbage-pail somewhere I can find it with an ole roller skate inside. I'll be awful good if you do.' She lay quietly a moment, wondering if that would be enough. She knew this wasn't the kind of thing you could ask the Relief lady for. She understood about Relief; it was the Government. It gave you food and coal, and if you died, so her mother said, it would pay for the funeral. But it didn't care about her and Johnny and coasters and things you just got to have.

* * *

Ruby hurried past the gate, walking sideways, as if to protect herself from attack, looking over her shoulder. Two big girls with rouge put crookedly on their cheeks sat on the gate, swung their legs and jibed at two boys. This was their way of flirting, a kind of bet-you-can't technique. They were all from the eighth grade. Ruby didn't know them, but she could tell by their size. She was in the third grade herself. Looking at them, she suddenly wondered whether she would ever get through all the rooms that separated her from them, all the blackboards, all the teachers, all the mornings with her stomach empty and growling to itself. She walked across the brick yard. There was a slide, overrun by children; they crowded up it and slid down it at the same time, the younger children stood in line waiting, with the patience of the weak, while some big boys directed the performance, shouting orders and yanking smaller children off, in mid-air, if they disobeyed. Children slid down head first, ran down, went down on their knees with their hands pressed together as if in prayer. The littlest ones crawled around underneath the supports and the whole thing seemed about to crack, crushing everyone in an uproar of arms, legs, bricks and torn tin.

The yard itself was square, fenced in by an iron rail, bricked, and behind it rose the square, dead, brick wall of the school. Aside from the slide there was nothing to play with or on. Some children, the rich or the clever, had old tennis balls, or chipped golf balls, and they batted these against the brick wall of the school, surging forward and backward like pennants in the wind, shouting. One very small child, named Alice, walked about with great dignity, and held a conversation with herself. If you stood near enough you could hear shreds of it, hints of the main plan: 'I beg your pardon, Miz Schultz, I certainly didn't mean to step on your baby ... if you can't give me thirteen dozen of the bestest eggs you've got Mr Hoffman I don't s'pose I'll bother, my family is very, very big, and eats most all the time ...' Alice bowed to imaginary people, busy adults like herself, talked, and looked about her with blind eyes.

Myra was playing post tag: she waved at Ruby, and returned to the game. Ruby scuffed her feet over the bricks and wandered around, trying to find someone she knew well enough to talk to. She sniffed the air a little, with pleasure; it was still cold, but the sun had come through and made lemon-coloured marks on the brick yard. It was March. The wind would stop in a little while, Ruby thought, and then it wouldn't matter not having gloves. The noise of the children on the slide beat around her, and she walked aimlessly, dragging her feet, trying to remember what spring was like. It got warm, and when it was warm it was nicer: you could play hopscotch, if you had some chalk to mark the squares with, in the street after supper while the sky was still light. You could sit on the front steps after school and do nothing and feel the sun on your back and watch the ants. There was also the sandpile she remembered, thinking hard; it was on the river, somewhere by a factory. She had found it when last it was warm weather, and it was as big as a mountain, and she had rolled in it and built castles and filled her shoes and then fallen asleep. When the water-wagon came through the streets, at the end of the day, you could run out and get a shower, and Myra had told her, but then it was too late, that in a park somewhere, there was a wading pool for poor children, and anybody could go and splash around. It would be warm soon, she thought, with great contentment, and maybe Mother could get a pair of shoes for her from the Relief lady, so the pavement wouldn't burn that one bare hole on her left foot and she could drink lemonade …

She stopped: no, there wouldn't be any lemonade. You had to have a nickel. She hadn't had a nickel as long as she could remember, not since Daddy had a job, long before he went away. She decided not to think about the lemonade, but just to think about the sandpile. It was scary because it was so high and lovely and soft and warm. She smiled to herself and dimly watched her battered shoes scraping over the bricks.

Suddenly, like thunder and like mosquitoes, she was surrounded by children. Girls, because the boys never descended to mere girls' fights. She was in a circle with children dancing all about her, jumping up and down and shouting. What had she done, she thought, frightened and bewildered: she hadn't been playing with anybody, she'd just been walking alone, thinking about her sandpile.

'Poor little Ruby, poor little Ruby,' the voices sang at her, sticky-sweet and cruel. 'Won't anybody play with you Ruby, won't anybody play with you cuz you're too dirty, cuz you smell like old rags … where's your Pa, Ruby, why don't he take care of you and get you some clothes … why don't you lissen to teacher Ruby, why're you always last in class, why're you always asleep Ruby, don't your mother get you enough to eat … poor little Ruby, nobody loves little Ruby …' The voices whined and chanted and the circle grew: other little girls thought perhaps it was a new game, and came to see the fun, and Ruby stood in the middle, blinking her eyes and staring, unable to believe that this awful thing had happened to her. What had she done, what had she done to any of them?

Then Myra came, Myra was bigger than Ruby and she shoved her way through the circle and stood beside Ruby, put her arm around Ruby's shoulder and said: 'Shut up youse, you're not so good yerselves.'

'Yah, Myra loves Ruby,' the voices said.

'She's my friend.'

'Funny kinda friends you got, your friends never wash.'

'Shut up,' Myra said. 'You oughta see where she lives, you wouldn't be so proud then. She ain't got nothing, nor her mother neither. And her Pa went away. Besides she's on Relief, and a lot of you is on Relief too, so don't talk.'

'Not me,' a little girl with curly blonde hair and a hair ribbon stepped out, her chin up, and very pleased. 'My Daddy works at the gas house, he works steady; we ain't on no Relief, and we're not gonna be.'

'Well,' Myra said. 'Perhaps your Pa does work Betty Perkins, but Julia's Pa don't, and Sadie's don't, and Jane's don't, and Ruth's don't, and most of your ole Pas don't. Mine don't. But anyhow Ruby hasn't even got a Pa what don't work. He's gone, and she's only got one room to live in, and nothing much in it. And I bet all your Ma's gets more Relief than her Ma does. I know my Ma does. We get $6.60 a week and she only gets $3.50.'

'Well, why don't she get some clothes from her Relief lady, and why don't her mother keep her clean? Ruth's mother only gets $4.20 a week and there's more in her fambly and Ruth's clean.' Ruth shone with delight at this tribute, and stood a little apart so that everyone could see her.

Suddenly Ruby shouted: 'Stop.' Her voice came out of her in a groan, harsh and deep, and they were all silent, astonished and a little afraid. She shook off Myra's arm and stood alone, her feet planted stiff on the bricks, her face white and the skin seeming stretched over it.

'Stop,' she said again. 'And you listen to me,' she said, 'all of you. Don't you never talk like this to me again. I'll tear your eyes out. I'll wait in the street for you, and kill you when you go by in the dark. You listen,' she said, 'Myra don't know what she's talking about. I got a purty house with lamp-shades and beds and a big white tub in it and 'lectricity, and my Ma gets $10 from the Relief, and we have chicken every Sunday, and I don't wear my good clothes here 'cause I don't want to spoil them, but I put on a coat with fur every Sunday and go up to the west end to see my grandma, who has a big house, and my ma beats me for getting dirty, I'm just dirty because I wanna be, and my Pa didn't go away,' she said. There was a pause, and even the children on the slide were quiet and the big girls stopped swinging on the gate. 'He's dead.'

She turned and walked across the brickyard. Her feet moved very well she was surprised to see. She held her head up high and stiff, and stared in front of her, seeing across the street, in red and gold, the sign of the A. and P. Grocery Store. She walked out the gate and no one spoke and no one stopped her, and turning, still with purpose and dignity, she walked up the street and lost the school from sight. Then she sat down on the kerb and put her face in her hands.

\* \* \*

After the soup and bread had all been swallowed and Mrs Mayer had put out the oil lamp Ruby called to her in the darkness, across the rags.

'Ma.'

'Yes.'

'Where has Daddy gone?'

'I don't know.'

'When did he go?'

'It's more'n a year, now.' And Mrs Mayer turned over on the rags, easing her back, turning her face to the wall, because these things didn't bear thinking about.

'Why did he go?'

' 'Cause he said it made him crazy to sit around here all day and nothing to do. He went every day to get work, but he couldn't find nothing, and then he just got so disgusted ...' For six months, Mrs Mayer thought. Looking and looking, and coming back at night with his eyes tired, and then, towards the end, he'd come home and his eyes were fierce and angry, and he wouldn't talk. Had Ruby forgotten, she wondered, how it was, towards the end; how he beat the child for no reason and how he'd shout at Ruby if she made any noise, and how jumpy and queer he was.

'He was a good Daddy, Ruby,' Mrs Mayer said, 'and when you was little he had steady work and we used to live in a nice place with three rooms and beds, but you wouldn't remember. They laid him off with a lot of others and then he couldn't find nothing. He useta work at the shoe factory. Can you remember how he looked?' Mrs Mayer asked. 'He was a big strong man,' she said softly, remembering his arms around her when they were young and he was being nice. 'When we went on Relief he went away and didn't come back for three days, and when the lady come to the house he sat and didn't say nothing, just said to me, "Gertie, you tell the lady what she wants to know." And when she left he went around the house like a crazy man and said he wouldn't let nobody come into his house and ask him questions. But she was a nice lady. I don't guess she likes to ask all them questions but she hasta. And then, when he couldn't find no work and we had to move all the time and fin'ly we got here, he just said he was going, he couldn't stand it, it would make him crazy. If he gets work he'll come back, I guess, or send us something …' Her voice drifted off. Work, she thought, remembering how it had been when he earned $20 a week and they had three rooms. She kept them nice then, but now she didn't have the heart, not in this place. They'd owned their furniture, but it all got sold the last year, when they were moving to smaller places, and finally the living-room set they'd been buying for five years got sold too. After that, she didn't much care, now she didn't care about anything: you just went on living, and perhaps Luke would come back some day, if there was work for people.

Ruby rolled around on her pile of rags and shoved some under her shoulders to make it softer. She lay in the dark, thinking about her father working, and how once they had had three rooms, perhaps rooms as she'd said this afternoon, with lamp-shades and beds and a bath. 'I wonder what'sa matter,' Ruby said to herself, doubtfully. 'I wonder what'sa matter with everything.'

* * *

Ruby trod the pavement as though it were rose petals, delicately, carrying her pride within her and smiling. In her hand she held a purple tooth-brush, covered by a glass tube. She put it up before her so that the light shone through. She had won it at school for deportment.

Miss Vincent had said that she was going to give a prize to the child who had the best record for behaviour during the week. And she said also that this was Hygiene Week, so they made posters about eating apples and drinking milk, and Miss Vincent talked to them about washing and toothbrushing.

Ruby had been deeply interested by all this. Especially by the pictures of the apples, which looked as good as or better than the ones at Schultz's grocery store or at the A. & P. She knew, though, that you couldn't eat them because of the Relief money; you could mainly eat bread and soup and sometimes pork and potatoes and things like that, or turnip greens, which she hated. She was more hungry than usual the mornings of that week, listening to her stomach growling over the breakfast of bread and syrup, and looking at the pictures of apples and fat milk bottles. Miss Vincent made a little speech about how good Ruby had been all week and gave her the purple toothbrush and said 'Use it every night and every morning.' Some of the other girls called her teacher's pet when she went home, because they were cross they hadn't won, but she didn't care. She stroked the glass covering gently so as not to break it and felt proud and important.

'Lookit, Ma. Lookit what I got.' She showed her mother the toothbrush and her mother asked, as she always did, with the suspicion of those who have nothing and don't get things easily: 'Who gave it to you? Where'd you get it?' Ruby explained about the prize and how they'd had lessons about brushing teeth.

'Well,' Mrs Mayer said, 'it's very purty and you can keep it on the shelf. I don't guess you can use it, because you haven't got any toothpaste.'

Ruby grabbed it and held it against her heart. No one was going to take the toothbrush and put it away; she was supposed to use it every night and morning, the way Miss Vincent said. 'I'll get toothpaste. You'll see,' she said. 'It's my toothbrush and I won it for a prize and I'm gonna use it, I'm gonna.' There was fury in her voice; this was the only thing she had of her own and she wanted it, she had a right to it, and she would keep it.

'All right,' Mrs Mayer said, soothingly, 'you get your toothpaste and use your brush and you can keep it anywheres you want.'

So Ruby smiled and held the glass case in her hand, patting it. It was the prettiest thing in their room, she thought, and at once began brooding on ways to get toothpaste.

'Well, you go on out and play, Ruby, I gotta work.'

Ruby had intended to go out and tell Johnny about her toothbrush, but she stopped and stared at her mother. What work? Doing the house was called doing the house, that wasn't work. Work was what you got paid for.

'Miz Burk, up on Elk Street, give me some washing to do for her,' Mrs Mayer explained. 'It's not much to do and she's gonna give me fifty cents. She's gotta baby coming soon so she can't do it herself. Fifty cents,' Mrs Mayer said again, with pleasure in her voice. 'We'll get some hamburger and some canned peaches and have a real supper tomorrow night, Ruby.'

'Oh,' Ruby said and sat down on one of the chairs to take time to imagine this.

'There'll be a dime left over. What shall we do with that?'

'Candy,' Ruby said instantly. 'Some heavenly hash like they have in the window at the Greek's.'

'Oh, no, we oughtn't to do that. We ought to get something nourishing. We could get a can of spaghetti for the next night.'

'Please, Ma. Please, Ma.'

'Now, don't be silly, Ruby, it isn't often I can pick up a piece of work and we gotta get all the extra food we can. I've walked around here till I thought my feet would fall off, looking for some washing to do or some cleaning, and you know it isn't often I get anything. You'll just have to wait for your candy till Daddy gets a job and comes back, I guess.'

Ruby wandered down the street, thinking how stupid grown people were. I'm gonna buy candy for myself as soon as I'm big and got a job, she said; I sure am. She wondered how long it would be before she was big enough to get a job. Johnny whizzed by on his coaster. She noticed that he had nailed a box on to the floor board and that it was full of something.

'Hey, Johnny, where you going?'

'Can't stop now, going to work. See you tomorrow,' he said and was gone.

It seemed very queer to Ruby that suddenly everyone was working, generally nobody had anything to do. She thought perhaps it's spread all over the city and got quite excited; saying to herself, I bet everybody's got a job now and soon Daddy'll come back and have a job and get me some toothpaste. She walked to Myra's house to see if Mr Herman, Myra's father, had a job, but when she got near the house she could hear Mrs Herman shouting at him, saying: 'Get outa here and stay out for awhile, will ya? You're just in the way, and stop picking on the kids. They ain't done nothing; it's you. You aren't much help around the house, you aren't, just sitting there and eating. If you haven't got anything else to do, go on up to the Relief and see if you can't get them shoes they promised for Louise.' And Mr Herman came out of the house, with a black, angry face, and started up the street, his shoulders hunched together and his feet dragging. I guess everybody hasn't got jobs, Ruby thought hopelessly, and never will, and Daddy won't come back.

At supper Mrs Mayer had more news.

'The Relief lady come today. She's got something for you.'

Mrs Mayer waited for Ruby to be curious and eager, and Ruby looked at her, questioning, expecting always and indomitably, some lovely surprise.

'She's gonna get you a pair of shoes and a gingham dress.'

'Oh,' Ruby said. 'Oh, hoo-wee ... they won't tease me then at school and can I be clean and purty,' she said, and her mother looked at her and thought: I had it better when I was a child, this is nothing for a child to grow up into.

'Yes, Ruby.'

'Is she gonna raise our grocery order this month?' Ruby asked.

'No, she can't do that; they got all their money already give out.'

'Well, you know Bessie Norton who goes to my school; she lives with her grandmother and there's only two of them, just like us, and she said they got $4.25.'

'Yes, I know,' Mrs Mayer said wearily. 'But it don't do any good arguing, and besides, I hate to. And I guess we ought to be thankful we're getting anything. Times like they is, we'd starve if it weren't for this relief. I can't get nothing to do, Ruby, so we better just take it and be glad it ain't worse.

'And she said that there canned beef,' Mrs Mayer went on, and Ruby wrinkled her nose, remembering it. One month the Relief lady had given them ten cans of it and she thought finally she'd rather not eat than go on with it, but luckily none had come since. 'She said it made the Golden children sick. It wasn't the beef, she said that's all right, but just they had to eat it twice a day every day for about two weeks becuz Mrs Golden's new on Relief and she don't know how to get along. And so the children all taken to vomiting, so they took them to the clinic and now they're getting milk and apples and it's all right.'

For a moment an idea, like a skyrocket, gleamed swiftly across Ruby's mind. She thought milk and apples, like the ones we put on the posters, and the soup tasted weak to her and she remembered it from many nights before, tasting the same way. Now if only I could vomit, Ruby thought, we'd get milk and apples. But then she knew she couldn't do it; she wouldn't know how. But it would be wonderful to have things like that for supper.

'Well, that's all, Ruby, so go to bed.'

Ruby took her toothbrush and laid it on the floor near her head, so that she'd see it first thing when she woke up. Presently, Mrs Mayer put out the light.

'Tomorrow night we'll have hamburger and canned peaches,' she said.

'Yes, and then I'll have my dress and shoes, and I already got my toothbrush,' Ruby said. She sighed gently to herself. 'It's not such a bad life after all,' she said.

Mrs Mayer laughed quietly at the child's voice and thought to herself that Ruby sounded like an old woman, comfortable in her fat.

Ruby saw Johnny getting on a street car and was filled with wonder. Where did he get the money? He waved to her and his face, flushed and pompous, gave her to understand he was going forth on grave business. She stared after the street car a moment and went on her way. She was going down to the river. Spring had almost come; a little grass pushed up tentatively on the bruised front lawns of her block; and the air, at noon, was gentle with sun. The thought of the sandpile now ranked first in her mind, with thoughts of candy and toothpaste, and she was going to the river to see if she could again find that golden slippery mountain, near a factory, where she had played in the spring sun, last year.

She said hello to some women who were drawing water from a spigot on the railroad tracks. She knew them by sight: they lived in the hand-built huts along the river front. Ruby had tried in vain to persuade her mother to move down here: it was so lively and exciting, with boats going by and all the little shacks lurching amiably together; and getting water at the spigot a quarter-mile away and chatting to one's friends was fun. Besides, she knew that everyone here was on Relief, and no one would shout mean things at her. None of the children looked any better than she did.

She stopped at old Maria's. Behind a shack, in a tiny littered yard, Maria's hut leaned wearily towards the ground. She had made it herself out of packing-cases and brown paper principally, and some said it stood up stiff with its own dirt. Maria was very old and very dirty and very proud. She had never applied for relief; she ravaged the garbage pails and ate stew made of dead cats; but one day some neighbours found her fainted of hunger and then they spoke to the Relief lady, thinking it was high time. Maria had refused to answer any questions and when the Relief order came in for groceries, she quietly tore it up and let it float out in small pieces onto the river. The neighbours argued with her but she said she wanted only to be left alone: that was the way she had lived and she could well afford to die that way. Ruby loved her because she would sit in the sun, not noticing time, and tell stories of gypsies and talk to her dogs as if they were human, discussing with them how they felt about life and what kind of funeral they preferred. She found Maria home, making a pillow out of a burlap sack she had salvaged. She was wearing a greenish-black broadcloth jacket with silken frogs and puffed sleeves, which dated from the last century. She greeted Ruby politely and invited her to sit beside her on the dirt, in the sun.

'How're you, Maria?'

'I am being robbed,' Maria said amiably. 'I don't mind that at all but I do mind having that woman always poking and snooping about and never, never leaving me alone for a minute.'

That woman was the owner of the shack in front of Maria's. Ruby always saw her standing in the yard combing her hair. She had black hair, straight and stiff like a paint brush, and Ruby didn't care for her face. It was too square and her eyes were like raisins and never laughed.

'What's Emma doing to you?' She lowered her voice because Emma, they said, could hear every word that was spoken all up and down the river front, and she was a bad woman to anger.

'Oh, she takes all my grocery orders; she makes me go to the store and get things, and then she takes it all,' Maria said.

Ruby looked at Maria in amazement; why wasn't she crying or hating Emma, why wasn't she doing something about it. That was the very worst thing that could happen to you, to have your food stolen: since food was the only thing you had.

'Do you hate her, Maria? I hate her, I hate her for you.'

'No, it doesn't matter about the food. I can get on very well without it. I go around and find things, and they give me the stale bread at the bakery … but she's so afraid I'll tell the Relief lady or some of the neighbours that she stays around all the time watching me, and I never have a minute. I'm going to have to move,' Maria said. 'There's a very nice cabin up above the warehouse selling for $4.00, but God knows where I'll find the money. However,' she said, 'and how are you, Ruby?'

'Oh, I'm all right. I just came down today looking for the sandpile.'

'The barge, you mean? Well, it's right up the river, about fifteen minutes walking for me. Take care you don't roll off and drown, though I've often thought it would be a nice way to die.'

'I don't wanna die.'

'No, of course you don't.'

'Specially now it's almost spring.'

'Yes, of course,' Maria said, 'now it's almost spring.'

Ruby got up and bid Maria goodbye, and said she'd call again. She wandered up the street, waving to women on their porches, stopped to talk to some boys who were fishing hopelessly, but with interest from the riverbank, looked with admiration at a new toilet Mr Holz had put up right in front of his house, in the centre of his river view, scuffed her feet, practised walking on the rails and hopping from one tie to the next, and sang to herself, with pleasure. Presently she came to the barge. It looked even more golden than she had remembered. Far below it the river ran smooth, thick, and grey. Across the flat water lay Illinois, with the trees sticking out of the river, and she could even see little houses, like Maria's hut, half standing in water, ready to float if they hadn't been so soggy. Farther down the river thin chimneys like asparagus pointed up into a sky made grey with their own smoke. And a little way up men were busy pushing boxes and sacks around the warehouse, and a string of barges floated on the water, waiting to be filled.

The sand barge was tied up alone; the sand rose like a giant golden loaf, steep up the sides and round on the top. Ruby slid down the bank and jumped the distance between the barge and the land. Slowly she crawled up the sides of the pile feeling the sand running down the neck of her dress and scratchy and warm against her legs. Her shoes were filled, and the damp top sand stuck to her hands and arms. She hummed to herself, thinking that now spring had really come, and soon school would stop, and she could play here every day all summer long. Perhaps she would even bring Myra and Johnny with her. Ruby sat on the top of the barge and surveyed the world. Those little match-boxes down the river were the homes of her friends; those funny small rabbits scurrying around were the warehouse men; she was on a par with the factory chimneys, for size and height she thought, and up here one could talk rather bossily even to God. She sat straight and began making speeches to the small inferior lives below her. 'Mizz Sanders, you fix it right away so my Daddy comes home and gets a big job, and we are moved to a fine house with 'lectricity ... Hello, Hello, is this the Green Street Drug Store? This is Ruby Mayer talking. Please send me a dozen tubes of toothpaste to my new house, the most expensive kind you have ... Well, Johnny, I'll give you $1 for your coaster, and I think you're making a lot on it ...

'Pooh,' she said suddenly and largely, and waved her hand to encompass the whole city, the entire world she knew, 'Pooh, for you. Nothing. You're nothing at all. You and your ole Relief and everything. Me, I'm queen of the sand mountain.' Whereupon she rolled down her stockings so that her legs were bare to the sun, pulled her dress up as far as it would go and opened it at the throat, lay down on her back, and went to sleep, dreaming of nothing more definite than light and warmth.

'Hey kid,' a voice shouted, 'Hey, you kid, come down from there.' She sat up, blinking at the sun, and saw the man standing with his head back and his eyes shaded, shouting at her. It made her furious. Who was this man to wake her up, to wake her up on the sand which was her own, and come into her private world like that, noisily bossing people when he had no right to?

'Why?'

' 'Cause that sand belongs to the Government, and nobody's supposed to mess it up.'

'I don't care. I don't know the Government.'

'You come on down, anyhow, or I'll come up and get you and give you a good beating for it.'

'Don't you dare,' she screamed. 'Don't you dare. You leave me alone. If you come up here I'll jump in the river and drown myself. I will so. Don't you dare come up here. It's mine. It's the only place I have, and I'm gonna keep it.'

'Hey, now,' the man said, in a different voice. 'Don't you do that, kid, don't you jump in no river. All right, you stay up there then, but don't come here again.'

He turned and walked towards the houses, and Ruby shouted at his back: 'I will so. I'll come whenever I want to. It's my sand. You tell your ole Government to stay away from me, or I'll drown myself.'

The man was out of sight, and slowly her heart stopped thumping with anger and the terrible fear that perhaps he would climb up anyhow, and she'd have to jump. She spread her legs apart, and scooped a mound of sand towards her, and began fashioning a house. This is my new house, she told herself, a very big one, with trees and a room for me, and a bed …

The water shone and went black as the sun set and wind furled the sand into ridges. Ruby climbed down, having waited until goose flesh crawled out on her legs, to be sure she was too cold to stay longer.

Mrs Baker saw her coming down the path, called street, and waved to her and said, 'Come on in Ruby, and have supper with the girls. Minnie May earned some money working for a lady, today, and we got canned tomatoes and pie.'

Ruby couldn't believe what she had heard. 'Did you say I was to come and eat with you?'

'Sure.'

Ruby stood in the dusk and teetered on her feet, and turned this new and amazing idea over in her mind. People did not give and receive invitations, that she knew of. She had always eaten at home in the room that was sometimes dining room, sometimes kitchen, sometimes both and bedroom as well, depending on where they lived. This, she supposed, was what you would call a party.

'I'm not awful clean, I haven't got on a nice dress,' she said, doubtfully.

'Neither have we,' Minnie May shouted from behind her mother. 'What do you think we are anyhow? Come on in.'

Ruby sat at the Bakers' table, and noticed that their oil lamp had a nice red shade; and that there were two rocking chairs and three beds in the room, and oilcloth on the table, and quite a few cups and saucers and plates and things. The food tasted good to her, and it was surprising to have something besides soup and bread for supper. Minnie May was fourteen, and the heroine of the evening, because she had provided the money for this feast. 'I gotta job doing some cleaning for a lady,' she said, and Ruby looked at her with awe, because Minnie May was smart, and big and could earn money. There was Ellen who was Ruby's age, but not very smart; she just sat at home all day and talked to herself. Everybody was nice to her, but she frightened Ruby a little, because her eyes looked blind, and she never seemed to hear anything that was said. Ruby ate and looked at the room with envy, whenever she thought the Bakers couldn't see her. And Mr Baker talked about how bad times were, saying to Mrs Baker, 'They tell me they're laying men off at the Chevrolet even now; and the shoe factory is gonna move outa town, and the box factory went bust; even them poor wops working at the spaghetti factory is getting fired.'

And he said to Mrs Baker, 'It's a terrible thing when the only person in this family can make a little money is that Minnie May, and her just a kid still.'

'Well,' Mrs Baker said, 'we gotta be thankful at least she can.'

After supper Minnie May said to Ruby: 'You wanna come with me to the Pentecost meeting uptown? It's kinda church, but not really.'

And Ruby, who never did anything but go to bed at night, thought it was surely Christmas, or a dream, so many things happening at once.

On the way, Ruby asked about jobs: 'Do you think I could maybe get something cleaning? We need money at our house awful bad.'

'You'd be purty enough if you washed your hair and face, and had a clean dress,' Minnie May said thoughtfully. 'You got a kinda cute little face.'

'Do you have to be purty to get jobs cleaning?' Ruby asked with despair, because she knew then she'd never find anything.

'I don't clean,' Minnie May said, with scorn, laughing to herself. 'That's what I tell Pa and Ma.'

'What do you do?' This was getting more exciting and mysterious as it went on, and Ruby looked up at Minnie May with admiration. That was a girl who knew how to get what she wanted. Smart like Johnny. But, perhaps, she thought, when I'm as big and as old as they are, I'll be smart too.

'Oh I dunno, I'll tell you sometime, maybe. And maybe you can work with me.'

The Pentecost church was just a meeting-room, with board benches and bare walls, and electric-light bulbs hanging from cords. They slipped in and found seats near some other children. A man was walking up and down the platform, like a caged polar bear, and also like a cricket, jumping and prowling, clapping his hands, saying 'Praise God,' as punctuation for his sentences, and the rest of the time rambling off into a shouted discourse, without sequence, to which no one listened. Ruby looked around and saw a lot of children she knew at school, and some of the river-front people. She wondered if they came often, because it wasn't very funny, this man just saying a lot of words.

Then people sang and Ruby was jealous seeing Betty Perkins and her sister, in clean dresses and hair-ribbons, singing on the platform. They sang songs that whined and twanged, and presently there was a collection, and the meeting ended.

Ruby was going home, but Minnie May said, 'Now's when the fun begins. You see,' Minnie May explained, 'there's always somebody wants to get the Holy Ghost, and now is when they start.'

They moved up front and watched. Women at one end, men at the other; two feet from the floor was a board, for praying. The women rocked, shouted, prayed; and a girl of about seventeen came forward: a process of hypnosis by noise, shouting the same things over and over, began. The girl aided by clenching her fists, holding her body rigid, and generally working herself into a frenzy. She wept and trembled, and the shouting went on.

'Why are they so mean to her,' Ruby whispered, 'what did she do?'

'Nothing, silly, she's getting the Holy Ghost. You wait, she'll pass out in a little while and begin talking funny.'

With their eyes wide and gleaming the old women bent over the girl, shouting at her: 'Sinner Repent; Open up your heart; Make ready for the Holy Ghost …' Their bodies swayed and curled like spaghetti boiling in a pot, and they shouted and leaned over the girl, their breasts hanging above her, their eyes evil and alight. Her face grew mottled, and her hair was damp on her forehead; the backbone made a neat line under her rayon dress as she bowed and tossed, in the agony of prayer. Ruby stood on the bench and watched with horror. It was too mean, why didn't they leave the girl alone, why did they have to go on shouting at her that way. She moved off, to escape the sight, if not the sound.

A little boy of four was sitting on a chair, looking at his feet. 'Do you like it?' she asked him.

'No.'

'It's awful noisy, isn't it?'

'Oh thas all right. Noise here, noise at home. Thas all right.'

She sat by him in silence, and was frightened. There was a man too, at his end of the praying-board, and the men took turns, shouting over him, exhorting and pleading; but their gestures were hammer-strokes up and down, not the writhing and coiling and twisting of the women.

Presently there was a shout and a silence; the girl had fallen backwards on the floor, in a faint. The old women waited, hanging over her, and suddenly her body came alive, and lashed against the floor, and strange words, senseless and jumbled, came from her mouth. 'She's got it,' Minnie May whispered. 'She's got the Holy Ghost. It's kinda scary don't you think?'

'It's awful,' Ruby said. 'I wanna go home.'

Minnie May and she walked out into the darkness, Ruby was relieved when they got out of the sound of those voices, and she blinked to forget what she had seen.

'Why do you go there, Minnie May?'

'Where else kin I go? You can't just go to bed every night, all the time. Gotta go somewheres. That's the only place I know it don't cost nuthin. That's why all us kids go. In summer you kin go and sit with a boy on the river,' she said; 'but it's too cold yet. Jest gotta do somethin. Anything's good enough if you ain't got the money.'

*  *  *

'Tim's sick,' Johnny said.

'What's he got?'

'Difteria.'

'Oh,' Ruby knew that was a bad thing to have; worse than measles for instance; you could probably die of difteria.

'They ain't got the money to give him what he should have.'

Ruby said nothing; of course they didn't. Mr Durkin didn't have a job either. Johnny said once to her that his pa never would have a job again.

His pa was a motor-man. 'They don't want street-cars anymore,' Johnny said, 'they want buses. He ain't any good with automobiles.'

They sat on the front steps and shivered inside their coats. It had stopped being spring; Ruby was still damp from walking to school in a fine wiry rain that streamed flat over the city all morning. Later the rain billowed in gauzy clouds. Now the wind came up, lean and sharp, and circled coldly around their feet and shoulders.

'This weather too,' Johnny said, 'It's cold in there.'

'We got some coal.'

'Yeah. Your ma already give it to us.'

'Shall I go in and play with him?'

'He can't play; he's too sick.'

Suddenly Johnny reached in his pocket and brought out a handful of nickels and pennies.

'Gawd,' Ruby said with reverence.

Johnny counted them carefully, it came to forty-three cents.

'Where'd you get it, Johnny?'

'From my business.'

'You gotta business?'

'Yeah. I'm a salesman.'

Ruby waited. Johnny was too wonderful, too smart. There was nobody like him, not even Minnie May.

'Remember, Ruby, when you saw me getting on the street car?' Ruby nodded, her mouth open, seeing the words before she heard them. 'Well, I was going out to sell. I get these dogs and kewpies and things made out of plaster – ain't you ever seen them, you know, at fairs or Luna Park, or beside the road sometimes. They're kind of ornermints. You put them on the mantel or on the table in the parlour. They're kinda cheap stuff, break easy and I don't think they're purty. But some women buy them. Well, I get them from a guy over on Maple Street, and I sell them for twenty-five cents and I keep five cents. First I took them on the coaster, but then I made enough profit to take the street car, and that way you can get out farther into better neighbourhoods.'

'What do you do when you get there; how do you start?'

'I just ring door-bells. You gotta be smart Ruby. Y'see these things ain't really nice so you can't take them to swell houses where people wouldn't want to put them in the parlour. Then you can't take them to houses like ours, where everybody's on Relief and ain't got a quarter. So you just have to pick the neighbourhood, where people got enough money, but not too much.'

'Yes,' she said marvelling at all this.

'I ring the door-bell,' Johnny went on, 'and I take off my cap and I say would you please buy one of these purty ornermints please lady. I'm taking care of my old sick mother.'

'But your Ma isn't old or sick.'

'I know, but they 'spect you to say something like that. Anyhow, she might just as well be; she ain't got nothing. Sometimes I say my little brother's dying ...'

They stared at each other in sudden fear. Johnny rose.

'I'm gonna buy him some milk and some apples,' he said. 'Wait for me.'

Ruby waited and thought about Johnny and how smart he was, and about Tim and difteria, and how it must be wonderful to work and make money and buy things when you wanted them.

Johnny ran into the house with his gifts and came out again, his face shining. 'I'll take care of them,' he said. 'They don't need to worry. I'll get Tim everything he needs. When my business is better I guess we'll move from this neighbourhood so he can be outdoors more and get some sun ...'

Ruby put her hand in his speechlessly, to show how much she admired him. Johnny swelled noticeably under this treatment.

'And I ain't like some,' he said darkly. 'I'm honest I mean. I get my money the right way, by working.'

'What ...'

'There's some I know, and you too Ruby, who gets it other ways.'

'How?'

'You know those Sweeney boys on the next block? Well, they gotta gang and they steal,' he said almost whispering.

Ruby shivered.

'Their Ma's will find out,' she said.

'Ma's! Christ, that don't count. It's the police.'

'Johnny,' Ruby said, after a silence. 'Lissen, I gotta have some money too. How'm I gonna get it? I'm too little to work, nobody will let me do nuthin'. And I gotta.'

'What do you want to buy?'

'Well, there's my toothbrush, and I can't use it.'

'Yeah, I forgot that.'

'And Johnny, I'd *love* some candy ...'

'Well, Ruby.'

She held his hand tighter; he was going to tell her now, and perhaps tomorrow she'd have all the things she wanted, needed.

'Well, Ruby, I know how some girls get money, and it's work too really, but then it's like stealing too, because if the police catch you and anyhow ...'

'What is it Johnny?'

'It's men.'

'What about men?'

'Don't you know? Don't you know about what men do? Don't you know about those women over on Sarah Street what sit behind the windows, and wave at men and walk around the streets at night?'

There was a pause; not awkward or significant, just a silence while Ruby thought hard, wrinkling her forehead.

She remembered Sarah Street, though it was not a place she played, and she didn't think she knew any children up there. Those women: and men. She had heard something a long time ago, the older girls talking at school in the playground, but the older girls always talked about something that you never listened to much, about clothes and boys and things that didn't matter. Something the men did with those women, she remembered dimly it had something to do with being naked and you had to be in bed and it was wicked, but she couldn't think what exactly had been said ...

'I heard about men once,' she said, 'but I don't zackly remember. I guess those are bad women up there anyhow aren't they Johnny? Not like Mrs Herman and Mrs Baker and Ma.'

'Well.'

'What is it anyhow? What's those women and men and things got to do with me? You said it was girls got money.'

'No, you can't do it Ruby. It isn't any good and you're too little. If you don't even *know*. And besides your Ma would beat you.'

'I don't care if Ma does beat me if I get the money first.'

'How about the police?'

'Oh,' Ruby said. 'Oh.' She hunched her shoulders against the wind and put her hands inside her sleeves. Then slowly she got up. 'No, I can't do it if it's like stealing,' she said, and walked up the front steps. She turned at the door. 'But I don't see why I can't have something too. I never have nuthin',' she shouted. 'Nuthin', nuthin', nuthin'!' and ran into the house with tears smearing dirtily down her face.

* * *

The sun got into their room somehow. It spattered feebly over the rags. Ruby woke up smiling. She pushed off the rags and crawled to her mother.

'Ma, wake up, wake up. It's my birthday. I'm eleven.'

'Is it Ruby? Well, go back to sleep now, it's early. We can't do nothing about a birthday anyhow.'

Ruby crept back to the rags and pulled them up around her and turned her face to the wall. She didn't cry. She had no courage left to cry. But why were there cakes in the bakery if not to eat them on one's birthday, cakes with candles. And there must be some children who woke up on their birthdays and got presents … I'll get them for myself someday, I'll get them for myself. Nobody will give me anything ever.

She didn't mention birthdays again; and all day long she kept telling herself, it isn't my birthday, it's only Tuesday …

\* \* \*

Ruby stood in front of the shoe store window and admired her reflection. The Relief lady had sent a new dress – it was pink, with white and yellow daisies on it – and a pair of new brown oxfords. Mrs Mayer, again and joyfully, had found some washing to do: Ruby wore new underwear and a new pair of short pink socks to match the dress. She twitched the dress where it stuck to her back with sweat, and turned her head, ogling over her shoulder, to see how she looked from the side. She put one foot out before her and stared at the smooth chocolate-coloured shoes, with complete soles, and no scratches; and her socks, like the pink cream filling of the bakery pastries, filled her with pride.

She moved into the shade of the shop doorway. Spring had been as brief as a hand-waving. It had fluttered softly for a week or two and gone. Now it was summer. People's heels stuck in the asphalt of the streets and heat ricocheted from the pavements to the brick walls of the houses. The air seemed to hiss like steam, at noon, and all day Ruby felt little lacings of sweat weaving about beneath her clothes. At night the room on the third floor, under the roof, was agony to endure. Finally, she and her mother sat on the front steps, saying nothing, just waiting for time to go by. Until at last they were too tired to notice and climbed upstairs and lay naked on the rags. They woke with their heads thick or aching and their mouths tasting like cotton. Ruby watched other children in the evening, playing hopscotch, and wondered where they got money for chalk, to mark the pavement into squares. During the day she walked about the city and licked her lips and felt her throat long and ragged with thirst, and sometimes she thought she would scream if she had to go on wanting ice cream cones and lemon pop and not getting them.

She had trained herself now bitterly not to stop at the bakery window, not to look at the candy store, or linger near the man with the little ice-cream wagon.

At the end of the afternoon when the glare no longer hurt her eyes she walked to the sand barge on the river, looked swiftly to see that no man was there to threaten her in the name of the government, and climbed up. But her thirst was always with her.

'Well,' she said to herself, waiting in the shade, having no particular place to go and nothing to do. 'Well, anyhow I'm not cold and that's something.'

And she thought, if my hair were pretty the way Minnie May's is, and if I could have big shining white teeth, from my brush, I would be very nice now with my new clothes. But, she thought, I don't want clothes and curly hair and things like Minnie May does nearly as much as I want roller skates and a jumping rope. It was funny about Minnie May anyhow; Ruby could remember how Minnie May actually had roller skates two summers ago, but now she just walked around and giggled with the other big girls and sort of teased at the boys. Ruby had seen her coming out of the ten cent store a few days ago and she showed Ruby what she'd bought: a lipstick. Ruby thought Minnie May must be getting silly or something; going and throwing money away on a lipstick as if she had a lot of it and there weren't things you really had to have. If you had as much money as all that you might as well get a bathing-suit so you could run out under the water wagon when it came through the streets. Perhaps Minnie May wasn't so smart, or perhaps it was just because she was older and people always got funny when they got older. Still Minnie May had a job. Perhaps, she thought, now that I have a new dress, I could get a job cleaning.

She cooled her forehead against the window meditating on this; after a few days she might make fifty cents. Fifty cents. She put her hand out in front of her trying to imagine how it would look with the silver half dollar in it. I could get, she started: then her mind balked. No, I won't get a cleaning job or anything. I don't get things, and I'd best just not think about it.

Hurriedly, escaping from herself and from that hated future without anything she wanted or needed, she walked towards the river.

Near the spigot she saw Minnie May and two other girls. Minnie May's hair was marcelled, very orderly and glued with wave lotion. She had on a fresh gingham dress, too, and a vast pink ice cream cone slid in and out of her mouth, slowly wasting away, but keeping a fine round shape as it went.

Ruby turned to go back. How did that girl manage she wondered, where was all this money coming from, Minnie May had everything. Perhaps Mr Baker worked now and then and didn't tell the Relief lady so he could give dimes to Minnie May. Well, she didn't have a Daddy to cheat the Relief lady. That was like everything else.

'ROO-BEE.'

'What?'

'C'mere.'

She walked towards them; they stared at her, Minnie May with her head a little on the side.

'She's awful poor,' she said to the others. 'Let's let her.'

'But she's too little, she's only about nine.'

'No, she's eleven. And that don't matter. They don't care, I don't think.'

'Her dress is nice,' one of the girls remarked, a dark girl with a chocolate ice-cream cone and a ten-cent store ring, signs of wealth. 'But her face is kinda dirty. And her hair.' She paused, in doubt.

'I bet we can fix her up,' Minnie May said. 'And she's really awful poor.' Then turning to Ruby she asked: 'Could you do with some money, Ruby?'

'Oh.' She couldn't say anything more. Perhaps Minnie May did know of a cleaning job then, or anything, anything.

Minnie May saw the way Ruby was looking at her ice cream.

'Here,' she said generously. 'Take a lick at it; don't bite, just lick it.'

Ruby rolled her tongue over the smooth strawberry mound and looked at Minnie May with love.

'Lissen, Myrtle,' Minnie May said to the one with the ten-cent store ring. 'You're only thirteen and that's only two years different, and Sally's only thirteen and a half. Lissen, let's get some soap and wash her hair and see how she looks.'

They agreed and turned towards Minnie May's house, with Ruby hopping around them, in a fever of happiness, saying: 'Am I gonna get a job, too, Minnie May, am I gonna get some money too?'

Mrs Baker lent them soap and they returned to the spigot. Myrtle and Sally made a circle, holding their skirts as a screen, with some difficulty so that the ice cream wouldn't roll off the cones. Ruby got out of her clothes and laid them on a box beside the spigot and Minnie May, who had eaten her ice cream cone in great bites, crunching the cone between her teeth, began on her hair.

'Bend over.' Ruby put her head under the spigot and the cool water ran over her body. Minnie May scrubbed and rinsed and soaped the hair ('Gosh, don't you ever wash it') and rinsed again. Then she gave Ruby the soap and Ruby, scarcely having to bend at all, washed and took a shower under the spigot.

'Jump up and down and you'll get dry quicker,' Minnie May ordered.

Ruby obeyed. She put her clothes back on to a cool damp body and Minnie May ran her fingers through Ruby's hair, drying it and fluffing it. From out of her bloomers she produced a little pink celluloid comb and combed Ruby's hair. It waved gently, and fell in a soft ripple over her forehead.

'Let's look,' Minnie May said, standing with her feet apart, critical. Ruby felt shy with them staring at her.

'She's pretty,' Sally said and Ruby blushed for pleasure. The small face showed up clear with faint colour in the cheeks. The lines of it were delicate and soft except for a hollowing in the cheeks, a little tightness, a little hunger about the mouth. The weedy hair was light and fine, and grew well about the face. She raised her pointed chin and stared back at them, feeling suddenly, now that she was pretty, much older and more important.

'She'll do,' Myrtle said. 'And we can say she's twelve anyhow.'

'All right,' Minnie May said. 'You can come with us tomorrow Ruby, but you gotta promise not to tell anybody specially not your Ma.'

'Is it stealing?' Ruby asked, because she couldn't do that, and again at once she saw all her hopes, everything she wanted, destroyed, lost. Her mouth drooped.

Sally laughed. 'Hell,' she said. 'It is not. You earn your money all right.'

Then everything was perfect and Ruby smiled at them, shining grateful. 'Can I bring Myra?' she asked. 'Myra needs a job too.'

'No.' They were quick and unanimous. 'And lissen, Ruby,' Minnie May said. 'If you tell *anybody*, even Myra, we'll twist your arm up in back – this way.'

She grabbed Ruby by the arm and wrenched it up behind her, and Ruby, astonished at this abrupt cruelty, didn't scream, but only said: 'Minnie May, Minnie May.'

'All right then, but you promise not to tell.'

'I promise,' she said, her eyes wide and tears in them from the pain that hadn't had time to bring tears all the way out.

'You can get your own cones,' Myrtle said, 'only you got to come down here and wash pretty often because if you aren't clean then maybe we won't get any work.'

Ruby promised that too.

'You meet us here at the spigot tomorrow about this time,' Minnie May said. 'About five. You can go by the drug store and look at the clock so you'll be sure to be here.'

The three older girls walked back towards the river. In the afternoon sun Minnie May's blonde hair glinted; she patted it elegantly and swung her hips a little as she walked. Ruby could hear them talking. 'We had to have at least one more,' Minnie May said. 'There's too many for us now. And she really is awful poor. That kid hasn't got anything. You see her ole man even went away so when he could p'raps pick up a job now and then, he ain't even here. Though, I must say,' she said, very important and old, the oldest of them all, 'I make a lot more money than my Pa ever does.'

* * *

She knew the cabin: it was old Lucy's. It sat between the railroad tracks and the river, isolated, half in the white territory and half in the black. It was bigger than negro cabins usually were: it was really a house, deserving the dignity of the name. It didn't leak, being firmly and entirely covered with tarpaper; it didn't even sag. Lucy had actually bought it: she was one of the early settlers here, having come in 1929 when things officially began to go bad for many people. Things had been bad for Lucy and her friends for many years, or perhaps forever, and she decided to buy herself a house in her old age before it was too late and there were no jobs left at all. She had worked as a cleaning woman at night, downtown in the office buildings and found her new home both healthy and convenient. During two years she paid for it out of her wages: then there were no more wages. She lived on Relief, easily. It was not much money, but it was sure. And there were always little ways of eking things out. Her house was an admirable investment; she kept it nicely and was praised by the Relief lady who was unaccustomed to seeing anyone in that neighbourhood tidy or possessive. She had rented a room to a man who became known as Mr Lucy, he stayed so long and obeyed her so well. But finally he left, and when she was looking for something else to provide the luxury money, she met a man prowling about the river front on obvious business and it gave her an idea. She thought it would be less trouble to rent her rooms just for a few hours at a time, and perhaps more profitable. She met Minnie May at the spigot and gradually, with no one ever saying anything first, this little affair had grown up. For several months now Lucy had been able to buy all the small things she needed; she was even putting away some money for repairs on the house, next spring. Like any good business woman she was thinking to herself, cautiously, of enlargements and improvements.

When they came near the house Lucy rose from a rocker on the front porch, smiled, said nothing and went away. She never stayed; if anything happened she didn't want to be there. The people who came didn't steal, anyhow; they weren't after that. She kept her money in a pouch hanging between her breasts and no one would notice it as a small bulge in the swelling uninterrupted, calico-covered mound formed by her bosom resting on her stomach.

'Why,' Ruby said, 'it's Lucy's cabin; are we gonna clean it?' with some wonder. 'And ole Maria lives right near here; we can go by and see her on the way home.'

'Gawd, isn't she dumb,' Myrtle said resignedly. 'Now you lissen, Ruby, lissen to me. You're not gonna go and see Maria and no one is gonna know you was down here this afternoon. If your Ma asks where you was you just say you was down at the sand barge like you always are. And don't you go waving at Maria. You just come down here quiet so nobody notices anything and then you go home quiet and you tell your Ma you was playing on the sand barge.'

'Yes,' Ruby said, thinking it all over carefully and trying to remember: not to speak to Maria, not tell Ma, sand barge … well, it certainly wasn't cleaning then: but what was it?

Minnie May explained her duties briskly.

'Ruby,' she said, 'today you can watch on the porch to see nobody comes. Somebody has gotta. You watch and if you see anybody you knock on the door loud enough so's we can hear. We each give you a dime from what we get: that makes thirty cents. The days you go inside you do the same, you give a dime to the kid who watches and you keep the rest. Two days a week we give everything we make to Lucy. That's the way we work it.'

'Yes,' Ruby said, in growing amazement. Thirty cents, she thought, almost fifty cents, for doing nothing but sitting on a porch. It didn't seem true and it certainly didn't seem right. Somebody would surely take it from her in the end, things didn't happen like that, not easily that way, not for nothing, almost free. It was like giving money away, and nobody would do that, ever.

'Come in and look now before they come,' Minnie May said.

The cabin had three rooms, the floors were covered with linoleum. There were three beds, one in each room, small iron affairs. They looked odd to Ruby; she felt something was missing on them. Oh, yes, they just had one sheet spread over the mattress and a pillow. No covering. Well, perhaps that was because of the heat, but still … And then who slept in them she wondered: there was only old Lucy living here.

The living-room had a table and chairs, and a lamp with a shade, and two calendars with pictures. Odd bits of furniture, not matching, not new, but all clean, sat rather uselessly in the other rooms. Outside, in a lean-to,

Lucy did her cooking. The only thing Ruby finally noticed or remembered were the beds like hospital cots, glaringly white and ready.

'Now,' Sally said, 'you get outside, they'll be here soon. I'll tell you when you have to begin watching for people we don't want.'

A man came up to the porch. Ruby made the note in her mind: 'a man'. She stopped thinking about him. He was a man like people's fathers, a grown-up man. He had no collar on. He said nothing to her and went inside. A door closed. She heard Minnie May's voice but no words; just the sound of her voice. Presently everything was quiet. Another man appeared, entered in silence, and before the door closed she could hear Myrtle saying: 'Oh, hello, you back again.' When the third man went in Sally came out on to the porch, and without greeting him said to Ruby: 'Now keep your eyes open, we don't want anybody else for a while.'

Dim things began to form in Ruby's mind. She sat on the porch and waited and tried to give shape and meaning to her thoughts. Things she knew or had known once, a long time ago, and not thought of particularly. Things about men. Something. Something Johnny had said too, about the women who lived on Sarah Street. The minutes went past smoothly and she sat on the steps, not daring to use old Lucy's rocker, wrinkled her forehead and tried to remember. Then the door opened, it didn't seem very long, and a man came out – perhaps the first one, Ruby thought, but they all looked alike, just grown-up men, the way grown-up men always looked. She stared shyly at her feet; he stopped, standing above her on the steps and said: 'Hello.' She looked at him but didn't speak. 'See you sometime,' he said, and walked down the railroad tracks toward the city. Minnie May came out. She was combing her glued, flatly-waved hair. Her dress was unbuttoned at the neck.

'I'll sit with you unless another comes.'

They waited. Ruby went on thinking, kicking up a little dust around her shoes, her forehead ridged and anxious. She wanted to ask Minnie May about the men but somehow she didn't dare. Minnie May, she felt, might be angry or laugh.

In an hour, or less, the other two men had gone and the girls sat together on the porch. They stayed there until after the sun had gone down and then Minnie May said: 'No one will come now, we better get back for supper.' She whistled rather loudly for Lucy, who was waiting to hear, and as they saw Lucy, square against the evening sky, humping slowly over the railroad tracks, they started walking home. Ruby followed a little behind the others.

'I got sixty cents this time,' Myrtle said.

'Lucky.' There was envy in Minnie May's tone. 'If we had a few more men I wouldn't let that Bill come. I don't like him. I don't like what he does; not like the others.'

Ruby listened, her mind churning with doubt, memory, wonder, and somewhere, vaguely, something like fear.

'Tomorrow,' Sally said over her shoulder, 'you can go in.'

Ruby thought waiting was good enough; she would be contented with thirty cents. But she kept silent; this was their work, they planned it, she was only to do what she was told and then have money – money …

At the spigot they stopped.

'Hold out your hand,' Minnie May said.

She stood with her hand out and each one put a dime in it.

'Be back here at five tomorrow,' Myrtle called, but she was shouting at Ruby's back. Ruby had started running; she was afraid they might change their minds and not want to give her money for doing nothing. And she had never had thirty cents; or not since she could remember. She ran up the street, half laughing, half crying, holding the dimes until she could feel their shape pressed into her hand.

For half an hour, tormented, she walked in front of the stores. Where was she going to start, what should she buy first? Now that she had money after this long waiting, after all the wanting and planning, she couldn't decide. With the dimes firm in her hand, and in luxury and pain of spirit, she walked between the bakery and the candy store and the drug store, saying, how will I decide, how can I decide? Finally, she bought a nickel's worth of heavenly hash, since it was evening now and she was more hungry than hot or thirsty. And a small tube of toothpaste for a dime, and then – fighting herself at every step but thinking I oughta, I oughta – she went into the grocery store and bought a can of peaches.

She walked home the longest way, slowly eating her candy, sucking it before she chewed it, letting it slip in an agony of sweetness from her tongue down her throat. When it was all gone she turned the sack inside out and ate a few squarish crumbs of milk chocolate.

She held the toothpaste in its cardboard box, with light and reverent fingers. She saw herself taking the lovely purple brush out of the glass case and spreading a pink cream band on it and brushing her teeth until her mouth was full of pink suds, and rinsing and brushing and rinsing … In the morning and at night, and she would have white shining big teeth. She had to feel the little box to be sure she had it, after all this time. The toothpaste ought to last all summer, she thought; I'll be careful of it and make it last.

She lied to her mother easily, surprised herself at how simple it was to make up a story.

'I was walking along Oak Street and a woman called me and said, will you take this package up to my daughter's on Olive Street, and I said yes, and she said, when you're done come back and I'll give you something. Her daughter gave me a dime (that's for the toothpaste) and I went back, anyhow, and she gave me fifteen cents, so I got the peaches for you, Ma.' It wasn't a very sound story but she told it with conviction and Mrs Mayer, delighted by the peaches, made no comment.

Poor Ma, Ruby thought, she has to work all day doing washing and only gets fifty cents, and all I have to do is sit on a porch awhile and I make almost as much. I guess I'll be making more soon, she thought, and the doubt came back and the brief flash of fear. But she looked at her mother, opening the can of peaches, and there was her toothpaste on the table, and she hoped it would be tomorrow quickly.

*  *  *

'I'll watch today,' Minnie May said, 'I'm tired.'

Sally led Ruby into the farthest room. She fidgeted a little, her hand on the door-knob ready to go. 'Ruby,' she said and paused. Ruby had not spoken since they came. This, she knew, was the work part. Sitting on the porch, and getting paid for it, was too good to last. She watched Sally. She wanted to ask questions and yet she didn't. I'll find out, she thought, what it is, may as well wait. I'll find out later, when the men come.

'Ruby,' Sally said again. 'Lissen. I want to tell you something. It'll hurt, Ruby. Sometimes it hurts bad but only the first time. And all you gotta do is think about the money and how you can get marcelles and lipstick, and go to the movies, and everything you want, afterwards. That's all you got to do. It don't last long. It only hurts the first time, really.'

What, Ruby said in her mind. What. What; what is this thing? What am I waiting for? She kept silent for a moment and then said: 'I don't want marcelles or lipstick or the movies; I want a jumping rope and roller skates mostly, besides cones, of course, and candy. I got my toothpaste already.'

Sally stopped, she was a little frightened of this. It wasn't right, somehow; Ruby was too young. Myrtle had told Minnie May but Minnie May said 'No.' Still, Ruby was young. Imagine wanting roller skates instead of marcelles or clothes.

'Well,' she said. 'Well. All right, get what you want. Now just wait.'

She closed the door and Ruby sat lightly on the edge of the bed, careful not to rumple it. She waited, her ears strained for the first heavy step on the front porch; but not thinking, just listening and waiting. The palms of her hands sweated. That surprised her. And her eyes ached from staring at the door.

Quite suddenly, before Ruby realised she had heard them coming, the door-knob turned. Minnie May came in; behind her was a man.

'This is Ruby,' Minnie May said in a funny voice, thin and nervous. 'Well,' she said and scratched one foot against her leg and hung on to the door-knob, swaying a little, uncertain. 'Well, g'bye.'

The man closed the door firmly. He turned and looked at Ruby; he doesn't see me, she thought, that's funny. He's looking at me but he doesn't know it's me. He hasn't even looked at my face.

'My name's Ruby,' she said helpfully, and then because he still seemed indefinite, strange in this room and not seeing her at all, though he was looking hard enough, she added: 'What's yours?'

'Hank,' he said. She jumped a little at the sound of his voice. Of course he would have a voice like that; it was silly to expect he'd have a voice like Johnny's. His voice was like Daddy's or Myra's father: a grown-up man's voice. And he was old too, old as anybody's father.

The man walked towards her across the room, slowly, a little doubtfully.

She didn't move, but felt her skin drawing back, felt herself pressing backwards on the bed. But his face looked all right; it didn't look as if he were going to be ugly or mean. She waited, staring up at him.

'What're you doing here?' he said.

There was no answer; that was what he should tell her, that was what she was waiting to find out.

'I'm gonna get some money,' she said in a thin voice, and the man laughed, relaxed, at ease again. She didn't like his laugh.

'Oh,' he said, 'so that's it? Like the others? Well, that's all right then.'

He sat down on the bed beside her and said: 'Now what?' But his voice was no longer hesitating and half gentle, half angry, bemused. It was a joking voice, a rough, easy joking voice.

She turned a little and looked at him, and he noticed that there were fine blonde hairs on her arms, soft, small, child arms, if thin. He picked her up and put her on his lap. Her arms hung limp and he said: 'Put your arms around my neck.' She obeyed, and suddenly the man found himself embarrassed; it was like visiting his sister on Sunday and taking his little niece on his knees. He told himself that he was a fool, these kids started young, they were all tarts and wanted the money, and hell, it wasn't any of his business, if it wasn't him it would be some other man, so what's the difference … But he told her to take her arms away, and told her gruffly. She yanked them away in terror. That sounded like Daddy's voice, remembered now in fear, long ago, when he had started to beat her for nothing, for no reason, just because she was there.

Hank decided he was wasting his time. For reasons he could neither name nor understand he was feeling cross and put upon.

'I'll call Minnie May or Myrtle,' he said.

'No, no, please.' If he called them she would get scolded; nobody had called her when she was waiting on the porch. That wasn't the way they worked it. The man just came in and then later he went away. If he called they wouldn't let her come any more. He was going to call because she was younger, that was it. People never let her do anything because she was too little. Her lips trembled trying not to cry; the man was going to call and she would be sent away and never get any money again. No skates, no chalk for hopscotch, no cones.

'I'm thirteen,' she said doggedly. 'I'm thirteen. I'm as old as they are. I just look little.'

'Oh.' Then suddenly, and Ruby unprepared, astonished, he began to pull off her dress. He tugged at it, pulling her around on his knees, hurried and ungentle. She was breathless and frightened and worried about her dress. 'Please be careful. Please be careful. You'll tear my dress. You'll spoil my dress. It's my new one, too.'

The man didn't hear her. Anyhow, he didn't stop. He seemed to be breathing strangely too. Or talking to himself or laughing or something. Ruby felt herself getting cold. She wanted to hit out at him and shout stop, but she couldn't do that. Minnie May was on the porch and Sally in the next room, and they'd hear and not let her come, and then all summer she'd have nothing, nothing.

The man held her up in his arms, the naked child's body, white and narrow, neat, soft legs, no hips, and no breasts at all, just two tiny points. Ruby stared back at him with wide eyes, all pupil, black and terrified, but she could not speak now if she wanted, or even scream. It seemed to her that this had been going on for ever. If she held her breath and was very quiet and waited, perhaps it would soon end and she could get back into the street, into the sun, on the sand barge, back to the things she knew about.

He tossed her lightly backwards on the bed and Ruby's hands, useless as flowers, waved up against him, and were crushed down. There was blackness in her mind, neither thought nor feeling, and she lay as dead until she began to scream. Her voice curved out, thin, wailing, fierce, and the man put his hand heavily on her mouth. The sound died and she began to sob without noise, her whole body shaking and bruised. She said nothing, did nothing, and the sobbing tore out of her quietly. The man rose, looked at her, at the bed, pulled his clothes about him in fury, threw a dollar bill on to her naked body, and ran from the house shouting at Minnie May on the porch as he went: 'You bitch, you goddam little whore,' he shouted, 'what're you trying to do here, goddam you.'

Minnie May, for a horrified moment, stared after him running down the railroad tracks, dragging at his clothes, cursing distantly.

She crept in to Ruby and watched her, lying on her back on the bed, with open eyes, the tears flowing down her face and her body retching sobs, in long silent gasps now.

'Ruby, what is it? What's the matter with you?'

From between the sobs, slowly, Ruby said: 'It hurts, it hurts.'

The house emptied and the other two girls stood watching with Minnie May, helpless, scared, not speaking.

They knew that you had to stop crying sometime; had to, that was the way it was. They could only wait. Finally Ruby lay on the bed, the tears drying on her face.

'I'll help you get dressed,' Sally said.

They didn't speak again. Ruby walked home a little behind them, limping, dazed, holding the dollar bill in one hand. She did not think and had no questions to ask. She walked carefully because she was afraid she would tear in two.

She hid the dollar bill in a hole under the front steps, looking first at the windows to make sure no one saw her, and she told her mother she had fallen from the sand barge, was sick, wanted nothing to eat, let her alone, let her sleep, let her sleep …

* * *

They did not expect to see her again. They had hardly spoken of it to each other, feeling that the picture of Ruby lying on the bed was best darkened and forgotten. Minnie May said once, briefly: 'I only hope she don't tell.' For two days they had gone about their business, sobered and stubborn. They did not see her on the streets anywhere, nor going to the sand barge: they asked no questions about her.

On the third day, just as they had passed the spigot, walking to Lucy's cabin, they heard a shout. Turning they saw Ruby at the top of the street, coming down the hill towards the railroad tracks. 'Lookit,' Ruby shouted. 'Lookit me on my roller skates! Lookit how fast I go!'

They stood silently and waited. As the speed increased Ruby crouched down, and her hair blew back from her damp forehead and her dress sailed out behind her. She did not look up, intent on keeping her balance, concentrated, smiling. And then, bumping off the curb, she stopped on the cinders, and stood up.

'I'm here,' she said.

They did not answer.

'I've come back,' she said. 'I bought these skates with the dollar. They're lovely. I go fast as anything.'

Still there was silence.

'I'll do it again,' Ruby said, her chin hard, staring at them. 'I'll do it again. Sally said it only hurt the first time.'

Minnie May looked at Myrtle, but got no help from her. Sally also waited, making no sign.

'I guess you can watch,' Minnie May said. 'You can just watch from now on.'

'No. I'll do it again. I'll do it the way you do.'

'You'll lose us our customers,' Sally said, coming alive at last. 'We can't have that. You'll lose us all our customers.'

'No, I won't. You said it only hurt once.'

They turned and started walking towards the cabin, without answering, not sure yet of what they intended. Ruby took off her skates and followed them. Her face was obstinate: she lowered her head, glaring at the cinders.

'All right,' Minnie May said, on the porch. 'All right, you can try once more. If you cry you have to go. You can't come any more if you cry. Go in today. We'll see.'

Ruby left her skates, crossed on top of each other, carefully, tenderly, in a corner of the porch.

She went back to the room, looked at the bed for one moment, wild and ready to escape. She shook herself and again her face set in obstinate lines. I know what it is now, she thought, I know what it is they want. That makes it easier … And then she wasn't sure; no, perhaps not, because ahead of time, before they came, she could think what was going to happen, how it would be. And all she thought now was: I hope it's quick, I hope it doesn't take very long.

The man who came in found a little girl with dark dilated eyes, staring at him, standing up, her arms stiff at her sides, her nostrils pressed out and the line of her jaw clear over gritted teeth. He stopped and looked at her a moment, startled, not knowing what to do next. But Ruby was ready.

'I'll take off my dress,' she said, whispered, urgent, hurried, her voice coming out between closed teeth. 'I'll take it off myself.'

Myrtle was on the porch in Lucy's rocker when she came out. Ruby sat on the steps, bowed over her knees, holding her arms tight across her stomach, and swayed a little to and fro, whimpering.

'What's the matter?' Myrtle said.

Ruby didn't answer. Minnie May had said not to cry. She held the tears back and hunched her body over.

'Did it hurt?'

'Yes,' Ruby said. 'Yes.'

They sat silently waiting for the others.

'Bill came again,' Myrtle said. 'He likes Minnie May but she don't like him. When I get older I'm gonna get married and go on Relief. I don't like this work. I'm tired.'

Ruby opened her hand and looked at the silver coins. 'He only gave me fifty cents,' she said.

'*Only*,' Myrtle snorted. 'Say, who do you think you are? I never got a dollar. You only got it cause it was your first time anyhow. *Only*. Lissen, that's a lotta money for kids. A big girl I know does this work says she gets a quarter, mostly. You oughta be glad. And lissen, you gotta pay your dime today, same's we do. We let you off last time, but you gotta pay today.'

Ruby looked at the money.

'I need it,' she said darkly, 'I need it. But I wish I could get me a cleaning job instead.'

\* \* \*

The newspapers said it was the hottest summer on record, and every day, braggingly, listed deaths by sunstroke, heat prostration. The people on the block suffered like animals, going leadenly through the days, their eyes aching and glazed from heat, thirsty, unable to sleep at night in the closed, airless rooms. The pavement burned through shoe soles, and the slight, unhealthy grass withered into a brown crust. Mrs Mayer endured this summer, as she had others before it. She said nothing, since it was useless to complain, and she looked forward to nothing, realising that the winter would merely be a change to enduring cold. She was only glad dimly, that Ruby seemed so gay and contented, since she had found that rich old woman uptown, to give her presents.

Ruby invented this lie, finally, with Minnie May's aid. It became a tax on her imagination to think up a fresh story every night, explaining away the sudden flow of cones, the chalk for hopscotch, the jumping-rope, and the various foods she brought home in bright cans. She broached the subject to Minnie May, asking how Minnie May got around her wealth. Minnie May had invented a legendary woman on Maple Street, for whom she did cleaning. But Minnie May was older, and Ruby knew her mother would not believe she had work. Then, one day, an old woman, who seemed incredibly rich-looking to Ruby, because she had on a real hat and proper shoes, actually spoke to her on the street and gave her a dime. From this incident, they elaborated the tale of a rich old woman living uptown, who had no children of her own and was lonely. Ruby said that she went up to see this lady every afternoon, and always came away with presents. It was hard for Mrs Mayer to believe at first: though it seemed natural to her that any woman would find Ruby sweet, and want to have her near. But, what she couldn't imagine was anyone with money enough to give some away every day. Ruby talked about the old lady's house, describing the lamp-shades, the beds ('with covers on them of pink,' she said, and then, breathlessly, risking everything, 'pink satin'). And, gradually, this mythical philanthropist took shape, became real, part of their lives, until Ruby began repeating her conversation in detail, and believing the story herself.

Slowly, she came not to notice her afternoon's work. It was only an hour or so, and she found that, if she thought hard about something else all the time, it passed quickly. She became casual and easy, if not friendly, with the customers. She never knew their names and never recognised them, even if they came back several times. Minnie May once complained of this, saying: 'You treat them like they was ghosts, or not in the room or something. You gotta say "hello" and their names at least.' But Ruby could not remember; she went through a routine automatically, and, as none of the men objected, Minnie May let the matter drop.

Ruby, now rich, now glutted with everything she needed, hurtled around the block on roller skates, played hopscotch as the light faded over the brick houses and the air cooled, sucked cones, luxuriously, drank lemon pop, proudly and busily bought presents for her mother: canned peaches, oranges, sometimes even a bottle of pop and once, daringly, she had spent her entire forty cents getting her mother jewellery at the ten cent store. Myra believed the story about the old lady and Ruby bought her cones, magnanimously, enjoying the reverence in Myra's eyes as she shelled out nickels. It was a lovely summer.

Johnny was going to have a birthday. Ruby had not seen him much this summer. He was working hard and often out of the neighbourhood, peddling his clay dogs and kewpies up and down the burning streets, until late at night. Things were not going very well. At this time of year people did not want ornaments for their parlours: they wanted coca-cola and bathing suits and electric fans. They sat on their porches in the dusk and rocked and fanned themselves with folded newspapers. Johnny was wondering whether he could contact some big business man who sold soft drinks. Then he could carry a box slung from his shoulders, with ice and bottles inside. That would have more sales, now. And the box wouldn't be much heavier than the basket with clay animals. He looked thin and weary. He didn't have to bother now with stories about his old sick mother; his own face was sales-talk enough.

Ruby went to the ten cent store and shopped carefully. She dragged her feet, elbowing people, touching things on the counter, thinking to herself about Johnny, and what he would like. Finally, she bought him a belt and a big bag of pink candy, and two handkerchiefs with J. in green machine embroidery, in the corner. She took the gifts home and made a package and greeted Johnny, early in the morning, before he started off on the day's work, jumping up and down and shouting, 'Happy birthday. Happy birthday.'

Johnny took the package. He held it a minute, without opening it, smiling at her. For two birthdays now, he had received no presents, and he had forgotten what it was like. Birthdays and Christmas: days like all the other days. His mother had kissed him that morning, which was rare enough, and said, 'You're a good boy, Johnny,' but that was all she could do. He held Ruby's hand and then leaned over and kissed her cheek quickly, a little embarrassed.

'Oh,' Ruby said and blushed, and ran back into the house. She stood inside the house, hiding behind the door, and watched him open the package slowly, and hold everything up to look at it. He whistled softly over the handkerchiefs. Then she hurried upstairs, to avoid him, as he came back to show the presents to his mother and leave them for the day.

He found her, that night, playing hopscotch with Myra.

'Lissen, come down aways with me. I wanta ask you something.'

'I'll be back, Myra,' she said, and walked with Johnny, feeling proud, possessive, delighted, his hand upon her arm.

They walked to the next block and sat on a stranger's steps.

'I been thinking,' Johnny said. 'It was nice of you to get me those presents. They're awful purty, and the candy's awful good.'

Ruby smiled in the darkness, and put her hand in his.

'But lissen, Ruby, where did you get the money?'

There was a pause. Ruby swallowed. Her voice came out rather shaky and high. 'From my old lady uptown, you know, Johnny.'

'No,' he said firmly. 'No, you can't have. There isn't anybody in the world like that, there isn't anybody gives you something every day, just to come and see them. I know. I seen a lot of people. Your ma believes it, but grown-ups don't know much. They don't get around. I know, though. Where did you get it, Ruby?'

'I told you.'

'All right.' He got up, sighed, and turned to go. 'I should think you could tell me. When you know we're gonna get married some day.'

'Johnny,' she said, 'come back. I'll tell you.'

She found it hard to begin. She stammered a little, and then, hopeless of finding any way to say it well, she blurted it out. 'I go every afternoon to Lucy's cabin down by the tracks, with some other girls. And men come and they do something to you, and then they give you fifty cents.'

Johnny did not speak. His shoulders bent over and he sat apart. He took his hand away from hers.

'Well,' he said.

'I had to have some money,' Ruby went on. 'You know. I had to. And there wasn't any cleaning I could do.'

'Yes,' he said. 'I know. Boys steal, and girls do that, if they hafta. I know. I wish you didn't, though.'

'Why?'

'Oh, well. Nothing. Only, I don't guess we can get married then.'

'Oh, Johnny.'

'Well, a man can't marry women like that. They just don't.'

'What kinda women?'

'Nothing,' Johnny said wearily.

'Johnny, I didn't know you'd care like that. I just didn't tell you cause Minnie May said not to tell, not anybody. But I don't see why you care, Johnny. It's just working. It's all I can do. I'm too little to get me a real job.'

'Sure. Oh sure. You better not tell anybody either. They catch you for that, just like stealing. The cops come and catch you. I know.'

'But how can they, Johnny? It isn't stealing. I don't steal nuthin.'

'I dunno how they can. They do. Specially if you're little. You better be careful, Ruby.'

She shivered. Minnie May had never said this. She didn't know the cops would care. It wasn't stealing. Her hands went cold. But if Minnie May hadn't told her, then perhaps Johnny was wrong.

'Johnny,' she said, and slipped her hand back in his, 'are you still sore? Aren't you gonna marry me when we get big? When I'm big I'm gonna get a cleaning job, and then you won't hafta be sore. Please Johnny. Don't be mean. I can't do anything else.'

She took his hand and laid it against her cheek, and said again softly, 'Please, Johnny.'

'All right. I guess I will, anyhow. Only you gotta do cleaning when you're big. You gotta stop this. I can't marry you if the cops get you, and you're in jail, can I?'

She hung on to his hand, frightened. 'Don't say that. Don't say that. You wouldn't let them, would you, Johnny?'

'I can't do nuthin about cops, Ruby. Kids like us gotta do what the cops say.' Then he put his arm around her, and said, 'No, Ruby, don't cry. It's all right. Come on back and let's play lampost tag.'

\* \* \*

The newspapers rarely mentioned deaths from heat now, and the sun sank earlier. There were shadows, like pieces from a jigsaw puzzle, over the railroad tracks as Ruby walked home. She had forgotten Johnny's warning. The days went on, each one the same, with delights enough. Nourished on ice-cream, washed under the spigot, smooth and content in spirit, she looked plump, fresh, and wore the meaningless general expression of happiness one expects in children. She bounced her new golf-ball up the hill, throwing it a little ahead of her, so that she had to run to catch up with it, and hummed to herself. The summer she thought would go on, the sun would slant over the barge as she lay dozing on the top, she would buy cones to lick slowly with her tongue curved and careful, she would play hopscotch in the evenings, and roar around the block on her roller skates. The summer would go on.

And one day, as she bent to put her roller skates in the corner of the porch, a hand came down on her shoulder. Not roughly, but quietly, finally. She straightened up, seeing dark blue pants, and above them brass buttons, and then a tanned policeman's face. She stared at him, her mouth open, with horror prickling up and down her back.

'Come along,' he said. Simply, nothing more, not ugly or mean, just definitely. She knew there was no use arguing.

'Can I take my skates?'

'No. You won't want them. Just leave them here.'

At that, something went wrong inside her; terror soared over her mind; helplessness; being caught; allowed nothing any more, nothing of her own. She wept with abandon, her head forward on her breast, and the policeman led her by the arm, because her eyes were blind with tears.

'She don't look like one,' he kept saying to himself, 'she don't look like one. She just looks like a nice little girl …'

\* \* \*

They were all quiet. 'The new girls,' the tall, bony woman had said, and the door slammed shut, and a key turned. 'This is where you sleep,' she said, and herded them before her, saying nothing, but just by her gestures showing that now you obeyed, now you did what you were told, and didn't talk back about it.

She pointed to their beds, and, as if hypnotised, each one went and sat down. 'You can stay there till supper,' she said, and left. Myrtle and Sally and Minnie May and Ruby. They sat with their hands folded in their laps, and stared ahead at the brownish concrete wall, with barred windows across it. There was nothing to do now. Except wait, wait, wait. Ruby whimpered softly, and the other three turned to look at her as if their heads were heavy, stiff, pulled on wires, and then looked away.

They went in to supper and met the other girls. Some were older, some must have been at least sixteen, Ruby thought. The dining room was bare like the dormitory, but had three long tables in it. On one of them, they ate. The oilcloth cover was stained, and, in places, had worn away to the brown, lining threads. For supper they had soup and bread and stewed apricots. She noticed the girls eating; they screwed up their faces and shovelled the food in, gulping it.

She discovered, to her surprise, that the girls almost always whispered, instead of talking out, though nothing they said was bad or a secret. 'You never can tell,' a girl with heavy red hair explained, 'they punish you for breathing.'

'They treat the coloured girls worse than us,' one girl told her. 'They don't beat us, but they do them. The food,' she said, 'gets worse and worse, till you think you'll puke if you hafta eat it. And there's nothing to do.'

'How long you been here?' Ruby asked.

'Three weeks. I'm waiting to go to court.'

Three weeks Ruby thought, three weeks. She tried to think what that would be in days, and it seemed to her unimaginable and terrible, to stay in this brown cold place, with bars before the windows, whispering, waiting, for three weeks. She looked out of the window at people in white clothes, walking carelessly on the streets, having all the streets they wanted to walk on. She reached her hand involuntarily through the bars, reaching it out to be free, grabbing at the air and the house warden came in and pulled her back and said: 'You can't look out the windows, nobody can, it's against the rules, go and stand on the line in the hall for an hour.'

This meant standing on one of the cracks of the tiled floor, not moving. It was the usual punishment, varying in length according to the crime. It was hard to do. She was tired when she went to bed.

\* \* \*

'I ran away,' it was the little girl with freckles, talking. She was thirteen, but small. She had a nice tweed suit and Ruby thought her teeth were wonderful, small, round, gleaming. They sat at one end of the long table, with their backs to the barred window. No one ever said anything about that; automatically they chose their places that way, to shut out the free world, and the bars before it.

'I ran away,' she said again. 'I live three thousand miles from here. None of you ever been there. The sea comes up on the beach in a big grey roll and makes foam all over. It's Conneckticut,' she said.

'It sounds nice,' Ruby said timidly. 'Water's nice. I like the river. There's a sand barge,' she did not finish, not wanting to speak of this place which was hers, had been hers, before.

'Oh, it's beautiful,' the freckled girl said. 'It's not like this where I come from.'

'Why did you leave then?' Myrtle wanted to know.

'Couldn't eat enough, couldn't get any clothes, nothing. My father don't work. He just sits around.'

They all knew about that.

'He useta work. He had a swell job. He worked in a store. We had a house with a swing behind and flowers. I had lotsa clothes; I had a pink taffeta dress for parties. But not now. Nor for a long time. And they're so crabby. Gee.

'It was fun coming,' the girl from Connecticut went on. 'Everybody was nice to us, me and my girl friend. We got rides all the way. We ast people for something to eat and they gave it to us. It was nice everywhere till we got here. Then they run us in. This is a hole, I mean.'

'Were you going to California?' the girl with the scar asked.

'Yeah. Imagine. They say you just get food off the ground, oranges and things. We didn't get there though. I sure hate this place. I never been in a jail before, and I don't wanna be again.'

'Me either,' Minnie May said, fervently.

'Did you hear those coloured girls yelling this morning?' the girl with the scar said.

'Yeah.'

'Gee, I'm sorry for that one they call Hazel. I listened to her, when I was standing on the line this morning. She was crying.'

'Why?' And Ruby thought why not, it's enough to make anyone cry all the time, all day long and all night. It's the only thing you feel like doing, here.

'Oh, they're gonna send her to the reform school for three years. Seems she's pregnant.' (Ruby rumpled her forehead, doubtfully, and Myrtle leaned over and explained, whispering, 'gonna have a baby, that means.') 'She ain't married to her boy and she was crying and saying: "How'm I gonna find that boy when I get out, how'm I gonna make that boy marry me when I get out, where'll he be three years from now. They don't do nothing to him, they just grab me. They're bustin' up homes here, that's what they're doing." She cried like that for an hour. Seems as if she loved that man.'

They were silent.

The days went on. Ruby tried to count. It seemed to her that weeks moved by, grey and unmarked. It was only four days. She began to get pale like the others, and the faint sun-gilding wore off. She lay about most of the day, feeling ill, wanting to roller skate, play hopscotch, run, laugh, roll in the sand on the barge. Her body felt limp and heavy and her stomach turned over, at every meal, with the soggy grey food on her tongue.

Gradually, though no one said these things publicly, but by whispering at night, from bed to bed, she found out why the other girls were there, waiting, like herself. Running away, stealing, going with men. She was surprised to find that others had thought of the same way to earn money: surprised and comforted.

One morning after breakfast, Miss Mayfield, the house warden, told them that they should get ready, they'd be going down to the clinic later. 'You four,' she said, pointing to Minnie May, Myrtle, Sally and Ruby.

They shuffled down the basement, hanging back, each one wanting the other to be first. Miss Mayfield, grey and sharp behind them, harried them with a voice like a scythe. 'That's enough, that's enough,' she said, 'pick up your feet and get along.'

The door to the clinic stood open. Inside a long hall, lined with benches, showed up dimly under dirty electric lights. There was a waiting-room; on one side negro women sat holding their children about them, hushing them, keeping them quiet and patient, softly. On the other side were the white women, hard-faced, shoddy, scolding their children, forgetting, calling to them. Some girls, about sixteen years old, sat alone and chewed gum and giggled with each other. There were a few children on the benches in the hall, waiting by themselves. Nurses came and went and in one room they could hear a murmur of conversation, brief professional talk, from the doctor to his patients. It was all dark, brown, with dead air. Not dirty, but used, worn-out, a place for the poor.

Miss Mayfield left them sitting on the wooden benches in the hall, and went to talk to the secretary in her office. The girls swung their legs nervously, and stared around them. Beside Ruby, sat another child. She was about thirteen and held a baby of three or so, by the hand. 'Now, Ruthie,' she would say. 'Now, Ruthie, just sit quiet dear and we'll go soon.' Her voice was a perfect imitation of a mother's or a nurse, except piping. Her hair was lank and unbrushed, and she smiled at Ruby suddenly, warmly, with the lovely unexpected friendliness of children.

'It's awful ain't it,' she said. 'We gotta walk up from the south side, takes us about an hour. They won't let you eat before you come for them shots, and we just wobble when we get here. We all come,' she said brightly, 'the two boys and Ruthie and me.'

'Shots?' Ruby said, startled.

'Sure, didn't you come before?'

Ruby shook her head.

'Oh, well, you go in there, and the doctor rolls up your sleeve or sometimes takes down your pants, depends, and they give you a shot. It's for bad blood,' she said helpfully. 'You gotta come or they 'rest you. Ruthie cries, so does Mickey.'

'Does it hurt?'

'Nah, not much. Not after a while. They say I got it from a man. I went with a man once. Did you?'

'Yes.'

'Well then that's what it is I guess. I guess you got it too. The man said he'd give me a bicycle, but he didn't give me nothing, he just went away.'

They heard a scream, short and high, instantly stopped.

Ruby jumped, turned towards the door and looked back at the girl next her, questioning.

She was shaking her head. 'It's Mickey,' she said. 'I don't know what'sa matter with that child. Sometimes he pukes too. It don't hurt him like that, he just screams 'cause he's scared.'

'Oh,' Ruby said in a tiny tight voice.

The nurse came out in the hall and said: 'Ruby Mayer, this way.'

She put her hand against the wall to steady herself; she was trembling. The nurse took her by the shoulder and guided her to the operating table. 'Just lie down there,' she said.

Hurriedly and not too gently the doctor examined her. She held her breath in tight and looked at the cracks on the ceiling. She had never been in a clinic or hospital before. It seemed to her that now they had her, the other people, the people like policemen and Miss Mayfield, they could do anything to her, send her anywhere, hurt her when they wanted, boss her and punish her, all the time without reason. And she couldn't cry, she couldn't say anything. She would just have to wait and hope the days would go by quickly.

'The same, they're all the same,' the doctor said. The nurse wrote something on a card. 'I'll just give her a blood test.'

Ruby remembered Mickey screaming. No, no, they wouldn't. They couldn't hurt her any more. It wasn't fair, she hadn't been as bad as all that. They didn't have a right, they didn't have a right. She wouldn't have people sticking needles or knives or things into her. She had never done anything bad enough for this, for the bars and the long days and the food and Miss Mayfield punishing them for nothing and the doctor hurting her and not caring, not seeing her, not knowing who she was ...

'No,' she said, her voice low and urgent. 'No you won't. I'm not gonna be hurt anymore.'

'It won't hurt,' the doctor said, taking the syringe from a tray.

He turned with it in his hand. Ruby looked at the long fine needle, with horror; the man would drive it into her, all through her, and her blood would spill all over the floor, no, no, they didn't have the right... She opened her mouth and screamed. 'No, no I won't let you, I won't!'

'God, what is the matter with these kids,' the doctor said wearily. 'They yell like we were going to murder them. Be quiet, you dumb child, this doesn't hurt, it only takes a minute.'

She struck out at him and he got angry. 'Hold her arms,' he told the nurse. Swiftly, his face irritated and cold, he stuck the needle into Ruby's arm. She shut her eyes and screamed in terror. The nurse pushed her to get up, and she went out in the hall, holding cotton against the little purple circle, making a muffled sound of crying, her eyelashes shining with tears.

'That's nonsense, Ruby,' Miss Mayfield said. 'You had no business making that racket. You'll just do without your play this afternoon, as punishment.'

Ruby wanted to laugh, stick out her tongue at Miss Mayfield and jeer. Play! that was their idea, their word. She knew what playing was, it was running, and sun on your face, and being free. Play! What kind of people were they anyhow.

\* \* \*

'Your mother's come to see you, Ruby.'

She was frightened to go into the house warden's office. Mrs Mayer would be there, stiff, angry, and she'd get spanked. She couldn't remember many spankings, but they had been good ones, when she got them. She put her hands behind her back and sidled in. But, when she saw her mother, bowed in the chair, ungloved hands red, empty and tired in her lap, her eyes glossy with tears, looking towards her, she ran forward and put her arms around Mrs Mayer's neck, climbed up on her lap and wept.

'Poor little Ruby,' Mrs Mayer said, patting the soft brown hair, rumpling it, bending to kiss it, her arms tight about the small shaking body. 'I'm sorry you hadta. I should of got you the things you needed, I should of, but I couldn't. If your Daddy had been here, working,' she said, and her voice ached, 'it wouldn't of been like this. We never had no trouble when your Daddy was working. My little girl,' she said. 'Little Ruby.'

Ruby clung to her, feeling safe. Her mother had come, and would take her home. She would climb up the steps at night and go to sleep on the rags and wake and find her mother and the things she was used to, around her. She would go back to school soon, and it was still sunny enough to play on the barge. She wouldn't go to Lucy's cabin because the policeman might come, but she didn't care any more about cones; she only wanted to go home, and know her mother was there, waiting for her, and she could climb up on her lap and be hugged.

She cried gently to herself, from joy, because the waiting was over, the long days and the bars and the cold, mean people and the things that hurt.

'Shall we go now, Ma. Everything's all right. I haven't even got bad blood,' she said, smiling, wiping the tears from her eyelashes with her hand. 'Shall we go home now, Ma?'

There was silence. Mrs Mayer held her tighter, pressed against her own thin body, and above Ruby's head, her eyes fixed on the door with hatred.

'I can't take you, Ruby.' Ruby's body went hard in her mother's arms. 'They won't let me take you home. They say I'm not fit to keep you. They say I should of known what you were doing, and if I didn't then I'm not a good mother.' Her voice stopped, as if there were no more breath inside; came to a stop from emptiness, as if there were nothing to say anymore, ever.

Ruby wept. She did not speak, but held her arms around her mother's neck, pressing her cheek against her mother's, sobbing. They were going to take her mother: they were going to keep her, alone, away, shut inside a house until she died because it was useless to live. Her mother couldn't do anything against them either. Her body was weak with crying: she heard the sound of her own voice, rising, crazy with fear: 'No, no ... no ...'

'You'd better go, Mrs Mayer.' Miss Mayfield stood in the door, impersonal as wood, and waited.

'Goodbye,' Mrs Mayer said. 'Goodbye, Ruby. Goodbye, darling.'

She lifted Ruby's arms from her neck, gently, and stood up.

Miss Mayfield took Ruby's shoulder, holding the thin bones tight in her hand, and pushed the child through the door.

'Oh,' Mrs Mayer said, stepping forward to catch Ruby, to lead her, to make it easier for her. 'Oh, don't – not like that.'

Miss Mayfield stood in the doorway and looked at her, not angry, not menacing: indifferent, dry, blank.

I'm not her mother any more, Mrs Mayer thought, they've got her. I'm not a good mother ... Miss Mayfield locked the door behind her.

Ruby, not even crying now, still and hopeless, leaned her head against the bars and watched her mother dragging down the street.

'She's going the wrong way,' Minnie May said. 'That's not the way to your house.'

© ROBERT CAPA / MAGNUM PHOTOS

# *About the Author*

**M**ARTHA GELLHORN (1908-98) published five novels, fourteen novellas and two collections of short stories. She wanted to be re-membered primarily as a novelist, yet to most people she is remembered as an outstanding war correspondent and for something which infuriated her, her brief marriage to Ernest Hemingway during the Second World War. She had no intention of being a footnote in someone else's life and nor will she be. Since her death there have already been two biographies of her.

As a war correspondent she covered almost every major conflict from the Spanish Civil War to the American invasion of Panama in 1989. For a woman it was completely ground-breaking work, and she took it on with an absolute commitment to the truth. 'All politicians are bores and liars and fakes. I talk to people,' she said, explaining her paramount interest in war's civilian victims, the unseen casualties. She was one of the great war correspondents, one of the great witnesses, of the twentieth century.

Her life as a war correspondent is well illustrated by two incidents. After Hemingway stole her accreditation, she stowed away on a hospital ship on 7 June 1944 and went ashore during the Normandy invasion to help collect wounded men; she was also refused a visa to return to Vietnam by the American military, so infuriated were they by her reports for the *Guardian*.

She was a woman of strong opinions and incredible energy. Though she turned down reporting on the Bosnian war in her 80s, saying she wasn't nimble enough, she flew to Brazil at the age of eighty-seven to research and write an article about the murder of street children. Touch-typing although she could barely see, she was driven by a compassion for the powerless and a curiosity undimmed by age.

# ELAND

61 Exmouth Market, London EC1R 4QL
Email: info@travelbooks.co.uk

Eland was started in 1982 to revive great travel books
that had fallen out of print. Although the list has diversified
into biography and fiction, it is united by a quest to define the
spirit of place. These are books for travellers, and for readers who aspire
to explore the world but who are content to travel in their own
minds. Eland books open out our understanding of other cultures,
interpret the unknown and reveal different environments as well as
celebrating the humour and occasional horrors of travel. We take
immense trouble to select only the most readable books and therefore
many readers collect the entire series.

All our books are printed on fine, pliable, cream-coloured paper.
Most are still gathered in sections by our printer and sewn as well
as glued, almost unheard of for a paperback book these days.
This gives larger margins in the gutter, as well as
making the books stronger.

You will find a very brief description of our books on the
following pages. Extracts from each and every one of them can be
read on our website, at www.travelbooks.co.uk. If you would
like a free copy of our catalogue, please email
or write to us (details above).

# ELAND

*'One of the very best travel lists'* WILLIAM DALRYMPLE

**Memoirs of a Bengal Civilian**
JOHN BEAMES
*Sketches of nineteenth-century India
painted with the richness of Dickens*

**Jigsaw**
SYBILLE BEDFORD
*An intensely remembered autobiographical
novel about an inter-war childhood*

**A Visit to Don Otavio**
SYBILLE BEDFORD
*The hell of travel and the Eden of arrival
in post-war Mexico*

**Journey into the Mind's Eye**
LESLEY BLANCH
*An obsessive love affair with Russia and
one particular Russian*

**The Way of the World**
NICOLAS BOUVIER
*Two men in a car from Serbia to Afghanistan*

**The Devil Drives**
FAWN BRODIE
*Biography of Sir Richard Burton,
explorer, linguist and pornographer*

**Turkish Letters**
OGIER DE BUSBECQ
*Eyewitness history at its best:
Istanbul during the reign of Suleyman
the Magnificent*

**My Early Life**
WINSTON CHURCHILL
*From North-West Frontier to Boer War
by the age of twenty-five*

**Sicily: through writers' eyes**
ED. HORATIO CLARE
*Guidebooks for the mind: a selection
of the best travel writing on Sicily*

**A Square of Sky**
JANINA DAVID
*A Jewish childhood in the Warsaw
ghetto and hiding from the Nazis*

**Chantemesle**
ROBIN FEDDEN
*A lyrical evocation of childhood
in Normandy*

**Croatia: through writers' eyes**
ED. FRANKOPAN, GOODING & LAVINGTON
*Guidebooks for the mind: a selection
of the best travel writing on Croatia*

**Travels with Myself and Another**
MARTHA GELLHORN
*Five journeys from hell by a great
war correspondent*

**The Weather in Africa**
MARTHA GELLHORN
*Three novellas set amongst the
white settlers of East Africa*

**The Last Leopard**
DAVID GILMOUR
*The biography of Giuseppe di Lampedusa,
author of* The Leopard

**Walled Gardens**
ANNABEL GOFF
*An Anglo-Irish childhood*

**Africa Dances**
GEOFFREY GORER
*The magic of indigenous culture
and the banality of colonisation*

**Cinema Eden**
JUAN GOYTISOLO
*Essays from the Muslim
Mediterranean*

**A State of Fear**
ANDREW GRAHAM-YOOLL
*A journalist witnesses Argentina's
nightmare in the 1970s*

**Warriors**
GERALD HANLEY
*Life and death among the Somalis*

**Morocco That Was**
WALTER HARRIS
*All the cruelty, fascination and
humour of a pre-modern kingdom*

**Far Away and Long Ago**
W H HUDSON
*A childhood in Argentina*

**Holding On**
MERVYN JONES
*One family and one street in
London's East End: 1880-1960*

**Red Moon & High Summer**
HERBERT KAUFMANN
*A coming-of-age novel following a
young singer in his Tuareg homeland*

**Three Came Home**
AGNES KEITH
*A mother's ordeal in a Japanese
prison camp*

**Peking Story**
DAVID KIDD
*The ruin of an ancient Mandarin
family under the new communist order*

**Syria: through writers' eyes**
ED. MARIUS KOCIEJOWSKI
*Guidebooks for the mind: a selection
of the best travel writing on Syria*

**Scum of the Earth**
ARTHUR KOESTLER
*Koestler's personal experience of
France in World War II*

**A Dragon Apparent**
NORMAN LEWIS
*Cambodia, Laos and Vietnam
on the eve of war*

**Golden Earth**
NORMAN LEWIS
*Travels in Burma*

**The Honoured Society**
NORMAN LEWIS
*Sicily, her people and the Mafia within*

**Naples '44**
NORMAN LEWIS
*Post-war Naples and an intelligence
officer's love of Italy's gift for life*

**A View of the World**
NORMAN LEWIS
*Collected writings by the great
English travel writer*

**An Indian Attachment**
SARAH LLOYD
*Life and love in a remote Indian village*

**A Pike in the Basement**
SIMON LOFTUS
*Tales of a hungry traveller: from catfish
in Mississippi to fried eggs with chapatis
in Pakistan*

**Among the Faithful**
DAHRIS MARTIN
*An American woman living in the holy
city of Kairouan, Tunisia in the 1920s*

**Lords of the Atlas**
GAVIN MAXWELL
*The rise and fall of Morocco's infamous
Glaoua family, 1893-1956*

**A Reed Shaken by the Wind**
GAVIN MAXWELL
*Travels among the threatened Marsh
Arabs of southern Iraq*

**A Year in Marrakesh**
PETER MAYNE
*Back-street life in Morocco in the 1950s*

**Sultan in Oman**
JAN MORRIS
*An historic journey through the still-medieval
state of Oman in the 1950s*

**The Caravan Moves On**
IRFAN ORGA
*Life with the nomads of central Turkey*

**Portrait of a Turkish Family**
IRFAN ORGA
*The decline of a prosperous Ottoman
family in the new Republic*

## The Undefeated
GEORGE PALOCZI-HORVATH
*Fighting injustice in communist Hungary*

## Travels into the Interior of Africa
MUNGO PARK
*The first – and still the best – European record of west-African exploration*

## Lighthouse
TONY PARKER
*Britain's lighthouse-keepers, in their own words*

## The People of Providence
TONY PARKER
*A London housing estate and some of its inhabitants*

## Begums, Thugs & White Mughals
FANNY PARKES
*William Dalrymple edits and introduces his favourite Indian travel book*

## The Last Time I Saw Paris
ELLIOT PAUL
*One street, its loves and loathings, set against the passionate politics of inter-war Paris*

## Rites
VICTOR PERERA
*A Jewish childhood in Guatemala*

## A Cure for Serpents
THE DUKE OF PIRAJNO
*An Italian doctor and his Bedouin patients, Libyan sheikhs and Tuareg mistress in the 1920s*

## Nunaga
DUNCAN PRYDE
*Ten years among the Eskimos: hunting, fur-trading and heroic dog-treks*

## A Funny Old Quist
EVAN ROGERS
*A gamekeeper's passionate evocation of a now-vanished English rural lifestyle*

## Meetings with Remarkable Muslims
ED. ROGERSON & BARING
*A collection of contemporary travel writing that celebrates cultural difference and the Islamic world*

## Marrakesh: through writers' eyes
ED. ROGERSON & LAVINGTON
*Guidebooks for the mind: a selection of the best travel writing on Marrakesh*

## Living Poor
MORITZ THOMSEN
*An American's encounter with poverty in Ecuador*

## Hermit of Peking
HUGH TREVOR-ROPER
*The hidden life of the scholar Sir Edmund Backhouse*

## The Law
ROGER VAILLAND
*The harsh game of life played in the taverns of southern Italy*

## The Road to Nab End
WILLIAM WOODRUFF
*The best selling story of poverty and survival in a Lancashire mill town*

## The Village in the Jungle
LEONARD WOOLF
*A dark novel of native villagers struggling to survive in colonial Ceylon*

## Death's Other Kingdom
GAMEL WOOLSEY
*The tragic arrival of civil war in an Andalucian village in 1936*

## The Ginger Tree
OSWALD WYND
*A Scotswoman's love and survival in early twentieth-century Japan*